When Somebody Loves *You*

BETTY LOWREY

ISBN   Softcover   978-1-949723-89-2

Printed in the United States of America.

To order additional copies of this book, contact:
Bookwhip
1-855-339-3589
https://www.bookwhip.com

Prologue

Laura Noble wanted to be a teacher but most of all she dreamed of marrying the boy of her dreams, settling down in a cozy little town and raising a family. They were a threesome, Richard, Tom and Laura. The problem was as they grew older both boys said they loved her causing a bit of friction between the two. While Tom's recklessness made her tingle with excitement, she saw Richard was like her dad, stable and trusted. She thought once the decision was made which one to marry, all her problems would be over but Laura was the tool used by another who felt life had dealt him an injustice as through the years he watched the three. What did they do to deserve a better life? How would Tom and Richard handle the situation he planned for Laura? What was there about one's upbringing that produced who they would become? Did the love their families seemed to have really make a difference? 1 Corinthians 13:4-8 may be the most important message this story of love could proclaim. "Love is patient, love is kind. It does not envy. It does not boast. It is not proud. It is not rude. It is not self seeking. It is not easily angered. It keeps no record of evil. Love does not delight in evil but rejoices with truth. It always protects, always trusts, always hopes, always perseveres. Love never fails."

Chapter 1

Florence Noble removed the last load of clothes from the washer and placed them in the dryer. It was time for the school bus to drop off Laura and Timmy. She and John had a serious talk with their daughter the night before for riding home with the Worthington boy. That meant her brother was left to fend for himself; they expected her to be there for him to give him the security he needed and to fend off the youngest Tellow boy who had a bent for bullying. The children on the bus were unaware of Tim's handicap, except for the Tellow boy who had seen him in shorts, the misshaped leg and the pliable brace, before he had corrective surgery this summer. Laura should be there in case Tim needed her.

At three forty, the bus pulled to a stop in front of the house, Timmy practically fell out the door dragging a book bag behind him. The bus driver sat hunched over the wheel, waiting. She wondered how many times each evening he waited for the little ones barely big enough to make the steps, the slow ones like Tim or those who could care less how much time it took for them to hit ground and then there were the bullies, who Timmy said stuck a foot out in front of them as they came down the aisle, and made them fall. This was the fourth day of the new school year. She walked out onto the porch, reaching down for his book bag while he pushed up the steps.

"Where's your sister?"

"She said she was riding home with Thomas Hargrove."

"Did you have any trouble with the Tellow boy today?"

Timmy grinned. "No, Laura took care of that last week."

"And how was that and why am I just now hearing this?"

"Laura said if you didn't ask don't tell, but if you did to tell the truth. She gave him a warning, if he bothers me again, she'll call in her friends and they'll take care of him." Timmy laughed. "That's when Richard and Tom came up behind her and she said, "These are my friends." He bent over laughing. "You know how tall Richard is and Tom put on his mean face."

"I'm not sure that was the best thing she could do but I guess it worked, didn't it?"

"Yeah, Mom, Laura's the best. Think what she could do if she was bigger."

That was the crux of the matter. Florence wanted the best for her children, but that meant they had to apply themselves. With Timmy's medical bills and saving for college for Laura, things were tight.

"You know what Mom?" He waited for her to turn and look at him. "I need to start saving for a car. I'm fourteen. Tom said he'd help me fix it up if I can find an old one like he's got. He paid thirteen hundred for his, now its worth twice, well it was more than that, anyway its worth a lot."

"Where do you find an old vintage car?" She couldn't understand. John's friends were driving around in the old cars they'd worked on, they said just for fun and usually a reminder of their first car and now the teenagers were scouting for the old ones, too. "What's wrong with a new Chevrolet or Ford?"

"Nothing, Mom, can we afford one?" With Florence silence, Timmy went on to his room.

It was late when a forty six Ford pulled into the drive. Red headed Tommy Hargrove jumped out, hurried around to the passenger side and opened the door for Laura. Timmy heard and came rushing through the room, caught last minute by his mother by the back of his shirt. "Let her come in, Timmy."

She sashayed into the living room, her laughter a last blessing on Tommy as he turned and headed back down the porch steps. Drama queen that she was, these days, Laura leaned against the door, swallowed the laughter and waited for the smile to leave her face. No doubt her mother would be waiting in the kitchen. She needed to make her own decisions but her mother didn't agree.

Florence stepped from the shadowed corner. "I thought I told you to ride the bus home."

Visibly blanching, Laura turned quickly to face her mother. "Did you mean that?"

"I think I made it clear. I believe there's a game tomorrow night, but sadly you won't be going."

"Mother, I'm almost seventeen years old. I'm going. You can't make me stay."

"Laurie," her mother slipped into her everyday name, "You have to abide by our rules. This is not the only thing. You have been staying out past your curfew, you don't want to attend church anymore and frankly, your ironing is stacked a mile high in your bedroom that needs dusting. What are you doing in your free hours?" Florence sank down into John's chair, her body weary and her eyes tired. "I can't do this, honey. One more mess up and I'm giving it all to your father. If you intend to cause problems and we can't work it out, then you and your dad will."

"I thought you liked Richard."

"That has nothing to do with you not riding the bus with your brother, and…" she stared at her child, "Tommy Hargrove is not Richard. You confuse the issue, young lady."

"They both like me."

"Which one do you like?"

"Richard has money, Mother, and class but Tommy is so much fun to be with, a bit on the wild side."

"Lord help us," Florence groaned. "You better let them both go, you will get in over your head and what do we do then?" Closing her eyes, Florence didn't want to think of the trouble Laura might face.

"I'm going to that game, Mother."

Florence saw the determination in her daughter's eye along with the dare. "We'll see." Turning toward the kitchen, she called back over her shoulder. "Clean your room and start on that ironing, Laura."

Alone, Florence thought about the two boys always vying for her daughter's attention, since Kindergarten. There was the time she and Julia found the three playing, Laura was wearing her white fairy Halloween costume; on this day it represented a wedding dress. "We need a preacher," Tommy announced as he and Richard stood on either side of Laura. "Why's that?" Julia asked. "To say who loveth this woman," the boys replied in unison, "We're all getting married." Julia replied, "You mean who giveth this woman." Tommy and Richard gave her a hostile look, "No, we mean who loveth this woman because we both do." They had laughed about it at the time but now it wasn't funny.

She had a strong feeling what she was seeing today in her daughter would be what carried her through life. She was strong willed and came naturally to it, sometimes fighting her battles alone. And Tim, was a good boy, he would learn a lot through having this handicap. He had learned quickly not to be brash or impatient. It was Florence job to steer them right. Sometimes it seemed she was more a monitor than a mom, keeping tabs on two teenagers. This was a new phase with Laura. Two boys competing against each other was changing the sweet girl Florence had raised. She would settle in time. She had to; life always told the tale of what a person was made of and Laura came from a line of strong women. Timmy steered clear of trouble and wanted what others his age had but Timmy was willing to work for it. She didn't think Timmy would present a problem; life would be smooth if he chose the right girl. She prayed he would find someone worthy of who he was. When Laura chose, she would stand firm in her decision.

Richard pulled his fifty seven Chevrolet into the cove of trees, waiting. Tommy would come speeding down the ditch road anytime and when he did there was reckoning. He had hardly cracked his book when he heard him coming. He waited until just the right minute and backed across the road. Gravel spewed and threw rocks through the air, as the sound of Tommy cursing filled his ears. "What tha," somehow he had managed to slam on the brakes and avoid Richard's car but that caused him to slide up into the break of trees that lined the edge of a four foot drop off formed by erosion of the ditch.

Jumping out of the car he came barreling toward Richard. "Are you out of your mind? You could get us both killed, not to mention tear up our cars." Tommy stomped around Richard, his eyes wild, his fist doubled. "Come on."

"I won't fight you…" Richard let his words settle, "Unless you keep causing me and Laura trouble."

"Hey, she chose to ride home with me. You got tabs on her?" Tommy gave his wicked laugh. "Oh, yeah, you're the great Richard Worthington, heir to the land magnate of Quinn corner. Right? And I'm just Mr. Worthington, seniors, right hand man's son." Tommy circled Richard. "That makes you…what?"

"One thing it doesn't make me is a man with a chip on his shoulder, such as yours." Tommy threw a right punch. Richard put up a hand and caught his wrist. "Tom, we've been friends since first grade, do you want to ruin it now?"

"Good Lord, Richard, you sound like an old man. You can drop that always do right attitude. We're the same age. "Tommy dropped a few curse words as his body heat began to settle and his mind clear. "Let's get this straight; you're not married to her. Laura has a right to choose."

"That she does," Richard agreed, "but it's you that's the problem, you flirt with anything wearing a skirt."

"But there's nothing wrong with that. It's a free world, you should try it sometime."

"Those girls over in Long town are not free, Tom. You'll go over there and get something and then you're back acting like

Laura's the chosen one, nothing too good for her when all the time you're playing around."

"We're not married." Tom tapped Richard's shoulder a few times. "Let's forget this and not let it happen again." His eyes held with Richard's, nondescript, the challenge didn't show through, nor his intent.

"What are you going to do about Laura?"

"You're in love with her, aren't you?" Tommy studied his friend. "Well, I'll tell you, I don't rightly know."

"What's got you in such a mood?" Tommy's mother sit a bowl of soup on the table. "Go wash up and help by putting ice in the tea glasses." She watched him slump out of the chair. "Is it that little Laura girl? I saw her getting in your car yesterday." For a moment she raised her head to stare at her son. "If she is Richard's girl, as I was told, maybe you should leave her alone."

Why?" He grabbed the handle of the refrigerator. "Will I cause Dad to lose his job?" He filled the glasses with tea, dropped a few chunks of ice his mother had placed in a bowl on one of the shelves and hurried out of the kitchen when it splashed on the floor, with his mother calling behind him, "try to remember ice first, then tea."

He couldn't stand the thought of another year in Walker. It was little more than a pit stop, if anyone could find it on the map. Right in the middle of farmland and Mr. Worthington's measure for the water lines going in, the pipe line for what they called gray water, meaning everyone's run off, whether baths or more dishes due to larger families. Walker was Mr. Worthington's father in law, long since departed; he had established the town right down to a one room church that served as school house in the old days. It was considered an honor to have the town named after you but to the two boys a hardship. The cemetery was part of the mix. Their fathers didn't have time to see after the graves but felt two boys their age would do fine. "You boys work together and prosper."

Tommy never lost sight of the fact Richard came from money while his own father labored for Richard's father. Once he made the mistake of voicing his thoughts and his father was sorely disappointed in him. "Son," he said, "what does it matter who I work for as long as it's good money?" Tommy was twelve years old at the time. Now, he was ready to leave home. Someday, he'd show Richard who was the man.

"It's embarrassing," he replied. "Makes me look bad." That day he decided someday he'd show them all he could do his studies as well as anyone and he intended to leave Walker and make a name for himself.

As he aged, voicing his opinion hadn't brought praise. "Well, then," his father replied. "Seems you better harness that other thing inside you that wants to be a ladies man, cause they'd come after you if you repeat what you told us at supper. You better leave the girls alone."

It was true, he was a bit of a ladies man, wading right in on the ladies whether they'd had their first kiss or not, he longed for them, plotted even, wanted interaction with them because they were different and right now little Laura Noble caught his eye over any of the other because she was like him, restless and she was a beauty. Olive skin, dark hair, dusky eyes, delicate but stubborn and iron willed; he smiled thinking of the many times they'd matched wits and the outcome was equal, you win some, you lose some. She made him feel like a man, taller than he was and that was a source of secret disappointment, it appeared he wasn't going to reach his father's height of six foot three. Right now he weighed in at one hundred sixty five pounds, five foot ten and one half inches tall. Of course, Richard was six four.

"Dad?" Laura pleaded but he wasn't changing his mind or perhaps it was her mother's mind. "Dad, I won't ride home with them anymore. Just let me go to this game."

John glanced up from where he sit at the kitchen table pouring over farm ledgers. "Laura, you can go to your room and next time pay attention to what you're told. It is all up to you."

She slunk off to her room, giving her mother the evil eye as she met her in the hall. Falling onto the bed she thought about Tommy and Richard, With Richard she would have security; Richard with his soft eyes.

How many times did she look up from her book in study hall to find his eyes on her? He would smile that content smile, tilt his head that familiar way and return to whatever it was he saw on the book in front of him. At games, when she was in the bleachers and he was on the court, during time out, he would glance to where she sit. She was always amazed he seemed to locate her immediately. Truly, Richard cared for her but did she care for Richard? Yes, a gentle protective kind of caring but was that enough?

Tommy. Rolling over she reached for her wallet, pulled the plastic sleeve that housed her pictures from it and flipped through to Tommy's. What was the relentless struggle about that went on between Richard and Tommy? Where did it originate? They'd all been in school together these many years. Tommy's smile warmed her heart but what he'd written across the bottom brought a moment of excitement. "Love you Babe." And on the back, "Come run away with me. Let's see the world."

She was asleep, still lying fully clothed across her bed when around ten Florence turned off the lights.

"Tell him you love me, Laura girl." Tommy chortled as Richard gave him a scornful look.

"Hargrove, you know you've lost. Go find yourself a play mate."

They were on their way to Winston, to play their most aggressive rival on the court. "You two need to cool down," Laura reminded them, "Coach said this is our most important game and you need to psyche yourself up to win. I overheard him talking to Stallings and he said if you two were at your best we'd win but if you get caught up in your own personal squabbles we don't have a chance."

"What did he mean our own personal squabbles?"

Laura couldn't say. It was embarrassing. Crystal was sitting behind them and she heard. "Not everyone is blind to the fact you two fight over Laura constantly. I suspect that's what Coach meant. Another thing, if you all fight on the bus another time they won't let us cheer leaders ride this bus. We'll have to ride the late one with everyone else."

"Well aren't you just little miss information?" Tom sat down by her and flipped her hair. "What you wearin' blondie? You smell pretty good."

Crystal preened. "Fabulous." Tom leaned closer. "I thought it was beans and taters. I'm hungry."

She slapped him. Tom reached for both of her hands and brought them behind her head. "I'll let you go when you place a kiss on my cheek where you hit me."

"That'll be the day," she retorted.

"You're decision," He said. "You'll be pretty uncomfortable after a while. It's twenty miles to Winston."

She thought about it. "All right. Stick your tongue out."

"Wow, Worthington, I scored. Watch her kiss me." He was grinning. "I didn't know you liked French kisses." He made a big to-do wiping his mouth and running his tongue over his teeth. "I knew you wanted me."

Crystal glanced up front. Their driver was talking to one of the team on the front seat. She looked over her shoulder to where their sponsors were snoozing away. "You'll have to come really close."

Tommy was willing to comply. "Watch this, Worthington. Learn something." Laura and Richard turned.

"Closer. Shut your eyes," Crystal coached. Tommy was feeling good. The next thing the whole group on the bus heard was Tommy yelling as a dribble of blood ran out the corner of his mouth." Everyone was looking. Crystal was sitting back to her seat, demure and ladylike while Richard shook his head.

"Unbelievable," he said. Tommy was digging in a duffle bag at his feet for a towel.

"You witch," he mumbled. "Worthington, she tried to bite my tongue off."

"I'd say you bit off more than you could chew that time, Hargrove."

Crystal was smiling like an angel. "Someone has to teach you macho men what's real."

The team won over Winston that night. The announcer for WTMV said it was because Hargrove and Worthington were playing like pros, teamwork at its best, but those two carried them to victory tonight."

Coach didn't understand when Crystal said, "You owe me." Nor, did he understand when he ask Hargrove if he'd had a tooth pulled the reason he had red drool in the corner of his mouth and Hargrove replied, "No, I've been playing tongue games." Coach threw up his hands. "What's tongue games?"

Hargrove worked hard keeping Laura entertained, firing up Richard in the process. Laura had gained enough experience to keep them both guessing and retain her lady like ways. She knew going off to college would help her decide which one she liked most, but Tom found the distance a challenge, after the first year. Richard remained faithful. She wished just once he would do something daring or out of his staid character, but he didn't and she accepted the fact he was loyal to her while hearing of Tom's escapades with the locals. Occasionally Tom would show up, start her heart to racing, take her somewhere special and then leave as quickly as he had come. They didn't mention those times to Richard. "He's too good a guy for us to rock his boat" Tom would say. Laura agreed but always felt she betrayed Richard even though all they did was have dinner and talk and then go separate ways.

Tom found Laura the girl most likely to make him happy but then if he married her he'd have to settle down. He wondered how long it would work, his dangling her on a chain, knowing the day she realized he was never going to change his ways, she'd cut him out of the picture for good. The day he showed up to tell her, that night he wined and dined her but it backfired on him, he found her to be the loveliest woman he knew he would ever know, he drank too much, she drank just enough to make her melancholy and the rest they vowed never to tell, because on his scale, he as usual had gotten a little out of hand. He was surprised when she sent him a wedding invitation. He had called her two weeks after their dinner to see if she was all right and she cried. "I'm marrying Richard," she said. "There will never be another man who loves me as he does. I don't ever want to hurt him."

"Neither do I," Tom replied. "Richard's the best. You are too, Laura." He stumbled for words to hang up and mumbled "when that day comes, I wish you and Richard every happiness. I'll always love you." He paused and added, "Both." When they said goodbye, he pulled the little black velvet box from his pants pocket and looked at the ring. "I'd never have been able to stay true to you, Laura. This was never meant to be."

Laura had known someone was going to be hurt from their threesome friendship, but she hadn't known it was her. Tom saying, "I'm not the marrying kind, Laura," had cut to the grain, but she would survive.

Now she was home. No more escape from Walker. Hometown was all right but she would be going to New Haven to teach Kindergarten classes, come September. Until then, she had time to get situated, plan a few ideas for her class room and in general soak up the atmosphere of her new job.

Richard, good reliable Richard helped her find an apartment, move furniture around in it and in general be there for her. "My mother," she was prone to utter when something went wrong and Richard would roll his eyes as if to say here we go again. Actually he found Mrs. Noble a fascinating woman, Laura could bite people in the butt as the expression went, if she were in one of those moods while Mrs. Noble merely gave a flick of the hand waving aside her daughter's impudence. "You don't know this, Laura, but you will miss me when I'm gone."

"How macabre, Mother, I hope you aren't thinking of leaving soon." A perplexed expression on her face, Laura would flounce around the rooms as though she meant it and he supposed she did. "I can't imagine life without you and Dad." Glancing up from opening another sealed cardboard box, she found Richard's eyes on her. "What's that expression about? Tell me what you're thinking."

Mrs. Noble had returned to her vehicle making it easier for him to reply. "I was thinking if you would marry me we wouldn't have to set this one up, we would be together." He eased up behind her, his arms around her as he pulled her close. "When are you going to give it up and say yes?" He kissed the top of her head, liking her in his arms. "Don't you tire of my asking and want to make it happen?"

For a moment, sadness washed over her. His goodness compared to her digression. That one incident would leave her with regret and haunt her the rest of her life. Almost, she wanted to tell him but the shame was too great. She turned to him laying her head on his shoulder, letting him hold her as he was happy and content. "I take that as a yes," he said.

"Maybe," she replied, "in time." She heard her mother return but Richard's arms brought comfort.

"You know, Mrs. Noble, I think it's time I met with you and Mr. Noble and talked serious business."

Within a month Laura said yes to Richard's constant proposal and now as she listened to the song being played, the one Richard always sang to her…the words touched her heart, "when somebody loves you, its for sure they're going to love you all the way, I'm going to make you happy and you'll make me a pappy come what may." A smile crept across her face. It all felt good and it felt right.

"You look lovely, darling." Florence was in her element, straightening the hem of the dress, touching the veil hanging from the bed post, peeping through the curtains to see if the neighbors had arrived. A light rain around noon promised a good attendance and that's what Florence wanted. "Yours will be the wedding of the year. This dress, wherever did you find it?"

Smiling, Laura reached out to take her mother's hand. "Let's sit, Mom, we'll be on our feet long enough after we take our vows. There are more pictures, but I told them only thirty minutes, and then the toast and cutting the cake." Putting her hands to her face her words were muffled as she said, "thank you for helping with so much. I wanted to do it all but I saw I couldn't."

The door opened just a crack. Then, John stepped inside followed by Timothy. "I hoped you two were in here."

Florence stood straight, "Is everything all right? No candles have exploded have they?"

Chuckling, John shook his head. "Nothing's wrong. We wanted this last opportunity to have a few minutes just the four of us because after today you will be Mr. and Mrs. Worthington. Right now we are still the Nobles." His grin said it all. "Can we do a group hug?"

"Dad you don't fool me a bit, I know that was you crying in the back hall." She put her arms around his shoulders. "Oh, Dad, you feel so frail, I mean when have we felt your top bones so prominent?"

"It's you leaving us," he retorted, quickly. "It's that Beauty and the Beast story Timmy watches."

"Really?" Tim was quick to reply. "You sleep through it." He turned to Laura, "By the way, your and Richard's friend arrived; full suit, quite distinguished, if I may say so. You can tell he's rich." He saw Laura's eyebrows peak. "Well he is and everyone knows. You'd think he was a celebrity the way everyone's flocking around him but Richard's got him in his corner so it will be all right."

"Who are you talking about, Tim?" Laura couldn't imagine anyone going to great lengths to attend.

"Mr. Hargrove. The girls at the door ask who he was related to and he said Laura Noble."

"I did not send him an invitation." Laura said rather quickly from the side of the bed.

"Darling. I did." Her mother offered. "I thought you forgot. I addressed the envelope myself." She gave a slight laugh, "When I remember how you were in your teenage days both boys wanting you to ride home with them and Timmy on the bus with that Tellow kid trying to bully him right after he had surgery, well, your dad had to step in. I knew you would want Tommy to be here for the wedding."

"What ever happened to the Tellow kid?" Laura changed the subject.

"He grew up and now he's a Baptist Preacher." John volunteered. "Talk about divine intervention." He stopped short of explaining what he'd heard. "Laura, honey, are you crying because it's almost time?"

"I wondered if I'd get through this without a bit of nerves." Timmy was handing her a box of tissues.

"It's all right," John went to her putting his arms around her shoulders. "Lean your head on old dad."

"Feels so good; like when I was a little girl, Dad, and you made everything right.

He chuckled. "Well, I tried but sometimes I couldn't so I just held on to you." He raised his head listening, "Isn't that our cue? Timmy, you and I follow your mother, right? And she will be escorted to the front."

"You're right, Dad. We go through the dining room and out the double doors." Timmy teased because there had been much discussion how much easier it would have been to be married in the church they'd attended their whole lives. Laura had insisted she would be married at home. "I told Laura it's a complete waste of that dress not to have this wedding at church…but no, we're here and the pictures will be in mother's backyard under the ivy covered gazebo. Right, Laura?"

"Actually," Florence spoke up from where she'd sat observing her family in their endless clatter. The last years the three had enjoyed each other's banter. "Actually, it is quite beautiful out there, the grass is a carpet and the sky is Laura's backdrop, not to mention the tent, the white cloth covered tables and her signature color has brought color to the whole thing. You did well, Laura. It's beautiful."

"Thank you, Mother." Laura smiled through tears. "I love you all. Thank you for being here for me."

"Right," Timmy nudged his dad, "We could have been fishing."

"We could have been cutting beans," John replied, "But the fellows said they'd see to that." His smile widened thinking of the men's request. It was their plan to shut down long enough to see Laura and Richard married saying they helped raise Laura. They planned to be watching from under the big oak where the white fence separated field and yard. John wondered if they'd remember as he wasn't sure they'd really meant it. Still, he'd left his own request with the servers if his men showed up to see they had refreshments. "Let's go," he said, hearing the music pick up. "Can't be late for your own wedding."

They made their way through the double doors, Tim and Florence being escorted to the front, while John and Laura remained discreetly hidden from the guests view. Laura saw Richard and his two best men take their places as Laura's two attendants stepped from one side of the garden and walked up the aisle. Richard's parents had been shown to their seats when the music first began. Melanie and Crystal looked beautiful in their red off shoulder dresses. Each carried a small replica of Laura's bouquet with lily of the valley and miniature red roses in addition to carrying a long stem rose to be presented to the mothers. Laura counted the seven roses cut from her mother's garden that morning. "A perfect number," her mother said. "What an honor to have grown those for you. What love," Laura had replied, kissing her mom as she held her two best friend's bouquets in her hand. Melanie's little girl was flower girl and Crystal's son Benjamin was the ring bearer. She mentioned them to her mother, "Aren't Crystal and Melanie's little one's sweet?" She saw the frown cross her mother's brow and then it was gone. "Is there a problem I don't know about?"

"It's really nothing except I care because Crystal is your friend, but there's a problem of some sort there, I heard it from a good source that little Ben has far too many bruises and the doctor has to report them," she sighed. "I hate to tell you this. Even Crystal has had a black eye, and wore her arm in a sling for a while." She saw Laura wasn't understanding. "Most people think it's her husband, Robert's bad temper." Determined to change the subject, she said, "What do you think Richard's fellows are up to?"

It had been a joke when Richard's friends from college, Joshua and Jonathan commented at recital they wanted to give something to the fathers and the minister ask what they had in mind. "Can it be a secret?" They asked and he agreed if it wasn't too outlandish and if the bride and groom agreed. Now the wedding party waited to see what they decided. All Laura knew was a bit of laughter had followed their decision and the minister saying, "I get it."

The music that accompanied the maids of honor up the aisle flowed into the song Janene and William Blue were asked to sing. The couple was new to Laura but Florence had become fond of the two through church and recommended them as the wedding singers. Accompanied by her father, Laura stepped into sight while they sang; standing on the rounded steps that led from the dining room into the garden. As her mother said, it was beautiful and this was her first viewing of the complete plan, white with a splash of red in the arrangements at each table. She loved it and now her eyes were on Richard and his smile.

Janene had begun the song, 'I look at you and there you are,' as William waited and then responded, 'we are a story steeped in old, when youth has turned to falter and problems would tempt us sore,' the next line they sang together. 'We will remember this day and our love and we will remember our vows and what we said.… we will guard this love…we will guard it with our lives.' It was their song but it was Laura and Richard's song, too. And then it was time for the walk to where Richard was waiting.

She had taken her place by his side and Crystal was relocating Benjamin when he stepped on Laura's gown and long veil, instantly his eyes darted to his father on the front row as Laura's followed. The expression on Robert's face gave her a moment of despair for the little boy. What she saw appeared threatening. Her eyes strayed to Benjamin's mother and there was fear reflected in Crystal's eyes too.

Laura bent down and placed a kiss on Benjamin's brow then smiled at his father sitting on the second row of chairs. Put at ease, she supposed, Robert smiled back. From that point on the wedding was blessed. Laura felt peace in a way she thought lost the last weeks, now her fears were relieved. The next song was to celebrate the love they'd found. After the vows, and the presenting of rings, the ceremony was coming to a close when the minister said to Laura's maids of honor, "you may now present the rose to the mothers," and then to Richard's groomsmen, "You may present your gift to the fathers to show appreciation." Joshua and Jonathan pulled a bill from their pocket, holding it up for all to see, as the minister laughed and said to both father's, "for some strange reason they thought it appropriate to present you each with a two dollar bill. You will have to ask them the story behind the bill." The Lord's Prayer was sung by Janene and Will and Richard and Laura were declared "man and wife, whosoever God joins together, let no man put asunder. Richard, you may kiss your bride."

"Beautiful ceremony," Richard's father said, "Welcome to the family, Laura." Laura placed a kiss on first Mrs. Worthington's cheek and then Richard's father. "Thank you, I will do my best to make your son happy." From the corner of her eye, Laura saw Tom Hargrove walking toward his car. Then Richard was calling to him. The two shook hands and Tom left. Laura breathed a sigh of relief.

It was late when Richard placed their suitcase in the back seat and glanced at his watch. "Our plane leaves in three hours, I hope we aren't cutting it short on time to drive to the airport."

Laura smiled and leaned her head against the neck brace of the seat. "We normally drive the distance in just a little over two hours." Richard smiled and squeezed her hand. "No problems," she finished. "Right?"

They spent a week basking in the sun in the Bahamas and returned to the apartment Laura rented on Jasper Street. "Let's leave the unpacking until tomorrow," Richard said. "I'm beat and I have to return to work on Monday and your school year begins."

"Are you just tired, or is there something more?" She studied him as he stripped to his shorts and climbed into bed. "Now that we're home you seem different, worried, maybe?" He shook his head. "No?" As weary as she felt she decided to let it go when he seemed to have something to say.

"I forgot to tell you, at the wedding, Tom had an appointment, the reason he didn't wait to talk with you but he said, "tell Laura should old acquaintance be renewed, he would never forget you." Richard yawned, "Isn't that a bit late, we were kids when we fought over you."

So, there was the reason he had become withdrawn. "That made you pensive and moody?" She slid into bed beside him, on one elbow staring down at him. "Does Tom Hargrove still intimidate you?"

"Laura, are you glad you married me?" His eyes held hers.

One hand on his chest, she leaned down to kiss his lips. "Do you have regrets? You ask me over and over and finally I said yes. Are you sorry?" For a moment her eyes were luminous with tears ready to spill over. "We are just home from our honeymoon, I don't understand this?"

"I don't know what to say," he sighed, pulling her onto his chest, his hand threading through her hair, "it suddenly came to me to wonder, why did you finally decide to marry me?"

"I had just moved my things back home and you helped me with this apartment, it dawned on me your kindness, your caring, and I ask myself why was I rejecting your proposal, it came to me how much I love you…what more can I say? It was only a few days when you ask me again and I said yes."

He seemed to relax. She felt the stiffness leave his body. "I won't ask again, Laura. From this day on our life together is built on trust." Turning on his side he pulled her into the hollow of his body. "I love you, Laura."

She lay there, afraid to move, her own body tingling with trepidation. She thought that worry was a thing of the past. They were married, no matter what happened from this day on, the past was gone, only the future remained and they would have a good life but the warning bells sounded and fear rose up to rob her of sleep. She would know soon enough if there were reasons to worry.

The next morning she unpacked the suitcases, pausing to inspect the one little reminder they'd brought back from their honey moon. Wrapped in one of Richard's T-shirts, a nativity set they'd both agreed on. They would treasure it through the years in remembrance of their first days together. "We'll enjoy it our first Christmas right on down to our last," they'd said. "What else could bring us such joy?"

Chapter 2

School began, Richard had returned to work in the family business and the days were good. A month passed and Mrs. Worthington dropped in mid morning on a Saturday. Richard had left for work and Laura was enjoying a cup of coffee. "I'm glad to see you," she said, "join me for a cup of coffee?"

"You know, Laura, I always wanted a daughter but after Richard, J.W. and I couldn't have any more children." She smiled the same smile laced with kindness as her son. "We are happy to have you."

Laura leaned forward to pat her mother in laws hand when a strange sensation hit her stomach. "Please, excuse me. For a moment there, I didn't know what was happening. I feel…" Rising, she raced to the bathroom and when she returned she said, "I don't know what that's about, I haven't eaten anything to turn my stomach and no one at school has a virus or cold, yet, but I was sick to my stomach."

Rather than look concerned, Julia Worthington smiled. "Dear, could you be pregnant?"

"Why would you think that?" Dismay sounded in Laura's voice. "Surely not, it's too soon. "She began to twist her hands together, as she ask again, "Why would you think that?" She felt deathly ill, rising quickly. "I must go back to the…."

When she returned, Julia took her by the hand and led her to the sofa. "Now, lie down and I'll place this damp cloth on your forehead. Don't worry if you are already pregnant. It happens. Practically happened to me, but I lost that little one in the second month. That's when the doctors began to work with me to make my body strong so I could bear a child."

Tears slid down Laura's cheeks. "Thank you. I'm shocked and don't know what to say." She closed her eyes tight. "What will Richard say? We haven't even discussed children…" A second thought crossed her mind, "and I have a class to teach. Will they let me teach if I'm pregnant?" A groan came from Laura. "I am so disappointed in me, Julia, I'm sorry you have to go through this with me."

"I'm honored. Please, if it should be, don't shut me out. Please allow me to share this special time with you." She saw the nausea rolling in on Laura as her skin became a pasty white. She held Laura's hand. "I promise I won't get in the way but I will be here for you."

"Oh, Julia, I am so sick."

Thus began an alliance between Laura and her mother in law. Richard left early for work, Laura dressed for school and conveniently finished morning sickness before she drove to New Haven to teach third grade. She wondered how her own parents would react because Richard's were wonderful. "I've got to tell Richard," she whispered on a particularly sick Saturday morning."

Julia checked on her those days, often arriving before Laura awakened, to straighten the apartment and start laundry. "Dear," Julia replied, "Before long he will notice and then you will see the cut of your man." Julia sit for a minute, just sharing time until the phone rang and she rose up to finish dusting.

It was her mother, "Can you come for Sunday dinner? We've been so busy here on the farm I feel I've not seen you in ages. I actually tried to call Julia and invite her and James Wilson but the phone just rings."

"Mother, Julia just stopped in. I'll let you talk to her." Laura smiled at her mother's refusal to call Richard's dad by his initials. Everyone else did, but not Florence Noble. It had to be his full name.

She heard Julia say, "I'll bring a coconut cake, Florence. No, no problem, as busy as you all are, it's the least I can do." Julia was gathering the dust cloths she always brought, stuffing them in a plastic bag and preparing to go home.

"Why are you so good to me?" Laura asked, hugging her.

"I told you; I always wanted a daughter, Laura, and now I have you and you are giving us a grandchild."

"I haven't told mom and dad," Laura scrubbed at the taste left in her mouth, "and I want to be sure before telling Richard. How far along were you when you lost your first baby?"

Julia picked up her keys from the counter, "I was into the second month but I knew something was wrong. You just feel it." Staring into space, she continued, "It seemed like I was walking on egg shells, not knowing why." She opened the door, "you can get a kit, Laura, or go in to the doctor for confirmation."

"I hear my teacher friends discussing a doctor who is affiliated with the hospital at the Cape but keeps an office in New Haven. That would be convenient since I teach there."

"Whatever you think, Laura. I'm sure you need to start the vitamins and what all is necessary to have a healthy baby." Opening the door, she stepped outside. "I'll see you and Richard tomorrow."

Laura spent the remaining hours ironing before Richard come home. She was just putting away the ironing board when he walked in. "Here, let me take that." Richard carried it to the back door closet. "So, how has your morning gone?"

"Your mother stopped by." He slid into the recliner as he beckoned her near. "We're having lunch with both parents tomorrow at my parent's home."

He chuckled as he pulled her closer. "It's nice the two get along, isn't it? I hear that's not always the case." Peering down into her face, he added, "They think the world of you."

"I hope I never disappoint them, or you."

"How could you ever do that?" He kissed her and gave a sigh of contentment. "This is nice." They sat awhile in comfortable silence until he said, "I probably should tell you, the owner of the big Hardware and lumber Company in New Haven has contacted Dad. He has cancer of the prostate and has decided to sell out because all he and his family have known is to run the business and see to the needs of the community. Long story short, he would like to spend time with family and sell to the Worthington Family."

Laura sat up. "How do you feel about that, does it affect you or us one way or another?"

"Only if we decided to move to New Haven permanently. That would mean raising our family in a small town atmosphere, when the time comes. I'm not sure New Haven even has a library."

"It is extremely limited in stores that I know." Her mind was chasing facts a dozen different ways. "Why is it the hardware and lumber company prospers?"

"Due to the distance for supplies, elsewhere, and Dad says the family has managed it expertly. There are a lot of people wanting to escape big city life and they're flocking to places like New Haven to live though they work in the city. Some are willing to drive two hours each morning and night to their job."

"That's a lot of hours on the road." She scooted off his lap and began to pace. "Have you checked it out?"

"Only in the sense of how many homes are presently being built and Graham Lumber provides supplies."

"There's a new sub-division going up on the North end of town, I pass by it every day." She took a deep breath, "I don't think our budget can stand that expense, yet."

"It might surprise you, if renting a unit is near what we pay rent monthly, it might be arranged."

"You read of this, couples who move too fast end up with all kinds of marital problems, finances are probably the number one reason."

"I'm curious, what would be number two?"

"Fidelity."

"Well we don't have a problem with that. Think about it, wouldn't you love to plan the home we intend to live in the rest of our life and where we'd raise our family?" The thought seemed to energize Richard. "After church and dinner with the folks, why don't we take a drive over and have a look?" He watched her think as she paced. He was coming to understand those little innuendoes that made her truly unique. He thought he knew her as a teenager but she was more than he'd seen on the surface that he loved. Deep down, Laura was a very fine person.

Sunday

"Three families in three different churches, now that really speaks of brotherly love, don't you think?" Richard laughed. "But here we are going to break bread together." Laura was quieter than usual. "Penny for your thoughts, or is there something wrong?"

"Not wrong, just on my mind. What you said about building a home. We don't have any idea what our style is, Richard. We have a miss-match hodge-podge apartment that actually turned out very well. It's…."

"Homey," he supplied. "Well, we could build the house and worry about all that style stuff later. What's important is the location and enough rooms that we don't have to build on in a couple of years when the kids start coming."

Richard slowed and pulled to the side of the road. Leaning his arms on the steering wheel, he sat there staring at Laura. "Hon, what's really bothering you?" She sat staring at the floor mat, her body had gone stiff and her mind was a dull mass, if it was a motor it was in neutral. He was holding her hand now. "I can tell something is on your mind."

She shrugged. "I need a vacation, I guess. We return from our honeymoon, happy but tired and I began a week of teaching twenty five babies, really, with more energy than Hoover Dam." She heard him chuckle. "I'm sorry I'm such a dud today. If we can go back to the apartment at a reasonable hour, maybe I can take a nap. I don't know why but I'm exhausted."

Patting her hand first, Richard put the car in gear and pulled back onto the road. "We can do that," he said. "Maybe seeing your folks will help."

Her dad was walking across the yard. She went to meet him and when they hugged she felt again the boniness of his shoulders. "Dad, are you all right? Seems like I feel something different in you."

"Nothing's wrong with me that time won't fix." He said, but she noticed he didn't look up. She stopped walking by his side, standing still until he turned. "What's wrong babe; did you pick up a rock? Why are you standing there?" He always called her babe when he was trying to comfort her.

"Dad, you'd tell me if something's wrong, wouldn't you?" Now she caught up to where he waited for her. "I feel it, Dad. What's wrong?"

He looked crestfallen; his face rearranged itself a dozen times before he spoke. "I didn't want you to know, yet."

"Is it you or Mom? What don't you want me to know?" Fear sliced through her. "I can handle it, Dad."

"It's me. Remember about ten years ago, I dealt with a few problems and we got that taken care of?"

"Yeah."

"It's back but this time there's a spot on my lungs."

"Now?" Harvest had just begun and it was a fast paced crucial time. "Will you be able to work?"

"I have to."

She felt a sickness in the middle of her chest, an ache she couldn't put down. "Dad, if I gave up the teaching job, I could help you."

"You just started, babe."

"What if I came after school?"

He reached across to give her a quick hug. "I always like you around but I think that might overload you." They'd reached the back door. "Don't let on like you know, I promised your mom we'd keep a light atmosphere since your in-laws are joining us."

"It doesn't matter, Dad, they'd understand." She wiped her eyes of the tears that kept trying to fall. "I'm the sucker here, I want to bawl my head off but for Mom I'll keep a happy face." She turned to touch his shirt sleeve. "Dad, I love you. Whatever you need, tell me and I'll do my best."

"You always have, Laurie, you always have."

It was later, they were driving to Newhaven when Richard asked, "What's wrong, Laura, you are too quiet."

"I have a lot on my mind." She wasn't ready to share the problem of someone so dear. That thought shamed her. This was her husband and he was giving her a puzzled stare. "Don't worry, when I'm up to it, I'll talk to you about it, right now with the fatigue I just can't. Please, try to understand."

"You underestimate me, Laura. I care about what concerns you and I'll always listen." But she had laid her head back against the neck supports and was fast asleep. For a minute he considered whether to turn back but she was sleeping so he went on. It did bother him that she seemed weary to the bone.

He had circled the new development several times, when not watching the roadside he hit a bump and it woke Laura. She sat up, looking around as she yawned behind her hand. "Have you found anything?"

"Surprisingly, I haven't. I thought it would appeal to me but somehow it just doesn't fit."

She was trying to digest his words when he said, "Let's just drive through and see what this town is like on Sunday." They were a good fifteen or twenty minutes into the drive when Laura saw a lane that led up a slight knoll to an old house with a barn behind it, the barn was near collapse, but the setting the house and barns claimed was beautiful. "Someone keeps this mowed, don't they?" Richard remarked.

"Look," she pointed to a swing made out of an old tire hanging down some twenty feet from a huge oak. "I always wanted a swing like that but dad said the limbs on our trees were not safe." She was smiling. He was pulling into the drive, the lane behind them. "Let's get out and walk around, you can tell the house is abandoned and the poor old barn is near falling."

"This is probably five acres. Most loans in real estate require a certain amount of acreage. What would you think if we sought out the owner of this property with the intention to build in the future if it looks like we'd be happy here in New Haven?"

"It's a beautiful property, but it may be pricey because of that. I can't believe someone hasn't snapped it up." The line of trees and the lay of the land did appeal to her.

"Most people want the convenience of a housing development, though one with more than a lot's space, I'd think. Who wants to be in hollering distance of their neighbour?" She laughed at his words. "You need to do that more often."

"What?" She tilt her head wondering what he meant.

"Laugh, Laura. You have become so quiet, lately, it scares me." He reached for her hand and led her to the nearest oak, leaning against it and pulling her against his body. They stood looking out onto the yards charm, the serenity of the place and he felt her relax.

"Is that true, that my being quiet scares you?"

"Yes, it does. I wonder, daily, whether you are happy, even though I said we'd go forward on trust, that's not enough, I worry whether you are as committed as…" She turned to face him. He studied her expression.

"I think I must tell you. I wanted to keep it to myself until I knew for sure."

His heart sank. "Laura, are you ill?"

She saw the color drain from his face, those soft eyes turn sad and she couldn't stand it. Taking his face between her hands, she swallowed and tried to say the words, knowing she alone held the key to why telling him was so hard. "Richard, I think I'm pregnant." He practically slumped against the tree. "You are thinking of a house and I'm still accepting the possibility that I'm pregnant, this soon."

Suddenly he was squeezing her so tight she could barely breathe as she felt the rumble of laughter build in his chest, until it exploded outside his body. "Is that it?" He lifted her up; hugging her all the while his arms seemed to multiply. "Oh, my goodness, I imagined everything, that you were going to leave me and once but only once the thought there was someone else…but why else would you leave me?"

Now he held her arm's length away. "Is that why you are so tired? If so, this will be a busy little baby, won't it? I bet it's a boy." His own exuberance, at the moment, was high on the scale while Laura had wilted in his arms. With all ease he picked her up and carried her to the car, kissing her on the way.

Amused at his enthusiasm, she could only succumb to the safety of this big hearted man's energy. "Could you carry me around school, you think?" She teased and that made him happy.

"What did the doctor say?"

"My appointment is next Thursday with a doctor Hutchens here in New Haven."

Placing her in the passenger seat, and leaning on the door he absorbed the information. "I'll go with you."

Suddenly she felt better. The matter she had held close to her chest, eating away, was now out in the open. There was no need for further discussion. He was happy. That was all that mattered.

The next morning Julia came as usual. "Just to check on you," she said. "How are you this morning?"

A slight smile accompanied Laura's words. "I told Richard I thought I must be pregnant. I didn't tell him you knew." Julia, as demonstrative as her son, grabbed Laura and hugged her. "He was happy," Laura managed to squeeze out. "And he's going to the doctor with me." Julia beamed, nodding approval.

Chapter 3

"So, you folks live in New Haven?" Dr. Hutchens was a big man, taller than Richard. "You don't?" He had glanced up from the clipboard to their reply. "Then what brings you to New Haven's Clinic?" He flipped his wrist to see the time on his watch. "Almost after hours, why's that?"

"I'm teaching at New Haven this year." Laura focused on the doctor. "My husband works elsewhere."

"Uh, huh." He lay down the clipboard, took her hand and found her pulse, then using the stet checked her ears, throat, and nose and seemed satisfied. "Preliminaries," he said. "I had Clara run the pregnancy test and it does in deed say you are pregnant. You appear in good health, therefore I will prescribe the vitamins we want you on and I'll expect to see you back in I'd say a month, unless you deem otherwise."

He shook Richard's hand and then Laura's. "In your mind, Mrs. Worthington, does anything feel out of place or other than the symptom of morning sickness you mentioned, are there things we need to know?" She shook her head, meaning no and rose up to leave. "Next time I see you folks I won't be wearing my white doctor's coat. We'll just forget I know you and start from there." He chuckled quietly. Addressing Richard who was a bit finicky and felt like a fifth wheel, he asked, "Do you have any questions? And, I or we won't know the gender until about the third month as far as I'm concerned."

They were quiet on the way home. "What are you thinking?" He finally asked her.

"To tell you the truth, I am dead tired and not thinking at all unless a reminder now and then this is real." She tried to scoot to sit straighter but the seat belt constrained her. "I guess I thought of the changes coming to our home." She stared at Richard. "What are your thoughts?"

"Making sure you like the property, Laura, before I bid on it."

"I do but to build is so expensive and I'm not sure about that."

"I've been saving since I was two years old and then my grandmother on Dad's side left me a small bit of money." Both hands on the wheel, he did a rap on the top. "That's my happy sign," he said.

Two weeks later, the big trucks drove down the lane where the old Emerson Farm barn had collapsed and when the gusts came, the old house fell nearly into the road but wind drove it onto the newly bought land Richard purchased. A part of history went with the two to the dump while the place was being cleared of all the debris in preparation for a new home.

Crystal was substitute teaching that week and came in to Laura's room. "Hey," the ever bubbly person inside Crystal gave Laura a hug. "Is it true, someone from Walker has bought the old Emerson Farm place?" She caught the slow flush of color on Laura's cheeks. "My goodness, girl, is it you and Richard?"

"Fraid so." A moment of embarrassment claimed Laura. "It wasn't my doing, but Richard was afraid if we waited it would be gone."

"So you are building a home here?" Crystal was nodding, "but why New Haven when you only teach here?"

"Worthington Hardware has bought out the one in Newhaven due to the owner's health."

"Well, girl, I'm glad you will be close enough for us to holler." Glancing at the clock Crystal started for the door. "It will be such fun, but I gotta go now. Bye."

They poured over book after book of house plans. "Remember, Laura, it has to be large enough for a growing family and I'd say you are pretty fertile getting pregnant on our honeymoon."

She flinched. "I had no idea," she said lamely. "I thought you were glad."

"I am but think how many couples struggle for years to be pregnant." He chuckled. "We're blessed."

Finally. In the second week they found a plan and the builder began the foundation. There was a spring in Richard's step. "I am so happy," he said. Laura smiled. If it weren't for her father's illness….

Two weeks later, the studs were going up. It was a scene of activity. Richard loved it. Laura's mind was on other things. She asked permission to go with her parents for her dad's appointment. Once granted it was her responsibility to find a substitute for the day she was away. She thought of Crystal. Instead of calling she decided to drop by her home. Crystal answered the door bell's ring. Startled, she could not help but notice Crystal's black eye. "Why Laura, come in. This?" She pointed up to her eye. "Just a little mother-son fiasco and I got the worst end of the deal, we were sparring, you know with boxing gloves. Don't worry about it." Laura saw Benjamin sneak out of the room trying hard not to look at his mother.

It did worry her. Still, she would leave the next morning with her parents for her dad's appointment in St. Louis. Richard worried whether the ride would hurt her. "No, I'm not that far along. I suspect our baby is the size of a tadpole swimming around." That made him smile. "Go to work, so I can dress."

They were quiet the first miles but the beauty of the landscape brought them around. "The color of the foliage is truly beautiful," John remarked. "I wish we could drive over on the East Coast and see theirs. But I do believe this is the nearest we'll see since this time of year is harvest for us."

"Maybe when you retire, we can go," Florence added. "Let's just thank the Lord we have this to compensate until that time."

"There's lots of things I'd like to do before I leave this old world." John's voice dropped lower as though he was talking to himself. "I'd like to take a driving trip back out west, Colorado, Nevada and maybe on up to, is it Idaho we like on our states, Flo?" Pausing a moment, he glanced her way and continued; "Now we saw the Grand Canyon but not the heart of it, it was windy and the guide wouldn't let us go."

"So we traveled through Death Valley going up into the Red Wood Forrest, "she offered, "Scariest ride of my life when we got up on that mountain and the sign said, "no vehicles without chains from this point, no turn-a -rounds and erosion to the road from this point on." Laughing she finished, "We had none of the mentioned items at the bottom of the warning sign, either, and suddenly there stood a couple we'd seen in Las Vegas and we each befriended the other, drew comfort from added number and made plans to leave after spending the night."

"What happened to the friends you made?" They were having such fun reminiscing, Laura was interested.

"They're the ones we traveled with the remaining part of the week."

Entranced in their lively banter and week's joy of travel, they were soon in St. Louis on the doctor's parking lot. From that point on seriousness sit in and turned to sadness. After the preliminary task, the doctor asked, "Do you hurt anywhere?" He sit on the stool, looking direct into John's eyes. "Now's the time to write the prescriptions, that take care of such, if you do." How many times had he been through this and he knew John would think, first to deny it all, except this man was different.

"How much time do I have, Doc?" They were two men respectful of each other, getting down to business.

"Two years, John. But it's up to you, your attitude. You are in general good health but if the spot on your liver is cancer, and the results will be back in about ten days, then we'll know. It has already set up camp in your lungs but when it goes to the liver there's little we can do. If you smoke, quit."

John stood, the doctor following suite, and the two embraced. One a man of the land who stayed behind, the other his friend who left the community, studied abroad, coming back to land a position where he ended up helping many from his home town. "Keep up the good work, Lawrence," John said.

"You do the same." He turned to Florence, taking her hand. "This man's a steward of the land, Flo. Help him take care of himself and you do the same." Next, he held out his arms to Laura, "Laura, I'm sorry we missed your wedding. I hadn't taken a vacation in years and our trip was scheduled when your invitation arrived."

Laura smiled through tears. "I'm glad you could get away. Did you enjoy your vacation?" Lawrence nodded. A man of composure, he ran a hand through his hair, the slight tremor of his fingers a glimpse into the true feelings he had for her father. Laura kissed his cheek and turned away, ready to leave.

"You want me to drive?" John was already sliding behind the wheel. Florence, tight lipped, sat rigid in her seat and Laura climbed into the back, choking on the misery of her thoughts. Nothing changed for the present and yet it had, they'd experienced the death knell; the end of life as they'd known it.

They passed through the suburbs, each noticing the practice and upkeep of the people, neither making remarks nor caring if one was well kept and the next sliding into disrepair as on and on they went finding the Interstate, gliding along, aware traffic was picking up and then slowing. It came to John, they had not eaten and there was a pregnant lady on board. "Laura, you hungry?" He took the first exit. "I know where we are and there's a good place ahead. Dinner is about to be served."

"I can take it or leave it, Dad," she replied. "How about you, Mom?" Florence nodded, afraid to speak, lest she cry. She knew, for months she would swallow her own sorrow to make life easier for the rest.

To her surprise, Florence warmed to the grilled chicken's moistness, the crisp salad and a new cut of potato wedges she wasn't used to and John was eating like a healthy man. Her eyes strayed to Laura's plate, "How are they dear?" Plump dumplings laced with chunks of chicken appeared appetizing enough but Laura was having difficulty. Reaching across, Florence took her child's hand, "Sweetheart, let's do this the best we can. We really don't know in this life who will be here longest, so it's up to us to make the best of each day, find our joy and keep it. That's what God expects and we are going to do it with his help." Fresh tears slid down Laura's face as she slid off her seat and headed for the rest room. "Don't let that disturb your dinner," Florence said to John. "It's always been in God's hands. She's pregnant. In a month or so, you'll see, Laura will handle this with the love she has for you. You're a blessed, Dad."

"Thank you for going with us, Babe," John hugged her, patting her head to his shoulder. "I love you."

"A lot of help I was," Laura's words were muffled. "You wouldn't even let me drive."

"Maybe next time," he replied. "I'll go back to Larry for a while, and then change over closer to home."

Her tiredness was as much emotional as physical. Laura drove to the apartment, left the door unlocked and climbed on the couch, laying her head on the pillows too exhausted to take off her shoes, leaving her feet dangling. Thinking sleep would not come, she drift off. It was time for the evening bell to ring; someone else would oversee the children to the buses.

Sleep does not keep time, nor do dreams allow happiness when one is sad. She was floundering in her own tiredness, trying to walk the hall of the elementary building and it kept getting longer. There was only the sound of the leather souls of her shoes clicking along. She would not sleep, her body was too restless. But she did. Aware of the drone of the refrigerator in the other room and the pendulum of Richard's grandmother's clock keeping time. She heard someone groan.

"Laura, wake up. Laura, Sweetie, it's me, Crystal." She knew that voice and the hand that was on her. "Laura, you're having a bad dream, love, groans and all. Come on, you've slept enough. Get up."

She tried but her body weighed a thousand pounds. Opening her eyes she saw Crystal and already sitting in front of the television at the far end of the room, Benjamin was watching Sponge Bob.

"I took the liberty of getting him settled for a few minutes. He's about as tired as you." Crystal pushed her bottom against Laura's legs and leaned to look down on her friend. "You didn't need that dream, whatever it was. Now…can I put something together for Richard's supper and let you rest?"

Giving a nervous giggle, Laura asked, "You cook now?" Sharing a room in college, Crystal's contribution was a lot of burnt offerings.

"I had to learn," she quipped. "Scorched food does not go over well at our house. So what shall I organize for the Lord of the Manor's meal time delight?"

"Thanks," Laura pulled to a sitting position. "Hi Benjamin," she called across the room.

"He won't hear you. He zones everything out. Bob Square pants is important, more than family, even."

"How did the day go? Were my children good?"

"Perfect," Crystal nodded, beaming with delight. "I loosened them up a bit for you. They had your stiffness." Seeing Laura's expression, she burst into laughter; full Crystal style with a snort or two. "I love those kids, you are doing a great job and I hope you keep me in mind if you need a sub. Robert approves of you and already has said if I could help anyone you're the one." She was completely unreserved, "hubba-hubba. He likes you and Richard, and my Robert is not one to be drawn in easily."

She left soon after. Laura folded the afghan she had somehow managed to wrap around her body and saw them to the door. Benjamin allowed her kiss on the cheek and that pleased her. Left to herself, Laura lay back on the pillow meaning to think the day through. Instead, Richard found her there and started the evening meal, prepared the table and sank into the rocking chair left from his grandmother's home and sat watching her sleep. A faint color had come into her cheeks but the shadow of tears shed remained.

"Oh, my goodness," she came awake hearing Richard drop the lid off the green beans onto the stove. "I won't sleep a wink." Getting to her feet, she stood for a moment as the world swirled around her. "I'm so sorry." He was chuckling. She became aware of the table sit, and the aroma of food in the air. He reached her just as she swooned. "I thought I was over morning sickness."

"Got news for you, it's five thirty three in the evening and it's probably the way you were huddled on the sofa. But I didn't dare disturb you, my dear, you were sawing logs. Snoring even, I got it on tape."

"You didn't." He was seating her at the table, kissing her, and handing her a wet wash cloth for her hands. He poured tea in the glasses and sit across from her. There was a rice-ham-vegetable stir fry, a fresh Caesars salad and fluffy rolls they'd found in a package in the stores frozen section. "It looks marvelous. To think I slept through the whole preparation. I guess this means I do dishes?"

In the next weeks when she visited the house sight, she asked "How in the world are you coming along this fast, Mo Jessup?" Laura, climbed the steps the builder had nailed together expressly for her. "They help us to," he'd reminded her when she protested his kindness. "And how do we move along? Well, there's a secret there we're keeping from the general public, those nosey creatures who come and stand and gawk and give endless suggestions how we could do better." A twinkle in his eye let her know he was teasing. "We do have the gawkers though, and the suggesters. Is that a word?"

"It is for us," she replied, her grin as large as his. "I enjoy your banter, immensely. We don't have much of that these days."

"I'm sorry about your Dad, Laura, he's a good man." For a moment he let the word sink in. Then, to dispel the gloom he took her hand and led her down a row of studs on each side of a four foot width. "This is your hallway and Richard said you don't want a long hall, so we have put a bath here, then across the end there are two bedrooms with a bath in between but we have to back track just a short hall here to the master suite." She stepped carefully over a piece of two by four.

"Careful there, I had my daughter's Bryan come in before he left for conditioning for the basketball team to sweep up. I said, "Now Bryan, Miss Laura's comin' and we can't have nothing in the floor to trip over. *Guess he missed a piece.*" Mo stooped, picked up the board and stacked it in the space between studs. "Oh, now I get it, we're nailing boards between studs in places you might want to hang a picture or something. And say, did you consider that first room just off the kitchen we discussed last time would make a fine office because you've got the pantry lined up across from the utility room as you come in the back door." Her expression was one of not knowing. Perhaps it was all a bit much to handle.

"Is it too much to absorb?" He stopped to wait for her answer. "We want this to be exactly as you wish. When the sheetrock starts going in, space will be defined and you can see where it's going."

"I studied the plan, Mo. You don't have to worry and if it appears too confined, give me a chance to move a wall if we have to before it's all battened down, but since the studs are in I can pretty much see the plan and I like it. I like how the wall turns there at the kitchen and where the refrigerator sets people won't be seeing my messiness." Mo was grinning as though he'd heard that before.

"Here's your master suite. What do you think? It's away from the other sleeping areas, looks out onto the back yard with its own little sitting porch and the bathroom is to die for. I have been privileged to build only one other in a rural home where the bath is as grand as this one will be. Man. My own lacks when compared to this and I have to keep a pretty good plan to show those who want to see before agreeing to my building their home and I don't blame them." He glanced at his watch wondering where was Richard?

Laura was drawn to the spot where the small veranda would look out onto the yard but there was a question as to where they would keep a nursery. "Ah, Mo? Did Richard tell you about the nursery?"

His grin was as large as the sink in the bathroom. "Did he, ever? Congratulations, again." Now, he opened one of a set of doors where the wall slipped into the room, "Ta-da." He spread a hand motioning her in. "Thought it was a closet, didn't you? It has a window, Richard said it must, but the idea is when all the children are grown you can turn this into another closet or dressing room, it's a perfect size."

She hugged him. "Right now, that's probably the most important room of all, to me."

"Richard said as much. Did you notice, this is the only finished part and the only one where we've hung the doors? Richard said, just do it because your focus is on the little one and he wouldn't have it any other way." Mo scratched his head, "By the way, where is he?"

"Didn't he text you?" Concerned, she took her own cell from her pocket as Mo fished for his. "That was around three, Mo. But he called me and said a truck had come in he had to help unload, one man is out on delivery." Mo was grinning as he pointed to his phone. The text was there. "You forgot to look, didn't you?" Mo was nodding. "Well, thanks for the tour. We have our second parent-teacher night and I'm headed back to school to prepare the room. I guess next week I can visualize the upstairs?"

"You bet. It's a large home, Laura. Is there a reason for the double suites upstairs?"

"It's more than I dreamed, Mo. But there's room for change as children grow and become teenagers, or if a parent moves in we might have to take a room upstairs and give up the master suite. I thought it seemed humongous compared to the homes we grew up in but Richard said let's build once and not have to go through the hassle of add-ons."

"I don't agree with the one running a home having to give up their space, Laura. That's where stair chairs come in, you know where they attach to the wall and the elderly or handicapped sit in the chair and it takes them up or down. Now that's just me." He let the thought soak in. "What do you think?"

"Well, that's an idea, then there's the basement with a walk out and plenty of windows. It may begin life as our social spin but there's such potential to this house. You're doing a great job…just one thing, do you leave behind a house keeper?"

Open house proved, as usual, nerve-wracking. The invitations sent home clearly said adults only but almost every parent ignored that part making it difficult to speak to them about their child's progress or need when the child was hanging off the parents arm or around the neck and as in one case strapped to dad's back because dad was nearly six and a half feet tall with the physique of a line-backer.

It was Benjamin claimed her heart. Crystal and Robert were almost the last ones. "We couldn't leave Ben with a sitter this late," Crystal explained and Robert was quick to say he just drove in from Mississippi; a delivery he had to handle himself. Laura noticed Benjamin walked with a limp as he took a seat on the back row, good kid that he was he had been prompted and she wondered if threatened. There was a brittleness about each one. Were they afraid she would see beyond appearance?

"We are having Benjamin moved to your class room." Crystal seemed to edge behind Robert as he boldly stated something rules were established that forbid parents from instigating such when their child was already fitting in with another teacher and group of peers.

"I didn't realize you could do that once the school year was under way unless there's academic reasoning, not that I wouldn't appreciate your child. Benjamin." She hastily added staring down at the floor.

Robert was laughing. "We ask for you in the beginning to be his teacher. I'm surprised they didn't tell you. Now we are demanding he be moved. His teacher isn't there on a regular basis. Subs mess up and since Crystal is your substitute, that means he will have one or both of you at all times." He willed her to meet his gaze. "We don't like our teacher missing and another one chosen."

"Mrs. Berry is missing because they have to regulate her meds and they need her there, the other thing is she is taking radiation treatments. We can afford to be graciously accepting of her situation."

"I beg to differ, hell we don't beg, I don't see Mrs. Berry's health issues should hold my son hostage."

His voice had risen. "I guess I haven't thought to see it that way," Laura answered softly.

A bit frayed around the edges, Laura was happy to be met at the door. Richard, pulled her close, gave her a peck on the cheek and then led her to the sofa. He had a glass of milk on the side table. "I don't figure you need any caffeine this late, do you?" He studied her a minute then asked, "Do you want to talk about it?"

"Do I look that bad?" She sighed slipping her shoes off and putting her feet up on the sofa. "One particular set of parents and to top it off, it's Crystal and Robert. I feel deeply that man needs anger management."

"It runs in the family. The reason I know is in the early days the family moved around a lot."

"They transferred Benjamin to my room and now I'll have to deal with Robert even more."

"The grapevine gossip says Robert has over extended himself. He will be looking for work elsewhere."

On Saturday morning, Richard let her sleep late while he worked on landscaping for the new house at the kitchen table. They were scheduled to pick out bathroom fixtures, the works and then move on to flooring. The granite samples were in, according to Mo and the tiles for any room. The reason, not that they were ready to install but needed to be ordered to be certain their first choices were available. But old habits die hard. Eight o'clock she came wandering in to find him.

"You are awfully quiet in here," she said, stooping to nuzzle his neck, knowing his hands would come back of her, and pull her closer to kiss her. He was quite the loving husband, considerate and always the gentleman opening the door, putting her into the car and she appreciated him. She supposed there were women who would give anything to have the security Richard offered. She had spent considerable time trying to figure out why Crystal stayed with Robert. Educated and trained in all the social niceties a girl could want Crystal was brought up by mid-class parents who also could not understand why she chose Robert but Crystal found him exciting and on the wild side when they were dating. Now she lived with what she had chosen if he didn't kill her first. Crystal could fend for herself, she supposed, it was Benjamin she worried about.

"Are you ready to pick out commodes, sinks, bathtubs and showers? Because they're all set up for us this afternoon, even the tiles, the wall racks. It's all ready and amazing and exciting at the same time."

She lingered with her head on his shoulder, standing with her body against the back of his chair. "Then I suppose I should wear clothes, right?"

He chuckled, "Well the guys probably wouldn't mind you in your house coat, they just do their job but those women appear a bit carpy, I notice if one gets a haircut they all do, eventually, and they don't like men not having to wear shirts or reading the scripture half naked."

"You know this how?"

"I was just lurking around the water cooler, listening to that sad story that's been going around for ages." She felt the wave of laughter move through him, punched his shoulder and moved away.

"You know, Hon, we might visit the church in New Haven and meet a few people. I'd say knowing a few reliable Christian folks would be a great help with this house being built, what do you say?"

She crossed back over to where he sit. "You mean," she began, then cut loose. "I should know what these ladies of the night are like on other days?" She thought for a minute. "No. I want a good reliable Christian friend and one I can count on if I want to discuss something whether holy or disturbing."

"Hmmm," he said, looking up. "You have my attention. Am I not good at any of those things?"

"Nope, not it. If I want to go out one night and dance and have a bang up good time without the alcohol, of course, but there has to be something besides eat and go to bed and I want you right there with me."

"What do you think is missing in our lives if you have those hidden desires? Is it me? Am I that dull and boring?" He pushed back from the table. "You've got my attention, what's going on?"

"It's crazy," she replied. "I'm exhausted. Concerned over Dad and now Crystal and Benjamin, yet I think there's something we are missing out on."

"Not to mention we are expecting our first child. Isn't that supposed to do the trick…I mean occupy your mind?" His expression was genuine confusement. "If you aren't happy, Laura, then I shouldn't be either."

"I think I'm just at odds with the world since Dad's been given such a sad prognosis. It's thrown me and I don't know how to go beyond it. I love you, Richard, with all my heart. But you can't give this feeling to me that I need to get through every day. It's like I know he is leaving and I'm already grieving the loss."

"Then we do need to search out a new church. Both of us are believers but we aren't exercising that faith. The Bible says to associate with believers, that way we lift each other up, we give and receive. Isn't that right?"

"I think that's how it works." Shaking her head, she leaned back trying to release the tension in her neck and shoulders. "I didn't mean to open a whole new can of worms." She walked over to Richard. He opened his arms and she walked into them, wrapping her own around his body, "What would I do without you?"

"I pray that's one thing we never know." They stood there awhile. "Since we are going to live in New Haven, shall we try the church and see if we like the pastor's way of ministering?"

"I've thought about that, probably some of my students would be there and it would feel right."

"Or, we could try that little adobe mission down on the corner. Just teasin.' This Sunday or next?"

"I think Sunday if we aren't' worn out from this afternoon's work." Hugging Richard, she left to get ready for the afternoon wondering about the choices they would make. Before leaving she and Richard looked through the rooms, the little apartment had become home, "I don't know if I can do this," She whispered. "What if I mess up?"

"The worse that can happen won't affect our love or our health, will it?" She shook her head, no. "Then we are all right, aren't we? We might have to use what we choose for awhile, but there's change."

She didn't know if she could pin down the reason she felt so gloomy. She believed she used to smile and joke around. Whether it was being pregnant was making her serious and an all around different person than she used to be, or, was it the sin she had done before marrying Richard that was eating her up inside? And the loss of one she loved so much dying, she couldn't eat as much because her dad was having problems and it saddened her knowing she must eat for the baby forming inside her body.

"Honey, if you are still worrying about deciding on the fixtures for the house, it's not that big a deal."

"I guess it's everything put together, Richard. We are young to be building a home of this proportion, aren't we? Then it's the thing with Dad's health and that terrible prognosis the doctor said, outright, he did not cushion his words with hope and I seem to dwell on that." She took a deep breath and then there's me…a baby growing inside of my body." For the first time she laughed, meeting his startled eyes. "I know, it is pure laughter, isn't it? To think a body can produce another, in the form of a little baby."

"I like that on you, Laura," He reached over to squeeze her hand. "That was pure music to me. Maybe you could try that, when you have moments of doubt just think of the baby and smile. That's what I do."

"Really?" She found that interesting. "I hadn't thought what was motivating you."

"It's not just the baby, which I'm very proud is on the way, it's us. You motivate me. I'm a happy man."

"Okay," she mustered enthusiasm, "Let's go in here and rock the boat. Sinks, showers and commodes, here we come." She threw a hand in the air and gave a three "hip hip hip, hurray!" They exited the car laughing. He picked her up to his height and kissed her firm on the mouth before sitting her down in front of two elderly women walking down the sidewalk.

"We're having a baby," he said, as though they needed an explanation and the two smiled brightly.

Three hours later, they exited the building, with a considerably long statement with dollar signs all over it. "My yearly salary won't cover that," she remarked. "Does it bother you?"

"Nope. My sweet little grandmother is covering this part of the construction and she would be glad."

"You're sure there's not something else you'd rather spend your inheritance on?"

"Nope. I'm good."

Glancing across the street, Laura thought she saw Crystal entering, with Benjamin behind her. She read Delta Emergency Services on the sign over head. "Give me a minute, I think I should check on Crystal."

She found Crystal and Benjamin sitting in the far corner of the room. "Crystal," she lay a hand on her friends shoulder and felt her flinch. "What has happened?" At her question, Crystal turned full faced toward her.

"My nose is broke. Probably in three places and Ben may have a broken arm."

"Why? What has happened we were inside the building and I haven't heard. Was there an accident?"

"The accident happened at home." Crystal's words were crisp and resolute. "Come off it, Laura. You know Robert has an anger issue and we," she glanced quickly to Benjamin, "we are Robert's hitting post. I may have taken it all these years alone, but Ben can't, I won't let him. So here we are."

"What happens next? Will you go home or have to go somewhere else?"

"We will have to be really frugal this first month but after that I will have my own money and can afford an apartment."

"Do you need money, Crystal? I have a little to spare." She thought a moment, and said, "You are welcome to our sofa if you like. You know when I rented I didn't realize we were getting married so soon and then I got ashamed of Richard asking so often and said yes, next thing you know I have him in the apartment and for us it really doesn't matter that there's not a second bedroom because we aren't there, but you are welcome to the sofa if you want."

"Thanks, Laura. We will have to learn to fend for ourselves, one way or another." She struggled with the cotton looped over her nose meant to soak up the blood. "I can't see what I'm doing; it feels as though it's slipping."

"May I do this for you?" Crystal nodded and Laura lift the cotton strip and placed it closer to her eyes. The blood was trying to clot up next to her cheek area and running free from a second break. "It looks terrible, Crystal. I'm so sorry this happened." She sighed deeply concerned. "Really, Richard and I are going to talk to the builder this afternoon, if you want to take Benjamin in out of the chaos, feel free. I'll give you the key if you think you might." She could see uncertainty written on her friend's face. "Here. This makes it easier to decide." She laid the key in Crystal's hand. "Just don't lose it, I've already misplaced one. Let Benjamin watch t.v.

awhile and if you are hungry there's food in frig. Mainly be safe, don't worry about us and we'll be home before dark."

"We may have a couple staying overnight with us. Crystal has gotten out and yes, I think it was as bad as we thought. Her nose is a mess. He must have gotten really rough before she could collect Benjamin and leave."

"I've seen Robert's anger. When that temper kicks in no one knows how far he'll go." His voice played out, leaving her to question.

"Would he blame us?" A streak of fear entered her thoughts. "Why would he blame us?"

"If we help her, Laura." There was a sound in his voice she hadn't heard before. She stared at him as he let his foot off the brake and pressed the gas pedal. The car shot forward.

"Have I upset you, Richard?" His lips had formed a hard straight line and he was sitting straight as a pin, his shoulders stiff. "I have and I don't understand how helping a woman who has been battered by her husband and whose child possibly has a broken arm at the expense of his own father is causing trouble between us. What is wrong with this picture?"

"Nothing, if he doesn't come after us. Think, Laura, for God's sake from now on think before you act."

"Are you afraid of him, Richard?"

"I'm afraid for you, Laura, for Crystal and Benjamin. When Robert loses his temper, there's usually hell to pay and I don't want us even remotely connected."

"Has he done something before that I don't know about?" Richard gunned the motor and they moved faster down the road, speeding out into the country lane, a mile from New Haven, moving past the Shining Light Church and Pastor Merkel's home where his wife and small son saw them pass by and waved.

"I heard an interesting piece of information yesterday," he spoke after a lengthy silence. "I'll drive past our turn and show you the next home. I don't think you've been further on the road, have you?" She shook her head, watching as a white fence came into sight edging the road and running each side of the property, while marking the drive that led through a line of trees much like bordered their lane. "This property belongs to Dr. Hutchens. It seems he invented some little device useful to his calling and has made enough money from it to build a home."

"Nice," she admitted. "You don't know him?"

"I only met him with you the day of your appointment. I remember hearing something about his invention, but not making connection he was the doctor lived in the next town over."

"We shouldn't have to compete with what a doctor does, especially a wealthy one," she said. "Let's determine right now we live our life as we wish but not catering to stay up with the Jones or as in this case the Hutchens." He nodded but didn't say anything. She could tell his mind was on Robert's history.

Mo was waiting when they pulled into the building site. "Come on in," he greet them as he pecked a kiss on Laura's cheek. "How you feelin', Hon?" He saw her eyes dart to Richard. "Don't worry, I won't tell anyone else, it's your story but if you are pregnant, then that might influence your choice on a few things. Let's start with the kitchen," he said. "Justa movin' on up."

It was when Richard received a phone call and went outside trying to find signal, Laura decided to ask Mo's opinion.

"Mo, have you worked for Robert and Crystal Carrington?"

He glanced up quickly from going through a stack of floor samples. "Yes, I did and I wouldn't recommend you become involved with those two." He gave a deep sigh. "They bicker continually. It becomes a drain on your spirit." He thought a moment and started to say something but then didn't.

She sensed he wanted to say more but thought better of it. "I hope we don't have that affect on you."

"No," he drawled the response out slowly, "I don't know if you know them very well, but it seemed to me and some of the men that he hit her, you know, roughed her up and we couldn't stand to see that little boy wearing bruises. She was as bad as the daddy, because she covered it up, tried to, anyway."

"You built their home?" Laura began to study the different floor samples.

"No, we remodeled the front of the house and installed a new kitchen and bath, the rest they did themselves and did a good job."

"What is it you aren't saying, Mo?"

"They don't pay promptly, Laura, and we have to meet our bills each month. It took them a year."

"I see."

"No, Hon, I don't think you do. The kind of temper that man has, he has no business being around kids."

The next morning, Richard roused Laura, "Hon, I think you better go through before I do, to the kitchen, in case Crystal is laying there half covers." Laura groaned. "Sorry, Babe, but I don't need any more excitement in my life." She padded into the living room. They were fortunate the sofa made into a bed. Ben was snuggled up close to his mother and she had her arm around him. Padding back, Laura nodded it was all right.

"They're still sound asleep. Yesterday was traumatic for them. I'm surprised Robert hasn't showed up."

"I would say Robert is dead to the world, drunk. Crystal knows his ways or she would be up and gone."

"Is today going to be worse than yesterday?" He nodded. "Why?"

"Because each day she isn't there, he becomes angrier. I hope she got the restraining order against him."

"She did and she mentioned going to her folks, except she doesn't want him showing up there."

"Let's get out of here, Laura. It all gives me the creeps. I have known about Robert's family all my life."

"What are you not telling me?"

"Nothing, except they are vindictive and use whatever they want to make things their way."

At the dresser, putting on her make-up, Laura began to fill a small bag with items she knew Crystal used. Foundation, mascara, lipstick, eye shadow, and cheek color. All were new except the cheek color but she put it in anyway. *You may borrow from my closet and here's twenty to buy Benjamin an outfit. She pinned the note on the small bag and laid it by Crystal. "Stay safe."*

They locked the door behind and left for New Haven Church by way of a stop for breakfast and arrived at Shining Light Church in time to be seated before the first hymnal was sung. The pastor came back to introduce himself and welcome them as the singing picked up. "We sing a lot of praise songs," Pastor Merkel said, "but today is old fashioned Sunday and we will be into the old hymns. Hope you enjoy."

Richard thanked him and reached for a hymnal and when the prayers were said and Pastor Merkel began his sermon Richard listened with rapt attention. "There but for the grace of God, go I," the pastor said. "How many times do we judge another, not knowing what's going on in their life, or what their history contains, we simply shake our head and say, "there goes a loser." What if in their sight, we are the loser. How real is God in your life, today? Are you blessed? Do you remember where your blessings come from? How is your prayer life? All these questions and you wonder where I'm coming from. Well, sometime next week you will remember this sermon and God will speak to your heart and you will take a moment to ask yourself, how real is God in my life? What can I do to make a difference and who do I rely on. All these questions will file through your memory…"

It was on the way home, Richard remarked, "I liked the pastor and certainly found singing the old hymns refreshing, what about you?" Laura was reading the church bulletin. "Did you find something interesting?" She had him completely turned off. "Babe, talk to me, did you like the church?"

"I noticed they are having a seminar, it says they do this yearly and there's a class led by an area psychologist on anger management. I was thinking it might help Crystal to attend."

"Don't you mean Robert?" Richard glanced her way. "Isn't he the one that does the battering?"

"Yes, but will he attend?" She stared at the passing landscape. "This really doesn't look much different than where we live, does it?" Suddenly, inside she felt restless and maybe a bit nervous over things.

"No, guess not." He sighed. "And for anyone that doesn't know, Robert doesn't look different, does he?"

"They're bringing in a couple from the Cape's big church to help with another part of the seminar."

"Who's teaching?" Richard drove into the apartment's garage. "Look, honey, Crystal's cars gone."

"Wherever she goes I pray for her strength and that he leaves her alone." They stepped out of the garage to the sound of the Methodist Church chimes playing Amazing Grace and stood listening.

"Have you noticed the little mission in New Haven?" Richard asked. "They say it chimes at various times, completely unexpected I'm told. No one knows the denomination, it just evolved under their nose and plays often in the night. New Haven is a different little berg. I haven't experienced their chimes, yet."

Chapter 4

He slammed the refrigerator door, nothing worth eating in there! One of the chairs was sitting slightly farther out than the others at the table, he kicked it in place. Reaching the top cabinet he felt around for the tall bottle. It was there yesterday. It couldn't have disappeared but then she might have emptied it and thrown it in the trash. He raised the lid to look and there was the empty bottle. He'd get her for that. Maybe he already had. How would she explain her nose, shattered bone, he was sure and that made him grimace a bit. She wouldn't make the neighbours believe much about that.

This was no kind of life. He would go after her and find her no matter where she holed up, her and his son. Benjamin, I'm sorry. He sent the words ahead of him. The kid didn't deserve to be treated that way. He'd done it but he hadn't meant to. It was natural for a child to want to get between his parents but he shouldn't have thrown him to the wall. For a moment he felt his son's pain. He shouldn't have done it.

He was going after them. They'd have gone to the doctor, he was sure of it. Crystal was too attractive to live with her nose crooked in the middle of her face. He shouldn't have hit her there. What he did was batter away, punching her face. What could she do? She was small and she did fight back but his was the strength. Lord, have mercy, she may have covered for his temper in the past, but this time…she said he'd gone too far and she was getting out before he killed her. Well, we'll see about that, now he had to think where she'd go, no money, no clothes and not her precious make up. What she had was their son.

He drove through the town, last of all to the doctor's office but didn't see her car. It was his guess there was a return visit to the doctor. He parked and went in. The receptionist was young, eighteen maybe, he guessed. He flashed his best smile. "I'm looking for my wife and son. Crystal and Benjamin. I think they had a return visit this morning."

"Oh, they just left. What a terrible thing to have that kind of accident but let me give you the free pass." She tapped the poster next to her desk stating the carnival was in town and there were free passes.

"Excuse me," he said. "You people offer a free pass to the fair grounds and rides." She nodded.

"My son would love that. Thank you." They beamed their brilliant smiles to each other.

He didn't find her car parked anywhere in town. If she went home to her parents they would encourage her to press charges. Where could she go that no one noticed her crushed nose? He'd stop at the package store and go home. It was his time to do as he pleased. Didn't he always?

He stayed in a drunken stupor, knowing he need sober up for Monday morning if he expected a load out, but too far gone to think was preferable over accepting the fact he'd hurt not only Crystal but Benjamin, too. The kid didn't deserve bad treatment but Crystal did and he vowed she'd pay.

He began the coffee around four in the morning. He'd drink a gallon if it would clear his head. First thing's first, find them before going down to the loading dock to his truck. He stayed in the shower letting the water stream over his body, waiting for his head to clear and then finding a fresh ironed shirt, the tapered western style he expected Crystal to keep on hand. "Throw away any with a spot on them, it's not good for my image," he said. "I've got to look my best, wherever I go and I do."

He checked his watch. Nine thirty five. If Benjamin was at school then she was near. Like a good parent of good intent he stopped at the office to receive clearance, flashing his million dollar smile along the way. He came to the Kindergarten building, marveling at the bright colors on the wall. Were they there the night of parent–teacher conference? He wasn't certain but he found Ben's room and knocked on the door. The teacher's voice sounded weak on the other side. He entered and found Laura Worthington's cool stare upon him.

"I'm here to pick up my son," he said. "I'm sure his mother told you."

She shook her head. "No, we haven't spoken. The office said Benjamin's mother called in that he was ill."

"I suppose you know where they are?" His voice became testy as his posture changed and he stood feet slightly apart, hands on hips as if daring her.

"The office said, Benjamin's mother is keeping him home today, he isn't well." Laura practically gritted her teeth. "I certainly hope he isn't in any kind of danger."

"No, we're on the same page there." He threw back his head and laughed. "Ben's a good boy."

"Yes, he is precious."

"That sounds like someone's heirloom."

"No, it sounds like someone's treasure, that they would cherish."

He stepped a few feet closer, a smirk around his mouth. "What would you know about anything?"

"Excuse me; we need to get back to the children's studies. I'm sorry Benjamin isn't well." From that moment on she ignored him. Finally he left and she took a deep breath of relief. As quickly as possible, she closed herself in the supply closet and sent Crystal a message. "He's been in our classroom and he seems determined to find you. Take care and whatever you need go back and take from my closet."

Weeks passed, Laura didn't hear from Crystal and Robert stayed away from her classroom. Then it was time for her father's monthly visit to the doctor who was his friend in St. Louis. "This time," her mother said, "you will have to drive. Your Dad's sick and I'll have to stay here to run the farm. Will the school let you off that one day?" Which meant she needed to find another substitute, Crystal was gone? From the school's list, she found one name and called it.

The young woman who answered the call was Dottie Williams, younger but more adept in certain areas. "Oh, so they have music in this room and act out the song? Great, I know just what to do."

"You live around here, Dottie?" She asked, thinking to check her out. But then Dottie replied, "No, I'm not married but I have a wonderful fiancée, I can't tell you what all Robert does for me." She smiled, happy and content. "He's asked me to move in with him but my parent's are against it. They think he's too old for me." Laura's mind was in overdrive wondering if Dottie's Robert was also Crystal's Robert.

A month had made a huge difference in the house project. "Mo," she loved to call his name, his eyes always lit up. "Mo, you are an excellent builder. Don't worry, I didn't come for anything other than to see the progress. So what's the plan here on out?"

"Well, we have a key for you. The doors are installed and with all the fixtures going in we can start leaving our work ready for the next day. Go check out the bathroom and then I'll meet you in the kitchen. It's going to blow your mind."

"I love the bathroom," Mo's pleasure was evident in the spread of smile on his face. He moved away from the door and she was looking into the kitchen. "Oh, Mo, how have you done this? It looks like something you see in a magazine."

"Well, I can't take all the credit. The kitchen planner knew her stuff and when we brought in that second crew, it seemed like everything took off. Every day we could see a major accomplishment."

"You don't always work two crews?"

"No, but then we realized your building project was going to lap over into the Jenson's and we had no choice. Of course it helped that Bert was finished in the Bent Creek area and could come here."

"It's beyond anything I would ever imagine," she leaned over to kiss Mo on the cheek. "You are just like Moses in the Bible, you get things done."

"That's my name," he said. "Can't do nothin' about that." They laughed together.

Richard noticed her smiling different times as she prepared the vegetables. He was setting the table and making tea. "You seem rather pleased about something, is it the new sub?"

Glancing up, she smiled, "No, it's the house. Have you been in this week? It's gorgeous." She sighed, wiping her hands on a towel she'd draped around her middle. "In the beginning I was skeptical and a bit apprehensive, I guess, I don't deserve a new house of that caliber. I'm still young and have time for us to work toward it but you made it possible having saved the inheritance left you by your grandmother. Still, it seems a lot to accept when I've done nothing to deserve it."

"Have you read the scripture, He who has much, much is required of him? Something like that, well, I imagine in time much will be required of us because we are blessed. We found each other to go through life together. That was a good beginning."

"Mo said with the second crew working, he's pretty sure we could move in by the middle of next month."

"Really?" He whistled. "I didn't realize they worked that much faster. I guess they've been together so long they have it down pat." He grimaced, "the thing is, we are moving supplies to the New Haven location starting next Monday and that's going to be a back breaking job, some of the items are large and heavy…but this location is going to serve the community even better than before."

"You seem enthused over the new location. Any particular reason why?"

"It's a different community, different ways. There, I can deliver things to the farmers, if needed and in general breathe fresh air. I can't wait to meet the backbone of the community. Just wait, it's going to be good." He was smiling like a little boy and turning the television on to watch the weather like a country boy. "We're going to have to hire more people, though. One girl came on board today."

The phone rang and she being closer answered. "Hello, Laura, how are you today?"

"I'm fine. Who is this?" Richard turned the television off dawdled his fingers at her and went outside. Through the window she saw him go to the company truck and raise the hood. Turning back to the phone, she said, "I didn't hear you."

"Don't you recognize my voice, Hon?"

She hung up. Before she could join Richard outside the phone rang again. "Hello?"

"Don't hang up, Laura, it's Robert. I'm trying to find Crystal and my son. Have you seen them?"

"I can honestly say I have not."

"Then have you heard from them or know where they are?"

"No, I do not?"

"If you're lying to me, Laura, you will regret it."

"Would you like to speak to Richard?"

He gave a wicked laugh over the phone. "I have nothing to speak with your husband about, Laura, but you and Crystal have always been pretty tight, so I'll be calling you again in a few days."

"Please, don't bother," she replied. "If Crystal hasn't called me by now, she won't. I know Crystal."

"Do you now?" His hollow laughter came across the line. "And I know you, Laura, so don't get any ideas of protecting Crystal. It's yourself you need to be concerned over."

"What does that mean?" She sounded indignant. "Just don't call me, Robert, I don't know anything."

"For the record, I believe you, but you need to show respect speaking with me. You see, I know your dirty little secret that you are keeping from your husband."

Laura's blood ran cold. Could he possibly refer to, no, no one knew and no one would ever know.

"Robert, I have no idea what you are referring to."

"Let's just say a little incident that happened about a month before your marriage to dear old Richard."

She hung up the phone, glancing at it as if it were a snake ready to strike. The timing, the timing, she tried to sort it out. How could he know? She had told no one. In a flash the incident Robert spoke of flashed before her eyes. He was bluffing, pretending to know something in order to make her tell what she knew about Crystal but she knew nothing. It was a hit that left her reeling. Why would anyone do something like that? She was almost relieved when he called back one last time.

"Has any sense come back into your head, Laura?"

"I don't know what you are referring to," she said. "And truly I have no knowledge of your family."

"Just keep your eyes and ears open, do it for me and I promise your good news won't be public."

"What are you talking about? Why are you threatening me?"

"Why, your one night stand, Laura and the baby inside you, does it worry you?"

"You monster, I …." She broke down, crying. "Why are you doing this?"

"I'm so wrong, Laura, don't you get it, my sins are public, I hit my wife and threw my son against the wall, but what did you do, Laura? Your sins are secret." He paused. "So who is the greater sinner?"

The happy light feeling left. For a moment her body reeled with nausea. She rushed to the bathroom, but only dry heaves happened, a miserable unable to put down sickness she had experienced only one other time in her life. Tears smarted in her eyes while a feeling of weakness spread through her body. What was she to do? What could she do? She had allowed herself to think no one would find out, but Robert was like the evil stepfather, he would tell everything he knew in order to hurt her.

Her encounter with Tom had been the last week of the summer job she had taken in Langston County, before she moved home with the hopes of a teaching position she had applied for in early spring. She had been foolish to think Tom Hargrove would be an honorable man, decent on a date, only there to renew friendship having dinner together because they had run into each other, unexpectedly. But the whole thing had gone South. He had become irritable, then possessive as she tried to cajole his bad temper. No, he hadn't changed. When she offered to see herself home, he had become obnoxious in front of the restaurant clientele. Embarrassed beyond words she succumbed to his seeing her back to the summer apartment, and that was the biggest mistake of her life.

"I promise I'll be good," he said, "just let me come in and make amends for my ugliness through dinner. I don't know what got into me."

"Perhaps you don't hold your liquor as well as you think," she offered, honestly. That further angered him. In their years of being high school friends she had not known his temper flared that easily. Richard tried to tell her but all she remembered was a flirty Tom that made her laugh.

What was she to do? It would kill Richard if he knew and if he tried to rectify the problem he might be physically hurt. Maybe the gravity of the situation pushed her into saying yes to Richard's constant marriage proposal, but she was in such need to be held and appreciated she wanted to be with him and she did love him, she hadn't known she loved him that deeply. Would he cherish her if she told him she was damaged goods? Perhaps he would abandon her. The questions were not new; she had not been able to settle in her mind what Richard would have done, given the chance. She lay on the bed, her head throbbing, her body drawn into the fetal position. Richard found her there, flipping a switch to flood the room with light. "Babe, what's wrong? I kept waiting for you to come outside. It's a pleasant evening."

"Wanted to," she muttered, "my head is killing me. Migraine I guess. I just feel sick."

"Can I get your medicine?"

"Can't it might hurt the baby."

He kicked off his shoes and climbed onto the bed, laying behind her, putting his arms around her as she settled into the spooning position of his body. "This is nice," he whispered, "but I'm sorry you're sick."

She made herself go to school the next week. The little children brought a sense of right to her troubled world. They sang the songs joyfully with their little faces lifted up seeing things adults leave behind and for a spell she was happy listening to them, returning the smiles they bestowed on her. But at home, when the phone rang she paused, a stab of fear slashing itself upon her countenance.

"Babe, you are nervous as a cat," Richard remarked. "What do you need to help you through this?"

"This what?" She had to get hold of herself. She was losing weight and that wasn't good.

"The what…I don't know except that you are skitterish and you weren't before. Are you worried about the delivery?" Richard knew something was different but he didn't know why.

"No. I don't know what that will be like but I know we will have only joy when the baby arrives."

He flipped the television on to the evening news. "In view of the rash of people in high places being pointed out as to having intimately abused women on their climb up the political ladder to success, we find eleven percent of college age women experience rape or sexual assault through physical force and further statistics show one out of five women face this threat. The effects of this unwanted act prove challenging to deal with and often lead to serious and prolonged side effect to the victim's life." Laura left the room. She didn't have to hear the story, she was living it.

They awoke the next morning wrapped in the embrace of last night. Richard chuckled, "I guess I could go to work as I am but they'd ask me how I got so rumpled." Leaning over he kissed her. "Are you any better?"

The radio came on, an old song was playing. He began to hum but on the second bars he was singing. "When you love somebody," He stopped. "Am I making that up, or is it a song? "You can't go wrong. I'll spend my life with you, happy and blessed, because I love somebody…" He laughed. "I made it up."

Chapter 5

Richard's crew finished the move from Walker to New Haven. Laura was involved with the children, watching from the sideline while knowing the move to the new house was moving closer. Often, as she listened to the children and saw their progress she wondered about Benjamin. Crystal hadn't called and she understood. If she didn't know anything, there would be nothing to report to Robert.

She had spent enough time worrying over things out of her control. She searched scripture for hope and strength to carry on. Quoting Jeremiah 29 over and over, helped to disperse those moments of sheer terror and the blackness of doom. This is God's world, she whispered within herself, devil take your evil and go, leave me alone. Watching Richard's enthusiasm and caring for her, she wondered that she was blessed in spite of herself.

They had been attending New Haven's Shining Light Church and she listened to people's impression of the pastor. "He listens to us," one lady said. "If I had anything bothering me, I wouldn't hesitate to go to him for guidance. This one knows how to keep a confidence. He and his wife suffered like the rest of us." Secretly, inside where no one could imagine a problem, Laura wished to be able to discuss her dilemma with the pastor but it was an awkward situation. She and Richard were visiting the different classes before deciding which one they would enroll in. They realized in choosing commitment would be a very large part of their life from that point on that no matter what happened in their lives those were the people they would share with as spiritual supporters.

She met several women her own age and listened to their conversation on the upcoming ladies seminar and the return of the women who would be leading. "Ellen Gates leads in scripture, have you heard of her?" Laura shook her head, no. "The other is the owner of Marigold, the shop in the Cape. Perhaps, you have gone there?"

"I was at college and worked a part time job, before taking the position here at New Haven," she explained.

"Well, with your new home, I'd attend if I were you, Marigold Langly helps us to find the right direction. For instance after the fire here at the church she was chosen to help us make the right decisions throughout the renovation and I think it turned out lovely." The pastor's wife touched her hand before leaving. "We are happy you are with us and if we can be of help in any way, please call us."

The song service was moving, the songs spoke to her heart and by her side Richard sang from his heart but it was Pastor Merkel's sermon left Laura's mind in a state of unrest.

"We find an antidote for the ways of the world in Matthew 5:44," Pastor Merkel began. "Jesus said, Love your enemies and pray for those who persecute you. Do good to those who hate you, bless those who curse you and pray for those who would abuse you, we find in Luke 6:27-28. We may find this exceedingly hard to do. After all, these are people out to get us." A low rumble of laughter followed. "They may be so intent against us they would kill us, or perhaps they are people who abuse others for the sake of entertainment, their own entertainment. None the less, whether the act is great or small we are to pray for them. What did the scripture say? Love your enemies and pray for those who persecute you." He walked down the aisle, his eyes on various ones of the congregation. "What do you do when someone abuses you? Do you call a friend to talk to them about the situation? Or, do you talk to God about what's bothering you? Maybe you need to talk to God and tell him why the abuse bothers you. Jesus was reviled, insulted, beaten in the worst form of abuse and he did it all for me and you, dying on the cross that we might have salvation if we would call on his name and ask forgiveness for our sin. Why wouldn't he want us to talk to him when we encounter the unpleasant ways of the world? But why would he want us to pray for those who would abuse us? Because he loves them and he wants us to love them too. Impossible, you say? That's why we begin with prayer for them, to let the Holy Spirit break us down where we see the need of someone else and quit holding our heart so close to our chest."

Laura signed up for both classes to be held three Saturdays. With a home to make livable and her busy schedule she could use help. Their routine was the same. A work week, Saturdays at a slower pace and Sunday's attending services at Shining Light and visiting their parents in the evening. It was the Friday morning before the first ladies Seminar when Laura glanced outside the window as she always did to check on the weather, the fog was thick and she dreaded the drive to school. Fog made her nauseous.

She left early, laying her phone in the seat in case of trouble. The streetlights kept her between the lines although oncoming cars spread the mist into diffused shapes and pressed the landscape into one never ending area of white. When she thought it could not be any worse, a vehicle rode up behind her, nearly touching the bumper, stopping to rev its motor and come pell mell to the driver's side of her car. Lord, help, she whispered, it has to be one of the upper classmen thinking I'm one of them. Back and forth the driver of the vehicle maneuvered from one side to the other, finally to pull along Laura driving and started yelling to her. With shaking fingers, Laura was able to let down the window and hang on to the steering wheel. "What do you want?" She heard the shrill laughter and knew immediately it was not one of the students mistaking her for one of them. "Why are you doing this?"

"Just want you to know the anxiety I feel not knowing where my boy is. Do you know, little Laura?"

"No." The vehicle dropped back and pulled to the back of hers. Laura felt the wheels resist and then she was moving forward not on her vehicles power but his. There was nothing she could do, when suddenly and as quickly as begun he stopped. Her vehicle moved forward on its own as they met an oncoming car and then he pulled to her side once more.

"Don't hold out on me, Laura. If you know, it benefits both of us because then I'll keep your secret." Rolling up the window she heard rather than saw Robert speed on down the road as the school drive came into view. Someone had thought to place burning flares on each side of the entrance.

She barely made it inside the building, thankful for the teacher's lounge just inside the door. She collapsed on one of the chairs, while the baby inside her was moving, evidently protesting her emotions. A hand or a foot raked across the interior of her stomach again and again as if to say let me out of here and all of a sudden a sound came from her throat, bubbling up, needing escape, laughter; this was what it was all about. For the moment she was safe.

Cupping her hands around her stomach, you cannot defeat me; silently she raised her hands to heaven. My God is bigger and stronger and better than yours, Robert, what do you know that I can't correct? But she knew, too, it was the damage his accusation would cause and they were new to the community not ignoring the fact the new business was going into effect.

She left the teacher's lounge shortly, finding one of the Senior boy's helping with the bus arrival, leading the younger children to the buildings in the dense fog. He came to her, "Missus Worthington, I was afraid for you but I didn't know what to do, then that man pulled back and quit pushing you down the road.

Do you know who that was, Missus Worthington?" She shook her head no, speechless that he was the one in the third vehicle. "It was our Miss Crystal's husband. You know she left him and he's trying to find her and little Ben. I hear he no longer goes to work, just drinks and looks for her all day."

"That's scary," she replied.

"Yes sum, it is, but he has a name for doing wild things and he can be downright rude to a person. So you watch out for him, he's a mean dude." She hurried to her class room trying not to look back.

That evening she prepared the meal, yawning and tired, whether from the morning's ordeal or not, she wondered all the more about Crystal. By now, she should have heard from her. She wasn't with her parents so where was she? She and Richard ate in silence; he had worked with large equipment all day.

"Do you mind if I go to bed after we clear the dishes?" He glanced up. "Do you mind if I go with you?" They went to sleep listening to the chimes. "They're nice," Richard murmured, "and unexpected."

The phone rang at ten o'clock. Laura roused to fumble around in the dark for the light switch to the lamp as Richard found the phone. A strange expression on his face he hand the phone to Laura. "What is it?" Already she was placing the phone up to her ear. "Mom, are you crying?" Richard was getting out of bed, shuffling into the bathroom. "Mom, what's wrong?" She listened. "Yes, we'll be there soon."

"What did she say?" Richard was already tucking the tail of his shirt into his pants. "I knew it wasn't good. Your mother is a strong woman. She never cries, just works out the problem. I want to be like her."

"Dad's hemoragghing. She called the doctor and he wants to put him in the hospital. Evidently the radiation and chemo are harsh on his system and the doctor is reluctant to stop either if they are to knock it out." Laura had hurried into a pair of jeans and a t-shirt and was stuffing the minimum assortment of make up into a small bag. "If you drive, I'll dab a bit of this on." She glanced around the room, "are we ready?"

"You better take a jacket," he reminded, "the hospital is pretty cold in the late hours of night."

With Richard driving, they were at her parents within thirty minutes. Florence, had put John's house coat over the pj's and was herself dressed and ready to go. "I pulled the car around, Richard, if you can help him into the back seat that will give me a minute to answer our men's questions about tomorrow."

Laura had stooped to be on his level. "You are going to be all right, Dad. This is just one of chemo's many set backs and today it appears useless to hear. "I love you, Dad with all my heart.'" She knew he wanted to smile and reply but he was trying not to do anything to set off the bleeding again. Laura glanced up at her mother's joining them. "Are you riding in the back with dad, Mom?"

Florence nodded. "Yes, and I heard from Timmy, he and his friends are just leaving the Cape. He will meet us at the hospital." She climbed into the car and scooted as close to John as possible. "Here, Honey, lay your head on my shoulder and maybe you can drift off to sleep while we're riding there."

The doctor was waiting for them, due to the fact he was the one on call that night. "Rough night?" He took John in the wheel chair from Florence and headed down the hall. "Just follow me."

Laura and Richard waited in the row of chairs outside of the room where they entered. Richard reached over to take her hand. "You doin' all right, Babe?" She nodded and he smiled. "I love you," he whispered. They had been there possibly thirty minutes when someone joined them, glancing up they found Pastor Merkel. Richard rose to shake his hand. "What are you doing out tonight?"

"One of our members that is a nurse here, recognized you as attending Shining Light a few times and called me." He sit across from them. "Now tell me what's going on?" When Richard finished telling him, the pastor said, "Let's pray."

"Lord, God, our heavenly Father, thank you Lord for this family that loves each other. Father, Mr. John is having a bad evening because of the treatment he is undergoing. Lord, we are asking you to take away the pain, to relieve the agony of his soul having to submit his life for troublesome trial and treatment. He's an active man, dear Lord, a farmer with a high calling to provide for others and we are asking Lord that you allow the healing to begin this minute, to flood his body where it sees need. Lord, to cut off any outside afflictions that occur because we know in all things there are differences of opinion or negligence when unnecessary acts happen, so Lord we are asking you keep this family tightly knit together, to heal his body, to watch over each one of the family and Lord to thank you that we can be with this family. We love you, Lord and praise your name for the healing that is on its way right now. Thank you, in the name of Jesus Christ our Lord."

The doctor met with them around two thirty in the morning. "We cannot say without a doubt it is the method in which your father is being treated that has caused the hemoragghing, but there's little else to blame the swelling on or the ulcerated sores. We want him to stay with us a number of days for observation and we can reduce the bleeding." He studied them, much as he had his patient. "I think you all should go home and get some rest. There's nothing you can do here."

"Mom won't leave," Laura said to Richard but the doctor heard and smiled as he said, "no, the wives don't normally leave unless they're dying." He started to walk away, but turned back, "From what I see in you, young lady, you probably won't either." Richard put his arm around her in a hug.

"We have your mom's car, that leaves her without wheels."

"I'll drive you home," Timmy volunteered. "Sis, what do you say we contact our old church prayer group?"

"With your family permission," Pastor Merkel offered, "I would love to give this to our prayer warriors."

Florene crept up behind Timmy. "I came to send everyone home," she said. "And to thank you for staying with me." She turned to the pastor. "Thank you for coming. These times are very scary."

A week passed with Timmy trying to run the farm by staying in touch with his parents at the hospital. Laura found it impossible to be of help in her stage of pregnancy and Richard was finishing supplying the new business at New Haven. Mo called one afternoon as the school day ended. "Laura, this is Mo. Just want you to know, tomorrow we finish the last coat of paint on the moldings. I've called the clean up girls in for the next day and then we will turn your home over to you."

Excited and yet subdued, she thought because her parents were away and her dad in no shape to bless their new home, Laura drove in three days later to take ownership. Richard would be along in time to sign papers and tell Mo goodbye. Curious, she walked down the hall, stopping at the door to the nursery. It was painted the lightest gray one could find and the white wood moldings at window and door popped. A rocking chair had been painted white, its cushion a muted blend of rainbow colors in the form of huge round dots. She had no idea if Richard or the building crew was responsible for it.

"Oh," what she saw next made her gasp a breath of fresh air. "I wanted one of these so bad, but didn't think we could afford it right now." She circled the new bed, complete with mattress.

Soft laughter sounded in the hall and Laura turned to find Mo, a big smile spreading from ear to ear. "Did you make this, Mo?"

"I did." He was wagging his head, joyfully. "I ask old Rich what color was your baby's bed and he said, "I don't know what color it will be because we don't have one." Mo, surfaced the pile of clothes she had taken into her arms to clear the only chair in the room, "I took it on myself to build one for you. This one is four feet long, probably last til the baby is four years old and that dressing table you haven't noticed is tall enough you won't have an aching back when you finish changing all those diapers. Now I built these on my own time and I'm sayin' they're a gift from me to you."

Laura threw her arms around him. "You are absolutely delightful Mo. If you and I weren't married to other persons, why I'd chase you down and marry you. You are that wonderful. Thank you." She planted a kiss on his cheek. They stood there admiring Mo's custom built furniture, "How are you at building furniture for all the other rooms?"

"You don't have furniture?" He seemed astonished. "With this house, no furniture?" He scratched his head, "That's near unbelievable." His countenance became more saggy and pronounced. "I'm afraid that's out of my league."

Her laughter was joyous. "We haven't taken time to shop, Mo, with Richard moving into the New Haven facility and my dad in hospital, there has been almost more to take care of than we are capable."

He pat her shoulder. "Life gets that way, Laura. I just want to tell you that you have been a blessing to work with, no complaints or having to redo, it makes my job easier."

"What am I going to do with you off working magic for someone else?" She asked. "I always look forward to seeing you." He thought that one over before he replied. She could see his mind working.

"I need to tell you, Laura, there's word going round that Crystal's husband has made a threat against you as to keeping the whereabouts of his wife secret. Now, that's none of my business but Robert can be downright dangerous and I know you all had the alarm system installed…the thing is, use it, when you come in turn it on and just take that bit of time to do so, it could protect you. Don't mean to scare…"

She interrupted. "You really think he would hurt me?"

"The person he is when he's drinking will, Laura." He paused a bit before adding. "He's spending all his time in Rudy's bar drinking, not working or keeping up their place and I know Crystal and Benjamin are in hiding. They're not with her parents because that's the first place he'd look."

"Why would he come after me?"

"Because they are not available. You are." He gave a deep sigh. "I hoped I wouldn't have to tell you but if he's using your name in the bar then that anger of his is building and one day he'll need relief."

"But Mo, I don't know where they are. What is he saying?"

"That you do know where they are and one day soon he's going to wring the truth out of you."

"Isn't that a public threat?"

"This is New Haven, Laura, not Washington D.C." He turned toward the kitchen. "Just be careful."

Moving in was full swing on Saturday; Saturday because Richard and Laura had jobs to go to through the week. They rented the trailer for moving; Richard and his two friends, Mike and Jerry loaded everything inside its enclosed walls and sped on down the road to move into the new house. "Son, I hate to tell you this," Mike said, "but in case you haven't noticed you have a lot of empty space. Guess what? You don't have any furniture."

"Shucks, so you noticed," Richard replied. "Well, maybe this afternoon we'll look for furniture."

"I have sandwiches, if you guys are hungry."

They shook their head, "If your man will take us back to our trucks, I told my wife I'd help clean the garage this afternoon."'

"I didn't dream we'd finish by noon," Jerry said, "man it must be not having all that heavy furniture we're used to. I think I'll make good on a promise and take my boy fishing if you don't need me."

Richard, taller than either, reached over to tousle their hair. "I'll take you back but we do appreciate your helping us. Laura can't lift at this point of the pregnancy and some of those boxes needed two men." Taking the keys to the truck from his pocket, he waved to Laura. "I'll come right back, Hon. So don't do anything you aren't suppose to…we've got the rest of the evening."

"What about the furniture?" Mike asked. "I'm a little concerned over the lack of, so to speak."

Laura went inside to their laughter ringing in the air. They were good friends.'

She was in the bedroom finishing putting away bed linens in the small closet behind the door that led to the bathroom. Crocheted doilies made by her grandmother were stretched across the bottom of the box to keep them flat. She had seen to their placement but now, restricted by outdoor clothes she could barely reach the bottom. It didn't matter, she wasn't planning to use them but she had kept the boxes in case she found more hidden surprises.

She was bent over her head down to the box when she felt someone move up behind her. Immediately she straightened, at the same time knowing whoever it was had clamped their hands over her face, twisting her around so she could not see in the old fashioned mirrors. "Settle down, little Laura," It was a man's voice, nipping her neck ever so slightly, with his teeth beneath her hair line, his hand splaying across her back. "I'm back to see you Laura. Don't even think of telling your man I was here, you don't want him to get hurt, now do you?"

"Why would you hurt Richard?" Her body was shaking and her voice was a hoarse whisper. "What have we done to you?" She heard his terrible laughter as he loosened his hold.

"Don't look at me little Laura." He was backing from the room. "You know where Crystal is with my son, don't you, Little Laura?"

"No, I don't. She doesn't want me hurt. I don't know."

"Lie to me and you will regret it."

"Please, leave us all alone. Get help. You don't have to be this way."

"What way, is that, little Laura? The way of being truthful, me against all of you or should I say all of you against me, higher up, better than me, driving me to drink while you sit on your high thrones looking down on a poor miserable truck driver?" He had come back. His anger burning hot, his hate driving him recklessly toward doing something even he would regret but there were no holds on his tongue.

"There's nothing miserable about being a truck driver." She felt the rise of resentment against him, her own rage forgetting his warning. "You make your own impressions, any work is admirable done well and we all benefit from each other. But you have a chip on your shoulder you use as an excuse to deem yourself inferior when you really don't believe it." She faced him. "You come into my home like some idiot madman, if I had a gun I could kill you for trespassing, instead I stand here seeing you for who you are and really what you are, a man who has such low esteem for himself you would stoop low. You bully someone else to make yourself feel strong but at the end of the day you're not strong, you're soaking yourself in a bottle to forget how pitiful you really are." She thought he would reply.

"Why are you here blaming me for your family problems, all I ever did was have a friend that went through life with me through years of knowing each other and respecting each other. She loved you. What did you do? Kill her love? And you come to me, threatening me? Does that make you a man?" She laughed, her own terrible fury of being invaded working its way out. "You are the only one could turn this around. Get the chip off your shoulder, stop drinking, go to work and be the man God wants you to be." She didn't care. She had forgotten reasoning. Now she faced him, anger written all over her.

:Oh….ho…oh, no," He sputtered, momentarily taken that he had listened to her diatribe. "You don't have the right to judge me, Miss Holier than Thou with your own sin, looking down on me because I drink?" His voice rose to inflect words, now. "Sitting in your ivory tower, wearing your rose colored glasses but I put fear in you, didn't I? Fear your husband will find out the baby you carry may not be his, fear he will realize you had a little fete' la' fete' with my cousin."

Laura blanched. Robert was a cousin to Tom Hargrove. It all washed over her, a flash through the brain that remembered everything she tried to deny. Before she returned to Walker when the classes ended, and she held a temporary job, they had run in to each other and he hadn't changed, flirty, handsome Tom flashing that million dollar smile, she had been smitten as though it were the witching hour and the stain would be forever on her soul. So frustrated and unhappy with herself, when Richard persisted she said yes and married him within a month of taking the apartment, knowing her life had changed and would change more as she tried to make him happy. It all rushed through her mind, assimilating who Robert was and how was it she had not known? Why had no one thought to explain it to her? It came in a rush, the answer, they thought she knew.

He saw it was his moment. "What now, little Laura? Find my wife and child and I'll keep quiet."

"This," she laid her hand on her stomach, "Is not your cousin's child."

"Can you prove it without running test, Laura?" He was up in her face. "I think not, and how will fine upstanding Richard handle this situation? What will the community say about their Kindergarten teacher?" His demonic laugh filled the room. "This little town is still struggling in the dark ages, it won't take lightly what you've done."

"Why would you destroy me and my husband, what do you gain from the act?"

"Satisfaction for myself and Tom and all the other stupid bastards born to poor families. We don't deserve to be left out; we deserve the life you have."

"My family works, Robert. My dad's father was a share cropper that cleared land in this area. Your family had the same opportunity. Give it up, Robert. Be the man God wants you to be. You have made your skills known and prospered but now you are destroying yourself along with wanting to destroy us."

"You have no idea what you are saying. You think you can talk your way out of this, but you can't. It's in my power to right a few wrongs and I intend to do so."

"It's within your power to be a man and to care about someone besides yourself," she said softly. "This may be your last opportunity in life to do something right..." She let the words hang between them.

"Now, you're laying the threat on me but it won't work. To you, I'm damned if I do and damned if I don't, but this is me. Help me find Crystal and Benjamin or I'll blow the lid off your secret." With that he turned and stomped out of the room.

A few minutes later she heard the rumble of an eighteen wheeler's motor as Richard came down the lane. She turned from the window, trying to control the shaking of her body, as she vowed from this moment on the alarm system will be on.

Fall harvest was completed. John's chemo and radiation seemed to have helped. He was no longer retching at bathroom commodes unexpectedly. There was a semblance of order to his illness now that the treatments were over but the whole family worried. Florence had dropped thirty pounds without trying and for her that was a milestone. "I've worked with weight my whole life," she said, "now, I'm not trying and it's falling off." She watched as John was making his way from the kitchen to his chair.

John tousled Timmy's hair. "You've done good, Son," he said. "I know it put you out of your comfort zone but you stepped up to the plate and I'd say you made a home run of the harvest. What do you say, Mother?" He reached up for Florence hand as she came from the kitchen to settle by his side.

"I think we have a wonderful son," she replied. "From here on we know we have someone to keep things going when need be. He says he's not going to college and wants to stay on the farm."

John tilt his head thinking as usual. "It's a hard life son but a rewarding one. I don't regret all the years we've put into it, do you Flo?" His glance to Timmy brought his son over to pull a chair closer to his parents. "I tell you what, we have had to work hard but we've worked together and that's been good."

"We can only wish for you and Laura what we've had and more but the truth is, it has been staying close to the Lord has allowed us to stay together and progress. Maybe we haven't progressed as much as some, but we know only our story. There were times of uncertainty that we could only trust the Lord."

Timmy listened to the two recalling times they'd thought they weren't going to deliver, to keep farming and raise a family on what they were making off the rented ground in those days. Now that they'd turned the farm over to him, the biggest problem he faced was whether he could handle the acreage by himself, or not. It chafed his spirit, sorely, to think his father wouldn't be there much longer. How did mom do it, sit there talking as though they had a hundred more years, when she knew time was slipping away. What he hoped for was a girl that would take him as he was and when one did to have the kind of marriage Mom and Dad experienced. Right now, he had all on his plate he could handle and if it weren't for Mom knowing the farm business too, sometimes he feared he couldn't take care of it all.

CHAPTER 6

The doors opened at ten o'clock for the seminar. This was the first Saturday. Laura rose from sleep wondering if she would profit physically to stay in bed and let her body rest, but her mind seemed to say you need this. The emphasis was to be on Godly women in the home and the work place. She lived both lives, she supposed and needed the fellowship of good reliable women, besides that the two coming to lead the Seminar were touted as being among the best.

"Morning, Love," Richard was dressed already to leave for the store and she dragging her feet. "Can I get you a cup of coffee?" He was up, pulling her chair out, ever the gentleman and good husband.

She felt cranky. How could he be smiling first thing of the morning? "No, can't have caffeine."

Pursing his lips just so and his eyebrows rose questioning, he already had a feel of her disposition. "Restless night?" She huffed air, putting her elbows on the table to cradle her head. "Headache?"

"No, Richard, just me trying to make some sense of whether to go on to the seminar at ten, or not."

Most men would say I think you should or something, she knew, but Richard just reached across to pat her hand. Silent. Oh, she hated the fact she felt at odds in side while he had his act together. "You should try this," she said, her voice petulant. She didn't know why she was whining. She just was.

'What can I do to help?" Tilting his head, he studied her. "Bring the car to the door? Help you dress? Pray for you and me and all those women trying to make decisions this morning?"

She glanced up, thinking a retort to his insensitivity justifiable but his kind eyes were on her. "Pray."

"Dear Lord, thank you for this beautiful morning. Thank you for Laura in my life. Thank you for all the things we take for granted. Now Lord, we ask you to watch over us today as we go through the hours help us to honor you by how we use them. Lord, as we encounter others, help us to be an example unto you. Now Lord, I ask a special blessing on Laura as she carries our baby and her body sometimes grows weary in this awesome miracle you are allowing us. Whatever you have planned for us today, Lord, help us to appreciate that you are the giver of life and love and all things good and help us through the rough times, Lord, for we love and praise you and thank you in your precious name. Amen" Finished, Richard kissed the top of her head. "Will you be all right if I go to work?" She nodded and he heard her faint thank you. Yawning, Laura followed him to the door, resting in his arms when he opened them wide to take her in as he always did before he left. "I love you," they whispered together and she began to feel relieved. Down the street the chimes were ringing out Peace in the valley, it almost seemed for her.

Fresh coffee fragrance waft through the air, as she entered the building. The concourse was streaming with women in all mode of dress, fancy to plain, dressy to casual. "Come on in," one of the ladies who greeted each Sunday morning came to her. "Welcome. Welcome," she said. "There's fruit drinks and of course coffee. How can I help you?" Laura smiled and said thank you, I'll be fine and the woman left her for another new arrival.

Leah Merkel came to greet her. "I'm glad you felt up to coming. When I was pregnant, I felt so swollen I was a candidate for world's biggest Mommie." They laughed together. "Bad joke," Leah said, "but truth. How are you?" She was guiding Laura to the juice table, pouring juice into two glasses and then to the pastry bar, "you've got to try this," she said, taking two crescent shaped rolls from the stack and adding fruit on the side of each plate. "Okay, you have the drinks, I've got the goodies. Let's sit over there." She pointed to the last table in front of the windows. "This spot holds a memory for me and my first seminar at Shining Light Church."

"It was a good memory?" Laura asked.

"Hardly, Levi had just gone through a revival here at Shining Light and I unable to become pregnant left him alone through the whole thing. Can you imagine a church having a revival and the pastor's wife is missing? Lord help us all."

"Tell me more. I've never heard of pastor's wives telling such a tale on their self."

"Well, the same women that are coming to lead today, somehow, well not somehow but by divine intervention, all part of God's plan, Ellen had been here helping with the music for the revival, with her husband of course. Then revival's over and I'm to lead in a Pastor's wives seminar…me…the one who has left her husband… and he calls to remind me…I feel I must honor that I said I would, so I come back and a little girl, Ellen's daughter, Ruthie is with Marigold, the one who led in the renovation of our church after the fire…well while Marigold is talking to the workers, Ruthie helps me set up in this room and she says, "Don't you think you should reverse the seating arrangement so the ladies look at you instead of out the windows?" Leah chuckled, remembering. "So we switch the chairs and tables and it worked!

"I'm still hung up on the fact you, a pastor's wife left your husband."

"Year after year we rejoiced over new babies to other couples, and that year it became a thorn in my flesh. I rejoiced with them but we'd been married years and I was barren. I wanted my own baby, too." She sighed. "God was working on the plan even then and I was racing ahead on my own." She smiled. "Long story short, soon after I found I was pregnant and we have Jeremiah Isaac Merkel. We call him Jim. We call him Jeremiah but mostly we call him ours, by the grace of God." She laid a hand on Laura's. "I want to hear your story. It's time to begin, but remember, we need to get together." Quickly she finished the pastry. "Ummm, that's delicious. But I must introduce our guests. See you later." She took a drink of juice, straightened her blouse and was gone. Laura felt a smile in her heart. It was good.

"Most of you know these ladies," Leah was saying. "Ellen Gates not only does speaking arrangements for the Lord in her Bible workshops for women, she also gives of her time and talent along with her husband as they lead the music in Revivals. Ellen is a RN by vocation and a godly woman to others whether it is in her home or by God's call upon her life to lead and inspire women. Marigold Langly, has endeared herself to us through leading the renovation of Shining Light Church on various occassions. She has her own shop, called appropriately Marigold, which we all love to visit in the Cape and she comes to us today to bring the light of scripture into our hearts because He who created us, created in Marigold a desire to teach us how to share his love through our surroundings. Ladies take a bow. Ellen Gates and Marigold Langley."

A special treat is in store for us, right now as Ellen comes to sing. Thank you, Ellen."

Going to the piano, Ellen smiled and began to speak, "You know ladies, sometimes our lives are so full, we forget to pray, or we pray out of the realm, not of holiness communing with our Lord, but out of the realm of natural things needed for the day, such as safety which is important for our loved ones, food for their bodies, health, happiness and success but how often do we with a contrite heart ask Him to help us? Do we ask him, Lord, give me more faith, Do we ask for strength to be a better person to love others, Lord, as you love me, or Lord let forgiveness come into my heart where others have hurt me, or do we ask courage to tell others about the one who cares for us?

She paused, letting the words sink in and then continued, "I'm guilty. And then God whispers, have you forgotten? Do you love me, Ellen, enough to put aside your needs for awhile and think about others needs? Sometimes," she took time to let her eyes slowly take in each person, "We need refreshing, we need to pause and let the Lord fill our cup." Sitting at the piano, now, Ellen played the introduction. "This is a song written by Richard Blanchard and made famous by many recording authors. The message for me is this, we are not alone, as women we seek the Lord. To be all that he has planned for us, we must seek the Lord."

"Like the woman at the well, I was seeking." Laura, would remember later thinking of the quietness, the ultimate attention directed toward the one singing for them, surely the spirit of the Lord was in this place. When the song ended, the women sat, it seemed each lost in their own thought and Laura's own was… Lord, help me remember to come to you for others, I need the refreshing of my soul.

The Seminar was both a time of enriched learning and a workshop to understand the skill they held within themselves. "You are unique," Ellen reminded them. "There's only one you that God has made to see the world through your eyes, your heart beat that you are willing to live your life according to his principles and show others the way and it starts with you, in your home, you are the master of your ship, second to the power God instills in you to do his will. He has put power in your hands. Remember the fruits of the spirit. Practice them daily and love others. If we love others as we love ourselves, surely we will make this world a better place to live."

Laura was driving home, lost in thought, the Langley woman had shown them boards with wonderful fabrics and paint colors and accent pieces. Laura gave her credit for willingness to pack and unpack after the seminar the many enticing ways available for decorating one's home and her information was free. At one point she had said, "I would work for free to help you if it were in my power to do so, but I still have bills to pay at the end of the day, therefore I try to work for my customers at a reasonable rate they can afford, rather than run on to a few who say I didn't know what to do and I made a mess." Everyone laughed and then she said, "that's when they come to me and the budget is half gone. You have to understand, licensed as a decorator I receive many discounts with my suppliers which I pass on to you."

Since she and Richard had no furniture to speak of and a house of empty rooms, Laura considered hiring Mrs. Langley. She was coming to the four way stop that led to their home when a red pick up truck cut her off. Laura slammed on the brakes nearly crossing the line of the road into on-coming traffic, when her car landed in the ditch in a forward pitch. It happened so quick, she thought to get out of the car before it ended up deeper or turned over. Cutting the engine, she scrambled for her purse and reached for the door handle just as the door swung open by someone on the outside.

The evening sun blinded her as the person led her up out of the ditch, his hand on her arm tight enough to make her wince. "I'm out," she tried to say, but the person kept moving her along, trying to get out of traffic she supposed and into his truck, but she resisted. Then he spoke and she knew the voice.

"Get in and don't give me any trouble that you or I will regret, because I will drag you through the mud if I have to."

Frantic, now, she tried to look both directions to find a way out. Passer-bys were waving and smiling at her captor thinking him to be the good guy helping a pregnant woman who ran in the ditch. Help me, she mouthed and they mouthed back something she could not discern. He was holding the door open. "Either you get in or I will throw you over my shoulder and deposit you there myself."

"Please," she was near tears and scared out of her mind. "You don't have to do this. Why are you doing this?" She saw him then. His eyes were blazing, his face red and there was a look of hate in his eyes. She glanced upward. God where are you. I need you. "I haven't done anything to you. Please."

"Shut up. You make me nervous and when I'm nervous I usually hit someone. Remember your friend?"

"I remember your little boy limping," she said, regretting the words the minute they popped out.

He slapped her so hard her head flopped to her shoulder. "Now, get in. That's your fault."

Through the haze and burning she wondered if anyone saw him hit her and if they did would they report it? The step up into the truck was high. Adding indignity he practically pushed her up and into the seat. "You even think of getting out, I will run you down," he threatened. Laura shrank against the seat.

He was at the wheel in a flash, throwing the truck into gear and moving across the line going the opposite direction than her home. "Where are you taking me?"

"Don't worry about it. If I say duck, you duck and if I say shut up, you know you had better."

She sat there tears streaming down her face. At first he only blinked and gave her a dirty look, but the tears wouldn't stop and it began to get on his nerves. She could tell he was becoming fidgety, using one hand to search under the seat until he finally said, "I have to drive right, I can't alert anyone that anything is unusual. Feel under the seat for a bottle and hand it to me."

She didn't ask what kind of bottle, she knew, he meant whiskey or beer and she'd guess the first. "There's not one," she finally said, lying, because there was one with no lid, empty, that given the chance she would use. Her mentality was so shaken she wasn't sure what she believed spiritually.

"I'm stopping up the road for fuel and you don't go getting any ideas. You understand?" He kept his eye on her the whole time he was fueling the truck and she wondered how he would handle going inside. She saw him motioning to someone. Evidently the person wasn't interested, then he took money from his wallet and held it up. A teenage boy came over. "Go inside, have Charlie look at the window and see that it's me. Tell him I want the usual and get yourself something, too. Tell him my wife is sick and I'm afraid to leave her in the truck by herself. He'll understand and make that pronto."

It wasn't ten minutes until the boy returned with a bottle in a brown paper sack and handed it to Robert. "Keep the change, Kid," he said climbing into the truck. "Tell old Charlie I said thanks." Laura thought she saw seven dollars in the boy's hand. "Easy come, easy go," he laughed his evil laugh, smirking at her. "You might learn a thing or two, little Laura." He pulled the bottle from the sack.

"I thought you couldn't alert anyone that something's wrong." She feared his driving if he was drunk.

"Well, now little Laura, a fellow can anticipate, can't he? When we arrive our destination, I'll have what I need but you won't, will you?"

She noticed he had some semblance of sobriety, possibly his first behavior was due to drugs that had worn off in the mean time. "Are you going to call Richard?"

"He looked at her as though she were dumbstruck. "Why would that be. Do we need him?"

"I need him and I can't imagine why you would need me."

Watching the view behind, through the visor mirror, he pulled quickly off the highway onto a foot path of sorts through the trees, except he was driving his truck and making wave in the water trenched roots. She counted the times he left the truck to hack up ugly green plants that blocked his view and obsured the path. Weary, he stopped after a length of time and motioned she sit across from him while he recouped his energy level. She closed her eyes and prayed help was on the way.

"Don't you value your life?" He was breathing hard but retained enough strength to look at her as though she were crazy and he was doing some great favor for her.

"Do you not appreciate my attempt to protect you from the wild, little Laura? Word has it there's a mountain lion loose in this neck of the woods. We could have walked but you would have tired out and I'd had to drag you to where we're going and I didn't fancy that chore, so I'm cutting a trail, a trail no one will think to look on because of the overgrowth." He laughed at his own brilliance, "and the truck's tire marks are conceled in the root water bed. Few people know about this little island in the midst of creation."

"How did you learn of it?" She must be alert and pleasant. Pleasant spoke volumes to him.

"Are you being nice, little Laura?" He appeared to consider her question. "I grew up in this area. My father owned a piece of land he inherited from his daddy's family." His voice became droll, "But my daddy gambled his away. Gone in the blink of an eye, he lost it, drunk and gamblin'. Our home gone, my mother crying, where will we go? My daddy drinkin' to forget what he'd done and my brother and me beside ourself that what we knew as home now belonged to someone else." He tipped the bottle to his lips and drank. "Now there's only me. Our sister died giving birth to her third child. My brother hung himself, out by the road, danglin from a tree limb where we'd talked about hanging a swing. Can you imagine that?"

She was silent. He didn't like silence. Silence made a man think and he did not want to think. "No words, little Laura. Don't you want to comment on the unrest of my soul, the tragedy of my family? Do you wonder if I have a mother, still? I do. She's in a nursing home and she doesn't know my name. The last time I saw her she thought I was her husband that lost her home. Do you know how it feels, little Laura when your own mother doesn't know your name? My family is gone and now my wife has taken our son. Gone. And you know where they are, don't you?"

She sat, mute, a shiver running up her spine. If she found opportunity to run, could she? The floor of the woods was woven with roots from the overhanging trees that seemed to flourish in their secret place. Add to that, there were cypress trees with knees visible, some a height she hadn't seen before. It was almost a wonder to be found in the midst of the rolling hills, a valley of sorts she guessed and wondered why she had not known it existed. "Are we trespassing?" She asked.

"So you are alive. I thought you had drift off to sleep. No, we aren't trespassing. I bought it back." He gave a tired laugh, all previous energy gone. "Were you thinking if we were tresspassing someone would come to help you? Well, they won't. I saved and finally I purchased my dad's land so my mother could have her home, but you know what? She had alzheimers and couldn't even stay on her own."

"I'm sorry," she said.

His terrible laughter rang through the trees. "I just bet you are. Sorry is a word used so many times a day, one wonders that it don't wear out. All right, get out of the truck, we have some walking to do, the truck can't go over those cypress knees. They've gotten out of hand with the wet weather. Just put one foot in front of the other and we'll get there." She must have looked as though she questioned him, he slapped his hand against the side of the truck. "I said, get out." The cold look was back on his face, he had managed to take her from the school but he was beginning to wonder what to do with her. "You should know by now, if I say 'hop' you had better hop. There are no second chances." In his hand was a strange tool, it reminded her of one she had once seen her father used to cut stands of cane.

She was weary from the seminar, something about talking social seemed to use more oxygen these days and now the emotional strain, she prayed she could keep up with him, he had taken off in a stride her legs could not match and evidently he was so inclined to believe she realized he would hurt her if she did not follow that he had nothing to worry about. She left her purse, the extra pound was too much to carry and she had no idea how far they were going. Once she thought she heard highway traffic but if he noticed he didn't let on. "Keep up," he barked. "I will not carry you but I'm not beyond dragging you, if I have to." She prayed. She hated his actions. She prayed forgiveness, hating his meanness.

She saw snakes and tried to gain the distance between her captor, if he had to he could cut them In two with the tool he was carrying. She feared they were the poisonous kind and was almost certain they were copperheads. She could not bare the thought of being bit; it would be too much for the baby. That made her sad, to think this was their first child and she might lose it because of her bad judgement going out with Tom Hargrove. She had asked the Lord to forgive her but this man with his giant vindaetta wanted her to pay because he thought she knew the where abouts of his son and wife. She didn't but the son or wife could neither respond nor know the circumstance she was in presently.

When she thought she could go no further, she heard his sigh of relief, and then his words, "There it is. My old home, little Laura, the one my daddy gambled away in a drunken ramble. I hated his drinking."

"And yet, you have a bottle in a bag, you drink every day and it turns you into a mean drunk." She saw his hand raise and shrank back. "just words to a song," she said, singing, "oh, Lord, how long until the sun leaves the sky, the world is our footstool of His magnificance and still we ask why.

"You better watch that smart mouth." He was stomping through the tall weeds that had turned brown and gone to seed to what was once a lawn she supposed. She tried to keep up, it wasn't a user friendly place. Two crumbling concrete steps led up to the porch that had siding half way up and torn screen hanging in swags that had finished the other half. "My Mom used to sit out here and watch the world go by." He pointed back to where they'd come from. "About fifty feet there used to be a busy road, then the interstate came in from Poplar and the people stopped driving by. It was a big disappointment to her."

Taking a key from his pocket he slid it into the solid wooden door and opened it up to a room that still held furniture. Peeling wall paper and a dank smell swelled and poured out of the room onto the porch. "I can't leave it unlocked, there's still kids trek through and if they think I'm in there they go on by."

"I've hid out in the bushes and made noises that they identify as a cougar or a mountain lion loose from the last circus, which as I recall was two years ago and I chased that animal, myself." His words wound down as he pinned his eyes on her studying her to see if the state of the room was bothering her.

She was taking in the lay of the house, a living room that opened to a bedroom one direction and a kitchen dining area the other. As far as she could determine a short hall lay against the backside of the living room entered by way of the dining area. "Your parents home had adequate space," she said. "Are there additional bedrooms?"

"Yes," he said, his eyes pinned on her, as he squinted ready to meet her question. "There are two more, but you won't be sleeping in either one. You have to be in my sight little Laura."

She drew out a long breath of air. "Why are you doing this? I don't know the first thing of why Crystal and Benjamin are missing. Have you filed a report?"

"Why would I do that, when you know full well it never pays to get the police involved."

"I don't know that, I've had few dealings with the Police. Evidently you and they are old friends."

He rose up to stand over her. "I told you to watch your mouth and so have you heard from your precious school." He listened as faint in the bacground they heard a chime. "See what's going on."

"It's a radio," she said," someone is looking for us, but there's no cell, if there were we could talk out."

"Which is exactly what we don't want." He held out his hand. "Hand it over. I've humored you long enough."

"Don't you want to know what's happening and if anyone cares that you have abducted me?"

"I don't know why I'm trying so hard with you? Every word out of your mouth goes against the grain." He pushed the phone into his shirt pocket. "I'm tired little Laura and need to rest. I've been up twenty four hours now, looking for my son. Can you imagine the heart ache, losing one you love? Not having the opportunity to right things that have gone wrong?"

He leaned in, his head a foot away from her, his eyes locked on her with an expression of hopelessness. In his eyes she recognized some of the truth to what Marigold had said in the Siminar. "We're going to talk about decorating our home and then we will add a rather taboo subject. No one ever thinks it will happen to them, but it does. We may all drink of the cup of depression at some time in our life…but today we will make it real. We will speak of circumstance, the cause and the antidote."

"I ask you a question," he thundered. "Can you slip down from your ivory tower and understand what I'm going through?" Anger slashed red across his face as he pushed her down into the chair. "Judge me, that's all the world does, judge me. I ask you if you understand?" He was screaming. "What's ever happened to you that scarred your world? You think you're entitled. That's what I hate about you people. You're too good for the likes of me and yet, you make mistakes, too. Does the world see when you people are adulterous, promiscuous whores?" Laura shrank back, cringing. "No, they see me, a drunkard. I'm labeled and no one cares."

She had to muster her strength and try another tactic. "It's not that you drink, it's that the drink makes you mean and you hurt your wife and your son." Her voice was equally loud and draining her to the bone but she had to keep on while she had his attention. "When you drink you become someone else, you put them down, you ridicule the fact they get nervous and make mistakes. Oh, no, you throw your son to the wall and he limps, what about the next time, will you break an arm, a leg or his neck?"

She saw it coming, tried to dodge but he was dead on target as his fist hit her hard, making her head reel as blood spurt from her nose strangling her as it went down her throat and her face throbbed, she wanted to kill him. At that moment she would wipe his world clean if there was a chance she'd win. She forgot all reason, her foot to his groin, her arms pushing up from the chair, her own fist aiming for his jaw she landed a good punch but he grabbed both of her arms, twisting her until the back of her body lined up to his front and his arms held hers to her side. "Stop now." She heard but her mind would not receive, she kicked until he spun her around. "I told you to stop." He was panting for breath. "I will tie you up to the point you cannot move a limb, do you hear me? Stop moving." He tightened his hold while she struggled until suddenly she remembered the baby. Fear claimed her now, not from his threat but afraid she had hurt the baby. She practically went limp as he managed to drag her to the bed in the other room.

"Get on the bed," his voice had gone from screaming to struggling for breath and cold reserve. She was drowning in defeat, afraid for herself and the baby and still a part of her wanted him to receive the punishment he deserved for taking her when she was nothing to his life but a mistake in judgement.

Chapter 7

At Five o'clock in the afternoon, Richard received the call as he was finishing his day at the store. "What do you mean I need to get my wife's vehicle off the road or it will be towed?" Consternation wrinkled his brow. He was already frustrated trying to reach Laura. Normally she would have dropped by the store after the ladies day at New Haven Church. But she hadn't made an appearance nor called to explain why. "Yes," he ended the conversation, lamely. He would call Bryant's Service to pull Laura's car out of the ditch and have someone drive it home. But where was Laura?

He and Jack Bryant arrived together. Jack was already wondering the best way to pull the car out. "Another foot and she would have slid into the deeper ditch," Jack explained. "Looks to me like she was cut off. See those marks? She hit the brakes pretty hard. Now look, here where the soil is wet from the last rain, two sets of tracks means someone joined her and I'd say the same one caused the accident."

A thread of worry crossed Richard's mind. "Why would anyone cut Laura off?"

Jack traveled the back roads of people's lives. He could name the problems of the local families on one hand. He wanted to think the citizens would act, if they had his knowledge but they were a complacent lot, not wanting anything to rock their world, easier to hide facts than acknowledge them.

"Listen, man," he said instead, "Think. Has your wife any enemies, anyone threatening her? Your wife is a very pretty lady." Jack had heard the stories being told down at the bar. Evidently this husband was unaware and maybe his missus, too, of those stories, being new comers. "All right, Mr. uh, may I call you Richard?" He stood straight, looked his customer in the eye. "Your wife is friends with Miss Crystal Carrington. Right?" Richard nodded. "Well, the grapevine says her husband believes your wife knows her whereabouts and he's got it in for your wife cause she won't tell him. Do you know about that?"

"I know Laura doesn't have any idea where Crystal's hiding out with their son." He was getting nervous, worried over Laura. "Laura thinks Crystal won't tell her where they are so Robert will leave her alone."

"I'm thinking it's the other way around," Jack replied. "These skid marks are from a pick up truck and I've pulled Robert out of enough places to about memorize the treads on his tires. You need to put out a call on the media, if anyone saw a woman leaving the scene of the accident from this location and who she was with."

"You feel that positive he would do something like that?" Richard was dumbfounded. "Man, I feel like a fool if all this has happened, and I had no idea and I'm pretty sure Laura wouldn't have either."

"It's too late to check with the school office to see if anyone's been hanging around causing trouble."

"What about the police?" Now Richard was very worried. "Don't you have to wait a certain amount of time to prove your wife's in trouble?" He had called home a dozen times and she wasn't there but this, this was so far out of his realm of thinking he had no idea what to do. New Haven was a peaceful town.

"Do you dare wait? Do you really care what someone else thinks? This is your wife, man and I get the feeling you are unsure it's the thing to do. If it were my wife I'd move heaven and earth to find her."

"Wait a minute," Richard riled for a moment. "I love my wife but she's so down to earth sensible I can't imagine this happening and she only went to a ladies meeting at the church, is all…this is Saturday."

"But you can't reach her by phone, can you?" Jack hammered away, he had a dreaded feeling. "I've lived around here all my life, the stories about Crystal's husband have circulated for years. He's an angry man, something went wrong in his childhood and shaped a man all bent out of shape. I'd make that call."

"I can't blame a man based on you identifying his tire tracks."

Jack pulled his own cell phone out of his shirt pocket. He pressed a preset number and then began talking. "J.R., this is Jack, there's been an accident down at the four way, I think you need to come down here." He turned back to Richard when he had finished. "Lord, God, man, and I say that prayerfully, you're wasting time with your hum drum sensibilities, this could be your wife's life."

A cold chill ran down Richard's spine. He felt sick, the thought of Laura hurt…he hit the highway, his huge frame laying across the line. Jack shook his head, glad to see J.R. arrive to help him get the man up.

Richard drove home. The Police Department wanted him there in case Laura came home from an innocent outing or, worse, a call came in that someone was holding her hostage. Her best friend's husband was thought to be the culprit. Home was exactly as he left it that morning, except Laura wasn't there. It was his job to tell her parents and his before the message for help was slashed across the evening news through the local channels. He prayed they didn't mention he got anxious and fell out.

Both sets of parents were in state of shock. He had dreaded telling Laura's family knowing her father was suffering more from the cancer these days. He was amazed the strength in the man's hands as he gripped Richard, staring at him, trying to discern if there was more than he was telling them.

They had come to him, understanding the Police Department expected him in their home. Julia, ever the home maker had brought food. "It's important to keep strength," she said, and maybe it will encourage us to pray more and worry less for our dear girl's safety. "Now, Lord," she prayed, "as we are together for our children, Richard and Laura, we come asking safety for Laura, safely and return to us, loving and kind as she left this morning. Let us bind the devil now that not a hair of her head is harmed. Should she encounter one who would mistreat her, let us give him to the Lord, chastise his soul that he feels remorse and shame if dishonor comes to either of them for our Lord, our God the one true God will not bless one who mistreats another in such a life threatening situation. Amen."

"Thanks, Mom," Richard hugged her, needing the creature comfort of reassurance only a mother can give in time of trouble. Laura's mother and Timmy groped for words to say, sitting quietly on the sofa with John when Julia turned from her son to pat their hands and said, "we're family, you don't need to say a thing. Our hearts are heavy together and our prayers are united in love to bring her home safely."

Laura wiped the blood from her face, trying to stop the flow from her nose as she continued to taste it in her mouth. He had wrapped the rope around her feet and tied it to the footboard post. She could do a half turn either way but there was no escape from the rope's entanglement at the foot of the bed. He, on the other hand, now sit in the old stuffed chair just inside the room, eyeing her with distaste that bordered on genuine hate. She had hurt him and would again given the chance. But he was on to her now. She had been docile, even quiet but their screaming had tired them both. If she slept, he would lay on the bed and rest as his body felt the hours bordering twenty eight hours now without sleep.

What was he to do with her? It had never been his plan to kill her but to scare her and in so doing gain the information he was certain she alone possessed. Where was Crystal and Benjamin? His head was pounding, he needed a drink but the fear of what he might do to her kept him away from the bottle that sit unattended on the dining room table. Maybe it was a mistake coming to the home place. Memories crowded in, blending with the present until he had a distorted view of what was real and what was not.

By now, her husband would have alerted the police. There was no way out for him. He thought by the time she walked through the vines and snakes she would be ready to give him Crystal's whereabouts. She insisted Crystal wouldn't tell her so he would leave her alone. Crystal wasn't with her parents. He had checked with them and spent a week watching their home. He wanted to tell Crystal he'd do better. He'd be the father Benjamin needed and if she wouldn't take him back he'd still take care of them. But then something would remind him of her abandoning him and the anger whipped harder and louder through his brain than any plan of redemption he'd considered.

Now he was guilty of abduction and the penalty for that was comparable to kidnapping. With her being pregnant the court would say he had exposed her to serious harm. What should he do? He couldn't turn her loose, she'd never make it out on her own. Where would he go? And he had used force. Why had she followed? Because he threatened her from the beginning. Force, confinement and bodily harm would be enough to send him to the big house.

He heard the voices now. He'd heard them when he was a child. His mother's voice speaking to his father, "Harlan, you don't have to beat the boys. They are good boys. They'd love you if you let them." Soft, whispering trying to show his father a better way. "Shut up woman. I don't need your words." And when she persisted, he'd hear the slam of his daddy's fist against her soft body, her whimper and the next morning she either walked with a limp or had a bruise on her face that deepened in the following days. "Momma, what's wrong?" She never complained, "I fell off the bed, Robert," or, "Wasn't that silly of Momma? I ran into the door." Then little Earl began to notice their mother's hands trembling when their daddy came home drunk. "You leave my momma alone," he'd say. How many times did daddy throw him against the wall until by the time he was twelve he shook like their mother, his head felt strange and the other kids laughed at him. "I'm not surprised he hung himself," he said to his momma. "Shh," she said, tears streaming down her face as she clutched him to her breast, "don't tell Daddy."

He bought the place back for Momma, as bad as life had treated her she loved the old house, the garden in the back where she grew vegetables, except the one year when everything was ready and their daddy went on rampage, destroying every thing she tended so patient and lovingly. That night his heart had blazed with anger. "I think I hate him," he'd whispered. "If he hits you one more time, I'll kill him." His mother had wrapped her arms around him, pleading, "for me, Robert, let it go, we can plant more next year, but I can't have another boy like you. He'd send you away or kill you first. Please, Robert." Her tears had wet the shoulders of his shirt. "I won't kill him, momma but I think I better leave."

He left. Taking a job in St. Louis, glad to be off the Interstate where he'd had trouble hitch hiking. He wasn't certain his job was legitimate. The restaurant served decent hard working folks by day but come eight o'clock the owner closed it down and the back room became a den of gamblers. He was the one sworn to secrecy to keep the drinks coming and his mouth shut. "I don't know why, boy," the owner said, "but I see something in your past recognizes the seedier side of life and if I pay you right, you won't get it in your head to be telling the wrong people…I think you understand if you did?" Robert nodded.

Three years and then he was almost eighteen when he went home to see his momma. She was sitting on the screened in porch in her rocking chair. Cataracts had claimed her eyes to the point she had to hear his voice to know it was him and then the joy lit up her face like the sun shining. "Where's the old man? Did he die?" The sun went out of her face as she pointed behind her. "He ain't well."

He sat the evening with her, until she said, "let's go in and fry some potatoes." The house was in such disrepair, he started picking up. "This is not healthy, Momma. I'll see if I can find someone to clean for you." It was all she could do to shuffle from the sink to the stove, her crippled body trying to deny movement. "Do you want to check on your Daddy?" He didn't but he went, anyway. The one who sired him lay on the old four poster bed, his hands a constant movement as though he were sewing or doing some kind of hand work. "Supper's ready," he said. No hello, daddy how are you, just, "supper's ready."

His father tried to raise up, his hands flailing as he brought them to the sheet to push off, his legs touched the floor as his upper body slid against the mattress until he could right himself. Robert saw he groped for something, possibly the walker against the wall and he placed it within his reach. It was his eyes, in the light, he saw them, a pasty bluish white and he wondered was he blind?

Now, he held his head in his hands, wondering why he was remembering. Why were the moments flashing through his brain as though it were yesterday? He was so tired. She was asleep now. He rose up and went to the bed, lowering himself easy and quiet on to the old mattress. His stomach rolled with hunger and he knew she needed food, but what he needed most was sleep. He was out like a light.

Someone was crying. A man. Laura awakened, listening to the sobs. Who was it? She started to rise, but found movement was restricted. The crying was there. Right there. She reached out a hand to touch Richard. But it wasn't Richard.

"Wake up. You're dreaming," she said it softly so as not to frighten him. "you're having a bad dream." The sobs deepened. Who could know his sorrow? She prayed for peace. "Momma, he hurt me, make him go away. Bring back my brother, Momma. Make Daddy go." He rambled for hours as the story of his youth spilled out and she had comforted him. It was instinct. She placed her hand on her stomach, was her baby all right? As though to reassure her the baby moved and Laura wept silent tears of thanksgiving. She withdrew her hand, coming from her own deep sleep, to remember she was tied to a bed, hungry, and her nose was swollen shut, therefore she could only breathe with her mouth open. She had no choices, only to lay there.

It all came back to her now. She had been abducted. She had walked miles it seemed although he said it wasn't and now her captor lay not three feet away from her, crying in his sleep in what seemed he was reliving the life he had lived in this house. She needed a bathroom and wondered if there was one? She was hungry but there seemed to be no food. How could she move with a rope around her feet that was tied to the foot post of the bed? She tried to rise up but fell back to the matress, tried again and on the third try remained in a sitting position staring at her swollen feet encased in the rope.

Glancing back to her captor she saw the phone lying loose in his hand. Dare she take it? Quickly she captured the phone, still sitting, she found she was able to locate the county sheriff's office. Hurriedly she typed. My name is Laura. I have been abducted. My husband is Richard who runs the new store in New Haven. Please, notify the New Haven Police. We are in an abandoned house somewhere that you have to walk through the woods to reach. I am tied up. There is no food or water and I am pregnant."

Robert stirred on the bed. Quickly she deleted her email, placed the phone back in his hand and fearing he was waking, closed her eyess as though still asleep. She didn't know, but felt he was studying her features in the dark. She did not move until a fresh flow of blood choked her on its way down her throat. The movement of sitting must have started the bleeding again. Now she coughed as he awoke and jumped from the bed as startled as she as realization of their situation surfaced his brain. Gripped in one hand was her cell phone. He glanced at the bars, wondering if there was signal and it showed positive. If he decided to abandon her he would have to send a message that she was alive and let them find her. He would be far down the road and her fate would be in their hands, not his.

J.R. listened to the ringing of the phone. It would be either the Sheriff's Department or one of his own men. He was careful who had his home phone number. The family must not be awakened every time a citizen of the town or county chose wrong. He tred into the next room before he spoke. "I'm here."

"J.R., This is Sheriff Denton's office. We received a text from a woman named Laura, it may be that lady you got the search going for. I'll just read it to you. Says she's been abducted, her husband runs the new store in New Haven and she doesn't know where they are but it's in the woods. We've sent ahead to the phone service. Maybe they can determine where the towers are because if she's in the woods there had to be one nearby, or else the text wouldn't have reached us."

"All right, I'll take it from here. We're going to use the dogs on this, treat it like a drug bust though thee's none involved. Don't know any other way to find her."

He dressed and went to the office. Already, his men had pins on the area towers that were near wooded acreage but they were dissecting the bit of information until only three pins remained on the map. As they stood discussing the likelihood of finding her quickly the second call of importance came in.

"J.R., this is Tom Hargrove, don't know if you remember me but we went to school together. I lived at Walker. My Dad was Mr. Walker's right hand man."

"Tom? I'm thinking. Seems like I do remember you. It's been awhile. How can I help you?"

"I'm thinking it's my cousin you are hunting. I heard the plea for help in finding an abandoned woman on ten o'clock news. Have you any thing further?"

J.R. decided he had nothing to lose. "We got this text," he said. "From a woman named Laura that says she has been abducted but doesn't know where they are though she had to walk to get there."

"I want to make a deal with you based on our past school years experienced together," Tom said in return. "I truly believe my cousin has messed up again and this time he went too far. Here's the thing, I can save you endless hours of search but I'm going to ask you not go against him with weapons, the man's had a rough beginning it seems he can't forget. He's slippin', I saw him last winter and thought I recognized a difference but its hard to pinpoint and we both had drank a little too much. What I'm trying to tell you, he's had a few hardships this year…if you could get him some treatment he'd be a different man."

"Abduction is next to kidnapping, Tom."

"And compassion and caring should be part of your Police Force, also." Tom was sweating, so dire was his need to tell the Chief forget it, but then there was the woman to consider. He gave him the address ; thinking Robert would have seen to the burial of both his parents, possibly on that acreage. Whether Robert was armed was the next thing. But if his momma's body was there, Robert would return.

"Is there a bathroom?" She asked, evident by the hoarseness of her voice suffering. "I've gone as long as I can go. Please." He was deciding whether to remove the rope from her feet. "I won't run. I promise. I'm too weak and tired. I couldn't. Please, is there a bathroom in this house?"

He pulled the knot and unwound the rope from her ankles. "Remember, you promised."

"Yes. Which way?"

He pointed. There were no doors she could exit, still he waited expectant, hoping she didn't try to escape. When she returned he pointed to the bed. "Lay down, as before. I will tie your feet, again."

"Robert, could we talk?" She was trying hard to appear calm when she was anything but calm. Her heart was tripping and her mouth dry as cotton. She was dehydrated but had she drank water throughout the ordeal it would have only caused more problem. As it was she had thought her bladder would explode.

"Did I hear you ask me if we could talk?" She nodded. "There's nothing for us to discuss."

"You talked in your sleep. I heard things, mostly about your childhood."

"I was probably lying," he said. "Now, get back on the bed before you regret it."

"You were asleep. Please, let me stand a few minutes. I need to, to allow my body to adjust."

"What do you have to say? You will tell me where Crystal and Benjamin are, after all this?"

"No," her no came as a wail. "I don't know where they are. Have you called her, her parents?"

"No." His reply was muffled. "I watched her parents house and went to see if she was there, But you didn't stand strong did you? You were supposed to tell them something and you kept it to yourself."

"What's that?" She was surprised at his words. His wife and son had left as abruptly as they arrived and she had nothing to do with it. She held up her hands. "I don't know what you are speaking of." He was resigned she had information. She felt a hundred years old as she struggled to get back onto the bed, climbing up the muscles in her legs burning. She hurt. He was wrapping the rope around her feet.

"I told you to tell Crytal I loved her and I promised I'd take care of her and Benjamin no matter where they are but you didn't tell her. I said I'd go to counseling if she'd just come home."

"You didn't tell me that." She was indignant. "You must have been hallucinating." How could she make him believe she never heard those words. "I remember vividly. All you've ever done was threaten me over Tom, who I had a meal with and you made your ridiculous threat that I was carrying his child. That was utterly unthinkable. If you are like that no wonder she doesn't trust you."

"Watch your mouth. I've had about enough of your goody two shoe ways."

Laura sat up. "I've had my fill of you. You are the most dispicable example of a man, if in truth you think you actually said that then why have you done this? This has ruined your life. You could have talked it all through instead of dragging me from the intersection where you caused me to wreck, then pushing me into your truck and later threatening me to go into a woods few would believe existed in our immediate world and now we are here in this forsaken house that has so many needs if you cared you'd do something but you are a victim of your own self pity. Crystal never had a chance with you, as beautiful as she is, you take away every privilege. You act as though you could do nothing to help this house for your mother while you really possess some strong skills…if you'd use them. I'm sick of you. Do you hear? I'm literally sick of the time you've made me miserable and stressed out and feeling sorry for you. But you thrive on it. You haven't worked! You whimper and whine and act like a spoiled brat. Yes, I'm sick to death of you putting your poison in my mind, trying to ruin my marriage. You undo those ropes. I'm walking out of here and as you so aptly deserve you can go to hell. God would love to have you in his camp but you have some preserved idea you are better than the rest of us. What did you call us some kind of whoremongers, was it? I've never gone against my husband's love. You," She eyed him with scorn, "you thought it manly to mistreat your wife and child. You are this tall in my eyes." She put her index finger to the thumb. Anger was feeding some energy she was expounding. "Get this shackle loose from my feet. Turn your back and I'll walk away and you go wherever people like you go. It will take me months to settle the ugliness that has happened where before there were no hard feelings. We didn't know you but neither did we dislike you. We hoped Ben was happy. How could we know?" She was loosening the knots her eyes on him. "I am finished being the scared little teacher, shoot me if you must and rot in prison. Or, look the other way or leave those are your options. And just for the record why did you call me little laura?"

A smug look came across his face. "Merely to intimidate you. Did it work?"

"I couldn't figure it out. I've felt anger for your ways and I've pitied what you suffered as a child and God forgive me, I've hated you at times but the hate doesn't last because I see your need."

"And what is my need?" He smirked. "Who made you so almighty smart you judge me?"

"You need God in your life. He's the only one can replace the sad hatefulness of your childhood."

He moved into her space so quick she felt his breath on her face. Twisted and ugly he screamed, "Shut up. Shut up. You talk about your God as if you know him but he never heard my cries. Do you think as a child when my mother was bent double in pain, when I bore the lashes on my back that I didn't call on God?" His eyes were pinpoints of fire, his whole body shaking. "Do you think I didn't know to cry out needing Him to stop it all? There was no one else, but he didn't hear me."

She was in such shock, she reacted laying her hands on his shoulders, putting her forehead to his. "Jesus, Heavenly Father, now, at this moment come into our presence. Father, touch this man, save him and save me." She felt the jolt of his resistance, time became nothing, she had no idea the hour or minute that passed, there was a war being waged of which she was not invested, she was merely the vessel of God's grace and the battle was not between him and God, it was the evil wanting to keep him prisoner and then there was a difference, the presence of all things right, goodness entered the fight and she felt him slump. She was uncertain what that meant his body losing its stiffness and he was quiet. Jesus? Within her being she called, Jesus. A feeling of peace came into her, spreading to every cell of her body. Her hands remained on his body, slipping from the shoulders resting now without thought on him as he gathered himself up. His face was different. The deep lines of anxiousness were gone. Almost, he seemed addled, until he spoke. "Little Laura, I don't know what happened but something did happen."

Laura was experiencing a newness of her soul, something she had not known before that the power of God was jolting when used for the good of another. She called on Him in desperation and he answered. "Would you have killed me, Robert? I never really believed you would kill me other than to leave me where I couldn't be found and that was my worry."

"You're not worried anymore?" His eyes met hers.

"No." She smiled and the stranagest thing happened, he smiled back, his eyes warm and at peace.

"I've never felt this before, Little Laura. What is it?"

"It's the love of God. Ask him to forgive you and tell Him you want him as your Savior. He will help you turn your life around, Robert. Don't lose this moment, give your heart to Him."

Tears stung his eyes. "I don't know how."

"Repeat after me. Lord Jesus, I want you to come in to my heart. I ask forgiveness for all the sins of my past. I confess my wrongs and I ask you to live in my heart and lead me the remaining days of my life." Robert repeated each sentence after her. "In Jesus name. Amen."

"What do we do now?" He had a longing to run, to put distance between her and the people who must be searching for her but now he had a responsibility for her safety.

"Will you be faithful to your commitment, Robert? Will you be strong and turn your life completely around and that means no more drinking because it turns you into someone you don't want to be."

"It is behind me," he replied. He handed her the phone. "Do what you have to do."

"When I see Crystal I will tell her you are saved and a new person. A good person."

They moved in quietly. In full protective gear, the men had been given warning not to linger in this one's sight and if he drew a gun, take him out. Dead men didn't tell tales. They hoped to find the woman alive and well. Hearing she was pregnant and no food or water, they brought both.

It was daybreak. They needed light to go through the woods. It was true, as the Hargrove man said. The land was marked by huge cypress trees and a swamp basin that held water year round. They didn't know what to expect. The pick up truck had been driven into the forrest and seldom did anyone venture in that far. In their minds anyone was fool hardy to live in the presence of all those snakes but the woods claimed a certain degree of attention, there were only three of these left in the bootheel.

Getting in and out without an accident was the thing, for they were in harm's way.

They found her, tied to the bed, a rope wrapped around her feet but he was gone.

J.R. radio'ed the base and the base called Richard. "Mr. Worthington, sir, we found her and she's none the worse for the wear. A bit dehydrated but no cuts scrapes or bruises having walked through that we can see. Will you come to headquarteers, Sir, and take her home?"

Richard was overjoyed. He grabbed his mother and swung her around. "Florence, our girl has been found," he embraced Laura's mother and shook her daddy's hand. "This has been the hardest thing I've lived through, them telling me to stay here when I wanted to be out hunting for Laura. But they said it could be her life if someone called and I wasn't there." He shook his head. "I don't understand any of it."

John had tears in his eyes. "I couldn't tell you how worried I was." Richard's father reached over to pat his friend on the shoulder. "God blessed us again." To his son, he said, "I guess you want to go alone?"

Richard grinned. "This time, Dad, I do. Y'all stay here and visit or nap and we'll be right home."

Laura was on the brink of pure exhaustion. The Sheriff said, "Mrs. Worthington, I suggest you see a doctor and get checked over as soon as you can. Be sure that baby is all right. It's just something most folks need to do. It's protocol as far as we're concerned but right now I'd say you could sleep through twenty four hours. You lost Sunday and this is Monday, so those kids you teach will be worrying and wanting to see you soon." He shook his head thinking she was one of the lucky ones. "When you're rested we'll do paper work." That too, he was letting slide because she was exhausted.

Richard picked her up and carried her to the car. "I was so worried, Babe, I never knew a person could put their self through such anguish. I was scared to death you were being tortured. Oh, Laura, did he hurt you?" She was asleep and it broke his heart just seeing her this way, maybe he didn't need to know. It almost seemed she was at peace, and yet she had been through trauma.

They arrived home and he carried her in. Under the lights they could see the grime from walking through the woods and her face was swollen and covered in blood. Julia was first to notice her nose was pitched at a wrong angle. "Florence, we got to clean our girl. She needs a good bath. Do we wake her and put her in the shower or wash her down ourselves?"

"Let's get the water just right and I'll get in the shower with her." Florence looked to Richard. "You'll have to carry her in and we'll take it from there." Laura's bath was something they'd never forget and in time they would laugh at what they went through giving it. Considering all Laura had experienced, her little baby was moving inside its mother like a tadpole in a ditch. The grandmothers reveled in its activity amd when some little dent raised Laura's stomach they rejoiced that all seemed well with the baby.

It was Julia mentioned her nose. "When my brother broke his nose we had an old time doctor and all he did was take a piece of plastic and tape it across top of his nose to keep the bone straight. You want to try it, til she goes to the doctor?"

"Might as well," Florence agreed. "I thought they'd insist she go to the doctor tonight." Before all was over, Julia was half in the shower with them but fully wet while Laura was scrubbed clean, her nose straightened and a piece of white plastic formed from a butter tub taped across the center of her nose and an ice pack placed on the egg sized lump on the side of her face.

"Richard," Julia called him back in. "You're going to have to go to bed and hold her and take that ice pack off after a few minutes then place it on that lump again, you understand that don't you, Son?" Julia thought a minute. "Now, she might wake up hungry as a bear, sweet or grumpy, and you can scramble some eggs and fix that bacon in the frig that's already cooked. She'll be happy." Julia was collecting the towels and wash cloths and Laura's dirty clothes. "Another job for tomorrow," she said.

"I can't come back in the morning if you all can manage. It's time for John's check up and to see if he's holding his own. I'm sorry but the appointment is important." Florence felt torn leaving Laura.

Julia turned to hug Florence. "Yes, it is, my friend and a few dirty clothes could never compare. We are all praying for John's recovery. We got a miracle here and we're praying for his miracle of healing. And this girl, here, needs her momma and daddy, just as much now as when she was three years old."

"Son," J.W. said, upon leaving, "You need to stay home with Laura until she gets on her feet. Don't you agree?"

"Yes, sir, I intended to approach the subject and as always you are ahead of me. Thanks, Dad." He watched their parents leave, thankful for the harmony between them because his mother was a force to reckon with and Laura's mom was just as firm, but Florence concern right now was her husband's health. Mr. John was showing the strain of the treatment, but the course of therapy alone was enough to kill him. Richard locked the door and went to the bedroom. Laura was so deep in sleep it concerned him, whereas it seemed not to bother the mothers at all.

"She's worn through and through, son. Physically, mentally having to deal with someone who took her captive and no doubt spiritually, too. It was a trial anyway you look at it. It had to be very trying." His mother's words circled his brain. Surely she wasn't molested she would have said, still he worried as he slipped into bed, replacing the ice pack that was supposed to relieve the swelling of her jaw and he wondered how that happened? She was pretty battered. His mind would not turn loose the questions. It was seven o'clock when she stirred. He had seen every hour on the hands of the clock. Thinking she was ready to face the day, he raised up on one elbow to study her face in the daylight. She didn't open her eyes but tried to snuggle closer to his body. Her face was a series of dark gray blue and purple bruises. For a spell, his thoughts lingered on revenge for a man that would hurt a woman that way.

According to the words of the Police Department, they had taken food due to the fact she hadn't eaten since Saturday noon but she had refused to eat saying she knew best it would make her deathly ill. "Laura," he said her name softly, lest he frighten her, who would know what she had been through and how she would react? "Laura," he placed a hand on her arm. "Babe. You have got to wake up and eat. The baby needs you to wake up, too." He looked up, to heaven, praying help me, Lord. "Laura."

She heard her name. But she couldn't reply. It was dangerous to make a sound. She was in hiding. "Laura." Was that Richard? He wasn't there. It was Robert, Crystal's husband. "Laura." She was hesitant. He promised the world but she worried he could produce. "Laura, the baby needs you to wake up." When did they have their baby? Her hand went to her stomach feeling the slight rise as she waited for the movement and then it was happening, the baby moved, her own little tadpole in its swimming pool of her stomach. She smiled. Thank you, Jesus. Oh, the bed felt so good. Delicious. And that brought her awake. The bed? Her eyes popped open. Where was she? It felt like home but she couldn't remember.

Slowly her eyes rounded the room, the long scarf wound over the windows, the opened blinds, a picture of a little girl with a watering can standing in the midst of roses. The dresser, a chest of drawers. She felt such joy, to see familiar things again. Surely they were hers and Richards. Where was he?

He walked carefully carrying the tray. He would waken her. There were scrambled eggs, bacon and toast and orange juice for two people. He prayed there were no new problems when she awakened. "Laura," he said, sitting the tray on the night stand. "Laura?" And she replied, "What, Richard?" There was a smile in her voice and his heart leapt with joy. "Oh, Babe, you are awake. I prayed you would be."

Laura tried to rise but her body resisted. She felt the flush to her face. "Oh," she was embarrassed. "It feels strange to be in this bed. I can't believe how thankful I am to be home where beds are clean."

"Do you want to talk about what happened since Saturday evening?" He sat in the big chair opposite the bed, "Or do you want to eat breakfast and then try to get through your experience so the Police Department can record it? It's up to you."

"First, I need to go to the bathroom. I think I nearly ruined my kidneys the first day," She was trying to bring her body around as she sat up. "If my body will just work." She had one foot on the floor but the other leg was giving her trouble following suite. "What's going on here?" She lay back, already feeling exhaustion.

Richard felt the unrest flash through his mind, how badly was she hurt and would she tell? "Laura, did he hurt you? Were you knocked down? That might be part of what's wrong with your leg movement."

"No, Richard, he didn't knock me down. For the record, Robert Hargrove did abduct me and keep me captive but he did not personally attack me." She sighed, her mind divided as to her captor and the new problem of her leg not moving as it should. "I think, in looking back, he was sorry he took me but he didn't know what to do about it. I couldn't help him because it was enough that he killed my willingness to be a docile prisoner by keeping me tied up so that in his mind I couldn't leave the house."

"This was at a house?"

"His parent's home. As I understand his father was an alcoholic and gambled and he lost their home, which Robert never forgave him and years later he bought it back for his mother who by that time had alzheimers. It's not a pretty story but I think it does shed some understanding on why he's the way he is." By using her hands on each side of her knee, Laura brought her other leg to sit normally.

"Do I detect forgiveness in your tone, Laura? I don't think he has achieved that. What he did was a federal offense." Richard's troubled voice was doubled by a mix of anger and sadness in his eyes. "I can't forgive the fact you could have been marred for life." He placed the tray on her lap and pulled away from her hand on his. "He heaped fear in our hearts and we don't understand why he chose you to make his big statement to society. It will be hard for me to forgive his harm to you."

She was no quicker in her thinking than the movement of her body. Later she would realize that was the moment she could have told Richard the secret keepings of her heart but would he have accepted her version or since she had been kidnapped believe the worst and remove his understanding and acceptance that she had suffered and still she would face the questions society would hurl her way.

They ate in silence, a slight break in their usual compatibility. What had brought on his line of question and why did she dismiss Robert Hargrove so easily? When she used the napkin she realized her face was swollen and hurt to the touch. "Would you mind handing me the little mirror, Richard, from the dresser." Without a word he reached for the mirror. Shock was her first reaction and then tears. "Oh, my goodness," she drew out. "Now I see why you think I was attacked."

Chapter 8

By the second week Laura's bruises had disappeared enough that make up covered the remaining shadow of discoloration. She returned to teaching stronger in body than had she returned the following week. It was the principal convinced her there was no need worrying the children whose minds were impressionable and that they might feel threatened they faced being kidnapped. Their concern for Laura was both comforting and a nuisance, though a sweet nuisance as they asked fifty times a day, "are you all right, Mrs. Worthington?"

She had been summoned to the Police station to give her account of what happened. She was thankful Richard was at work. An assault with intent to harm had been filed against Robert stating he used force and had abandoned her while restrained. "It doesn't look good for him," the Chief of Police stated. "His cousin has called asking we drop the charges, due to the fact the man has a recent history of illness. His words are that his cousin is suffering a mental break down after the loss of his wife and child." He studied Laura, his eyes penetrating her stoic countenance. "Are you aware he lost his wife and child?" One of his men had interuppted at the very moment she answered, "yes, sir." She shook off the possibility one day she might have to explain her reply. Truth was Crystal and Benjamin had left him.

The new ownership of New Haven's most prominent hardware celebrated a grand opening on the first weekend of November. "James Wilson has gone all out," Florence remarked. "I guess I never thought about you moving away from us." She sighed. "I know, it's a thirty minute drive but with your Dad sick it seems more." Heaving another deep breath she settled down in one of the big overstuffed chairs. "I don't know what's wrong with me, I seem to be grieving and no one has died. I'm relieved you are all right…it's just I have this sadness inside me…."

"I think you are grieving, Mom, over Dad's being sick and the doctor saying two years has to weigh on your mind, even if he is Dad's friend from High School." She dropped down by her mother's knees. "It bothers me, too, Mom. How do you think he's doing right now?"

"Relieved the crops out, but wore out every night. It's all he can do to get his shower and crawl in bed." She wiped a tear from the corner of her eye. "I usually can keep my emotions in check, hidden even but seeing him sad makes me more so, too. And Tim, is trying hard, Laura, he's taken on more that he thought he could but it's the same sadness wearing him down and he's young. He shouldn't feel it so strong."

'He's got a girlfriend, now, Mom. Maybe they will go places and have fun. Like you said, crops out and he's got enough money to do a few things and if he hasn't I'll fund him."

Florence laughed. "He's probably got more than both of us. He certainly is no spendthrift. I thought he was saving to go to college but then he said, no, he was saving to buy a tractor and get started in farming.'"

"'Mom, why don't you and Dad, Timmy, too, come to church with us Sunday? It would do you good to meet some of the people

Richard and I will be speaking about time to time and that way you can put a face on the names. These are wonderful people and it might give you something to think about. Pastor Merkel and Leah are down to earth people and good leaders at Shining Light."

"I used to wonder if ministers and their families had problems like the rest of us," Florence replied, "Your Dad said they are regular people. I think serving on the deacon board he probably knows a few things the rest of us only suspect. Still, they seem to be on a first name basis with God and have perfect lives. Of course I only know about the ones we've had at our church."

Laura laughed. "Well, Leah surprised me. She said once the church was having revival and she left Levi, Pastor Merkel. I couldn't believe it. I did, she said, everyone was having a baby but us, and my nose was out of joint. So I guess they do have problems but it's good they are on a first name basis with God."

"Do they have children?"

"One little boy with a name as long as he is tall." Laura started to get up. "Mom, you are going to have to help me out of this floor. That wasn't part of the plan but my big belly makes me lose balance."

"Oh, Honey, you aren't big at all. I gained sixty pounds with you. But yours is all baby."

She was driving to New Haven when Richard called. "I'm headed home," she said. "Mom's a bit sad, Richard. I guess Dad's been at the store with you and your dad, hasn't he?" She listened to Richard telling how her dad won the second place prize. That new coffed machine, he said. Reckon he'll use it? "I don't know, I guess he was putting on a good front, wasn't he, as though he was well and going to live forever?"

"That's about it," Richard agreed. She felt so sad she pulled off the road and had a big cry. During her time on the side of the road, her phone buzzed. She studied the number. It was unfamiliar. The message displayed two words. Thank you. She deleted number and message and pulled back onto the highway. She was in constant prayer these days. "Prayer makes a difference," Pastor Levi said. She was counting on it. For some reason the sermon he preached the

Sunday before the women's Seminar came to mind. No doubt it had a bearing on her experience during the time of abduction.

"Please, don't judge me until you have walked a mile in my shoes," he said on that Sunday morning. "You think you know my life's history, you don't. What you know are the horrible things people say trying to make entertainment in a small town atmosphere that is reminiscent of New Haven. My story has not been written and if it were you wouldn't read it. My daddy was an alcoholic, my mother lost her way when he became abusive and beat her over the smallest incident. It made him feel like a man, but to me it reduced him significantly. You ridicule my backward ways, but I'm not uneducated, I don't want people seeing my mentality as something they joke over. Given a chance, I will rise to greater heights but I must have a chance. When you sit in church wearing your best Sunday clothes, praying to your God think about me, I never had the privileges you do. But please don't judge me until you have walked a mile in my shoes. I received this letter through the mail this week. Does it belong to you?"

His eyes roamed the congregation. "Someone is reaching out. You sense the anger, the hurt but what can you do about it? What can I do? I don't know who wrote the letter. One thing we can do is this, prepare ourselves for a time when God puts someone in front of us who needs him. That is the need. We all need the Lord, but if someone by God's design stands before us, what can we offer that person? Can we love them? Are we prepared as scripture says to fight the good fight, to supply God's word? Are we equipped to act in our Saviour's name? The time may come upon you unexpectedly. What will you do?"

She hadn't realized until this moment, through the mix of emotions she had felt being taken and the walk through the woods, God had a plan and if he hadn't surely she would have been bitten by one of those many snakes. She shuddered, remembering. Other things had taken priority and though she would never have suspected she could react with boldness, in anger she had and the anger had turned to compassion for one who was hurting, turned by God's grace, not through anything she posessed. Now she was thankful she and Richard had attended Shining Light Church and the seed had been planted that Sunday morning. She must pray for Robert every day because the devil would try to rob him of his commitment to the Lord. Thank you Jesus, she whispered. Thank you I'm safe and whole because of you. Look, she wanted to shout to the world, I'm no one special but I'm God's child. Look, what he can do?"

Cutting through the forrest made sense, but it also made it more dangerous taking him deeper into the infested water. If they ever drained the basin it would be a choice spot, except for the snakes. Strange the snakes didn't seem to leave and he wondered why? Evidence of someone spraying the undergrowth made him question the feasibility of the act. He owned the acreage. This morning, however, when it was cooler and he was diving into his cache' of things he found the old alumni sweater he had worn to the games. In those days it seemed the "in" thing to wear. He tore the emblems off the back and front, leaving a pattern that could not be erased that made him appear like a homeless victim. He felt the pockets of the sweater, there had always been a photo of Crystal unless someone removed it.

He knew when the sheriff's people showed up, not one ventured into the forrest. Fear of snakes, he chuckled, me too. But he knew which ridge to take, backtracking near Laura and the incoming team from the Police department. They would confiscate his truck but surely turn it over to Crystal in the end. There was no way he could drive a marked vehicle. He would find a Mission and get different clothes, then he had no choice but to hitch hike to where he knew he could find a job.

The nearest town took care of the clothes need and he purchased a phone that he could easily discard if necessary. His first message bore two words. Thank you. He would spend the rest of his life being grateful God heard his prayer but already he recognized the devil was trying to pull him back into the blackness his soul had known. The bottles along the road teased his mind, while his thirst built. He was lucky a driver wasn't afraid of him. "You got a gun?" He asked and when the answer was no, he said, "Load up. I'm on the way to St. Louis, should arrive around five this evening." The noise in the cab prevented conversation. He dug in his heels and slept.

Shining Light Church

They waited in the car until they saw her parents pull into the church drive. Laura watched them getting out. Tim was at the wheel with his girlfriend in the passenger seat. Her dad stood, finally, stretching as he tried to rid his body kinks. "Dad looks pale," Laura said. "Doesn't he?"

"Yes, he does but he's made the effort to attend so let's don't say anything negative." She went to meet them, embracing both with a kiss on the cheek.

"You two are looking mighty dapper," she said. Her dad tried a slight bow but it was too much. "I'm so glad you came. Come, I want you to meet Shining Light's pastor Levi."

"Good to see you, Laura," he said, are you feeling better?" She nodded and introduced her parents.

The welcome was made and the song service began as Timmy and His girlfriend slipped into the pew.

"Oh, I like this," Florence whispered. "The old songs are so full of meaning." She squeezed Laura's hand and then patted John's. She saw the tears in his eyes but he was singing, Rock of ages cleft for me.

"Rock of Ages," Pastor Merkel began. "Do you know the Rock of Ages? Should Jesus come today, are you ready to go, to leave this place?" There were several amen's. "Let us stand for the reading of the word."

"First Kings chapter nineteen, to set the reading, Jezebel was angry with Elijah because he had slain her prophets and she promises he will very soon be as dead as her prophets and Elihah knowing Jezebel's wrath believes her and flees. Now he leaves his servant behind and goes into the wilderness but soon tires out and sits down under a juniper tree and asks the Lord to take his life but twice an angel of the Lord comes to refresh him and tells him you are going on a journey. Let us pick up in verse nine." Elijah came thither unto a cave and lodged there and behold the word of the Lord came to him, and he said unto Elijah, what doesn't thou here, Elijah? Verse ten, Elijah says I have been very jealous for the Lord God of hosts for the children of Israel have forsaken thy covenant, thrown down thy altars and slain thy prophets with the sword and I even I am the only one left and they seek my life to take it away."

"Here we find whether Elijah is truly alone or thinks he alone remains. Verse eleven. God said, Go forth and stand upon the mount before the Lord, and behold the Lord passed by and a great and strong wind rent the mountains and brake in pieces the rock before the Lord; but the Lord was not in the wind; and after the wind an earthquake; but the Lord was not in the earthquake. And after the earthquake a fire; but the Lord was not in the fire and after the fire a still small voice. And when Elijah heard it he wrapped his face in his mantle and went out and stood in the entrance of the cave."

"You may be seated. We know if we read the rest of that passage God is changing kings and prophet. Elijah will be replaced by Elisha, but the thing Elijah learns is he is not alone. God tells him in verse eighteen, "I have seven thousand in Israel whose knees have not bowed to Baal nor kissed him.""

"Did you notice? God came to meet Elijah, Why are you here? He knew but he asked. Neither the wind, the fire or the earthquake affected Elijah, he did not cover his face but hearing the still small voice, Elijah covered his face. The elements of wind, fire, earthquake may have terrified him but he was untouched; it was the still small voice of God's love, Elijah recognized God's tender mercy and covered his face."

"That voice spoke to his heart. Today, God's mercy and grace speak to us through the cross on which Jesus died. That still small voice has the power to take possession of our heart, to live within us, to become our rock. Elijah worried over being the minority but our God who sees in secret that which we do not, comforted him. "Elijah, there are seven thousand I know who have not bowed to Baal."

"Now, casting aside your worries listen to that still small voice, I am your rock of ages, no matter what you face believe in me, I am with you." Pastor Merkel looked on the people of Shining Light Church, "do you know your rock? Have you heard that still small voice. Is your belief in the God who will save you?"

On Sunday, In St. Louis, Robert found a place to worship. It was a seedier part of town, but he noticed the sign hanging over the door. God's people meet here. He watched the neighborhood leave their homes to gather in that old storefront building. His was a room on the second floor of his bosses home, neither elegant nor threabare, somewhere in between; because the boss kept a low profile.

"You in trouble, Robbie?" He'd ask, shaking his wooly head, not expecting an answer. "Come on down to the new restaurant. You'll be surprised. Same old job, eh, Robbie?" Cuffing Robert, he said, "Welcome back. I can always use a man like you. You understand what you see but you don't talk. Dead men don't tell tales, now do they?"

The restaurant was all silver metal and matte black trim, with wide spanse of mirrros everywhere to make it appear larger. "Steppin' on up, huh, Robbie boy?"

"Elegant," Robert agreed, eyeing the stark white table cloths with stiff matching napkins. "What do you do…. have a cover charge per person? I mean someone has to pay the laundry bill."

"You got that right." Boss moved behind the counter. "Not a lot of action here 'til say twoish, men in for a drink, women skirtin' real life and lookin for a little tease on the side, then hurry home to the kids and the dull husband, but after hours, we rock."

"Dull husband? I'll remember that."

"Did you marry, Robbie?"

"Yeah, it's on the rocks." Thinking of Crystal and Benjamin made his heart ache. He was in the wrong place, all that booze, but here he would go unnoticed. He had to be strong. She better be praying as she said she would. Maybe he'd be the light in the darkness. He glanced up to the boss studying him.

"Don't have to talk about it, if you don't want, son." The Boss turned toward his office.

"You seem to know the Boss," a fellow named Red remarked as theyi were getting ready to open. "Long time?"

"I was young, ran errands for him."

"Guess you heard his only son was killed last year."

"No, I didn't stay in touch."

"Bad deal. Drug exchange on the street went wrong, the kid was caught in the crossfire."

"Hate to hear that." Robert glanced across to the Boss's office. The door was shut.

"He didn't come in for a week. We ran the place best we could. Homey was in charge of money. Counted it every night and hid it somewhere besides the vault. We knew if there was a break in that's what they'd be after. Great chef that Homey is, no tellin' where he hid that money."

"Maybe in the potato bin."

"Don't take it lightly, ten thousand dollars in a week's time ain't chicken feed."

Robbie whistled.

Red nodded. "Yeah, lot of speculation goin on. Where'd it come from? What do those after hour folks do the day timers don't?"

He figured he was free labor for the evening hours but nights he was handed three hundred cash. That times six nights a week and a free room to sleep in, he figured he'd have wheels in no time at all. What to do about the situation at home weighed on his mind as he slid onto an old movie seat with one side of the arms torn loose. If she dropped charges it wouldn't be so bad, but would her husband let her?

"Welcome." Hand extended, "I'm Elijah Samson, the preacher here at Mission on the Street. Most call me Samson. Make yourself at home, we worship the one true God and pray blessing on your life, brother." Samson was aware he was studying the sleeve of tatoos on his arms. "No need to cover them up, are there, Brother?" Robert shook his head speechless. Samson was unlike any pastor he met before. Long hair in a braid down his back, wearing knee shorts and a red T emblazed with the words He Paid It All beneath Jesus on the cross but the most interesting thing was the tatoo of the cross in the middle of his forehead. "It's real," Samson said. "It doesn't wash off." He flexed his arms forward, "Did you see these?" Stripes. "By His stripes are we healed. Now, you see the serpent? The old devil would destroy us all if we allowed it. That's what we're about here at the Mission on the Street, we don't let him."

For lack of a better word, Robert said, "amen." Samson shook his hand again and moved on. The room was almost filled when the musicians came from the back to take their place behind the pulpit. Seeming to strive for a degree of respect they were all dressed in clean white t shirts and black cargo pants. He would find they were the backdrop for their flamboyant pastor, Samson. Just as he decided this was not the church of his Momma, the band began to play. A young man with a ukelele stepped up to the mike and lead in singing. I'll see you in the morning with a smile on my face, the music was fast paced and the musicians were expert. He settle back into his chair. The old Rugged Cross and I'll Fly Away came next and by then he was feeling the sincerity of the congregation. They may not have much at home or on the street but here it was about what they gave and what they received. They sang with their heart and listened with their mind. It was something he felt inside, himself. Here, they worshiped in truth and they sought God to bring them through whatever they faced next. He was one of them.

The singing ended and Samson stood before them.

"This morning, for some reason the Lord has changed my sermon. I planned the message around Isaiah forty five verses twenty two and twenty three where God says Look unto me and be ye saved; all the ends of the earth for I am God and there is none else. I have sworn by myself, the word is gone out of my mouth in righteousness and shall not return, that unto me every knee shall bow every tongue shall confess." Samson quoted the words, peering out into his group of people. "But the Lord tells me someone needs to hear his word from Psalm ninety one.'"

"Joy will hand out the leaflets with the words written on them, for you who do not have a Bible, just hold up your hand. For you here for the first time we welcome you. Joy is my wife and we pastor Mission on the Street through the united in spirit churches of our city."

"Psalms ninety one, verses one through seven reads as follows. "He that dwelleth in the secret places of the most High shall abide under the shadow of the Almighty, I will say of the Lord, He is my refuge and my fortress; my God; in him will I trust. Surely He shall deliver thee from the snare of the fowler, and from the noisome pestilence. He shall cover thee with his feathers and under his wings shalt thou trust; his truth shall be thy shield and buckler. Thou shalt not be afraid for the terror by night; nor for the arrow that flieth by day. Nor for the pestilence that walketh in darkness; nor for the destruction that wasteth at noonday. A thousand shall fall at thy side, and ten thousand at thy right hand; but it shall not come nigh thee." Let us skip to verse eleven. "For He shall give his angels charge over thee to keep thee in all thy ways."

"Someone in this group, and no, I don't want you to hold up your hand, you know who you are. You have been through a quagmire of problems, perhaps you are even running from the law. You believe in God the creator but you have been doubting your faith based on what has happened to you presently."

"Maybe you have had to dwell in a secret place, fearing being found, whether you have pulled away from family friends or society, you longed for knowledge that it would all be all right. You tried to summon your faith but it was weak. I'm not to blame for the problem, you say. It wasn't my fault and whether it was or was not, still you need the Lord. Psalms ninety one reads almost like a prayer. You want safety. You want a real life and you want to trust in Him. Gone are the days when you practiced all manner of wrong doing, now you are His. That's why verse eleven tells you He shall give his angels charge over thee, to keep thee in all thy ways. He knew where you were when you were hiding in that secret place thinking things over. Right now, he is speaking to you, saying trust me.

I know the temptation is staring you in the face to do wrong but you gave your life to me. I will cover you as a hen spreads her wings and covers her chicks. But you must trust me. You will grow stronger In my care. Whatever you face, trust me and don't give up."

"First, if anyone needs to come to the altar and pray, come quietly, now. If anyone does not know the Lord, come to the side of the Altar where Joy waits. And lastly, if you need someone to pray with you, come sit on the front pew and our members will join you and pray with you. As the music is played, come."

Sunday in New Haven

They were filing into New Haven's newest restaurant, built on the edge of town nearest to the Interstate. The little restaurants in the heart of town were owned by families that attended church and did not cater for Sunday business. They felt the need to rest in order to open back on Monday.

"I haven't been here," Florence remarked as they were seated. "This is really nice and I enjoyed the church, too. I'm thinking New Haven will grow with you and your new business, James Willson. How do you feel about it."

"Well," he replied, "The hardware was already here, but Richard felt if we brought in the lines we sell over home, it would prosper and thus far he's proven right. I hear there's talk of a walking mall coming in the spring. Word has it will locate across the road and face this restaurant and I suspect those flags are there for that very reason. Different colors mean a different line, water and so on."

"Could New Haven reach the size of the Cape?" Julia was listening as she studied the menu. "We've all been just a spot in the road for so many years its hard to believe progress is coming to this area." She glanced across to Laura's dad. "What are you having today, John?" She laughed. "Seems you and I order about the same every time."

"I'm thinking the chicken, Julia. They tell me it takes three days for beef to digest. I may not have that long."

Julia laughed but Florence scolded. "What a thing to say and there I spent the whole evening ironing your shirts." Everyone laughed, but the sound was hollow as all were concerned for John.

"I truly don't know what to think of their generation," Laura said to Richard. "Doesn't it seem a bit morbid?" There were actually tears in her eyes. Richard pat her hand and shook his head.

"Well, honey," John added, "I don't know. Sometimes I feel I'm going to make it and others I question. Only God knows the answer. Didn't you feel any of that when the fellow made you walk through those woods?"

"I try to put it behind me, Dad." She felt a twinge of remorse but why open a new can of worms?

"But I can't this one, Laurie," John wore a sad expression. "We don't know what's going to happen and you didn't either. I think the prayers of the people turned your situation around; I'm hoping mine too."

"What's the last word on the abductor, Richard? Has the Sheriff's office closed it or keeping the case open? I meant to tell you, Son, someone in the store mentioned this Robert is Tom Hargrove's cousin."

The following week, the grapevine news said Crystal and her son had returned to New Haven.

"Why would they do that?" One of the teachers ask, "If it is as rumored her husband beat the two of them, why would they come back for more?"

"The Sheriff's department needed to know what to do with his truck. Surprisingly it is paid for."

Laura listened, trying not to bring attention to the fact she was still present. She wanted everyone to forget she was abducted, being careful not to leave themselves open to such, just leave her out. I hope he doesn't return, she thought. I'm not sure I could deal with it. The thought was followed by a still small voice speaking silently. Did you ever experience such hardship, Laura? Do you remember the sadness of his life? Did you agree to pray his life would run smoother having faced his demons?

She hurried home that afternoon, pulling her shoes off at the door and sitting in the old rocker with an ottomon to elevate her feet. Not realizing how weary the weekend had made her, Laura drifted off to sleep. She awoke to Crystal leaning down to stare into her face. "Haven't we done this before?" She asked, "or is this dejuvu?"

Crystal laughed, beckoning Benjamin from across the room. "Come here, sweetheart, Aunt Laura is awake." She hugged Laura. "How are you muffin? You look ready to give birth and isn't it supposed to be a couple more months?"

Biting her lip she tried to stop the drool that had formed just inside her lips, this wasn't real or was it…Crystal was saying, "Hey, wondergirl, are you all right? You look a bit unscrewed."

"I couldn't figure if I was dreaming or you were for real. I'm embarrassed, I must have died to the world."

"Lucky me that you left the door unlocked. Haven't you learned a lesson about that, yet?"

Laura opened her arms to Benjamin. "Hey big boy, I missed you." He grinned and went back to watching television. "How is he? How are you?"

"We've recuperated. Robert's missing. The Sheriff's department said they can't find him and either we come get his pick up truck or they'd sell it." She laughed, "Well, something like that is what he said."

"You look good and you sound happy. Are you?"

"Yes, actually Benjamin and I seem to have healed, I'm working from home and meeting the bills, so life is better than before and we are settling back into the house. You won't believe what I've found out."

With Laura waiting, Crystal did a little dance. "I found out all that worry I've done whether we can make the house payment or not, the house was paid off last year when Robert was getting all the overtime."

"You didn't know?"

"No, we didn't talk about it. You and I did."

Yawning, Laura frowned trying to get a hold on the conversation. "Let me get this straight, how many times did you mention to me you were afraid you'd lose the house if the payments weren't made and today you tell me Robert was paying for it all along but you two did not discuss it. Why?"

"Things had gotten really bad and we didn't talk about important things. I didn't want to do anything that upset him."

"Crystal, why was he easily upset?"

"I don't know."

"He was your husband."

"So?" Crystal was returning to her old self. "Why would you care, Laura? You have all this?" She spread her arms and circled. "Have you ever wanted since you married Richard?"

"No. The question is, have you wanted since marrying Robert? Evidently he paid off your home and you didn't even know it. Did anyone tell him they were happy it was done because that's a "biggie.""

Crystal stood hands on hip. "You can't brag on someone if you don't know what to brag about, can you?" Her eyes were changing to a hard expression. "Whose side are you on, anyway? Isn't he the one who abducted you and walked you through that snake infested jungle."

"Speaking of sides, I've always been on your side but I've also been broad minded enough to think things through. Ever since the abduction I've wondered what set him off, why me and what makes him tick."

"What's to think? You have wounded me, Laura. So what gives that you would consider Robert for any reason. He beat his wife and son. End of message. What does a woman do after that? I got out with my body intact and my mind working and you're lucky you did the same."

"I know that, Crystal. Your news is a bit stunning in the fact that you didn't know."

Crystal slumped down on the sofa. "Is it? Remember my battered and broken nose? It has taken three months for it to feel like my nose again."

Laura was pointing to her own. "But you didn't wear a piece of plastic stretched across your nose to keep the bone in place covered by a huge bandaid. My nose met his fist, too."

"He did that to you?" Crystal was adequately startled. "Oh, my goodness. I didn't know." She was digging in her oversized purse. "Here it is." She brought out a professional brace of sorts. "This is what they stretched across my nose." She sighed dramatically. "I kept it in case I ever needed it again."

Laura rose and shuffled to the back of the sofa. Opening the drawer of the sofa table, she brought out the strip Julia had formed from a plastic butter tub. "Only in New Haven are the doctors so behind times to use these." They began to laugh, Crystal coming to wrap her arms around Laura. "I've missed you but a few minutes ago I was mad as the dickens at you."

"I know it wasn't the first time, heaven knows, nor the last, either, I'm thinking."

"At least we're laughing. I cried a lot when we left New Haven. Did you cry when you were abducted?"

Laura thought a moment. "I had tears but I didn't cry much; I felt I had to keep the strongest faith that I would come through that ordeal. The swamp or whatever it's called with all those snakes was enough to make me watch my step."

Crystal was hugging her again. "Oh, Laura, I'm so sorry. If he could only change, but he won't."

Laura was silent as she walked back around to sit on the sofa. Crystal slumped down beside her. "You still care for Robert?" Crystal nodded, all the earlier stance leaving her. "Then, if you do, it's up to you to do something about it."

"What? You know we've struggled these last years, before that it was great but I can't have Benjamin in an environment where he has to fear he might be hit when his dad's temper gets out of hand. A child shouldn't have to live like that. Mine won't."

"I agree. How do I ask this…is your marriage worth enough to try to talk to Robert, after all these months…see if he would do counseling, whatever it takes, Crystal. I don't know what couples do in this situation. Pray. Enlist others to pray. If we are held accountable to someone we try harder, don't we?"

"By being accountable, do you mean like the church? It's people praying for you?" She put her hands to her head, worrying with her hair. "That's so open, everyone knows your business. It's embarrassing."

"You wearing black eyes wasn't embarrassing?" She glanced across at Benjamin engrossed in some television program. "Your son thrown against a wall, tell me that didn't bother you."

"Oh, yes." She wrapped her arms around her body, it was all too much sometimes, and right now she was vulnerable. "If, mind you I'm saying if because I know Robert he will be hateful but if he would be there when I did the asking maybe it would happen…I don't know. I'm not sure, at all."

They sat in thoughtful silence until Crystal turned to her, "Do you have any idea what it's like, smiling when your heart is breaking, acting as though no word hurts you when its offered by an old biddy that has no idea at all what they're saying to you. When they live in their make believe palace and you live in the real world and you've just been insulted, slapped around and stayed because you have no place to go and you don't want the world knowing your business, anyway."

"No, I can't imagine. Robert threatened me with an issue that upset me to no end and in my own foolishness I nearly caved in thinking he knew what he was talking about until one day I realized he didn't. He was bluffing and I took the bait but he also was vindictive toward me because I was your friend."

"I've had time to think about that, he was jealous of our relationship, maybe because of his own insecurities but girl, we go along way back. I was not giving you up, my friend."

Laura watched as the old Crystal was returning as she stood and began to pace the floor. "So," Laura asked, "Where do we go from here?"

"Well, this person and her son has to go home. He will be back in your room tomorrow morning. I hope he has stayed up with the class as we took his books with us and we've worked on them everyday." Ever exuberant, Crystal leaned down to hug her again. "Thanks for everything, Laura. I love you."

With the closing of the door and hearing Crystal click the lock, Laura wondered when is love enough? Richard loved her but was it enough to forgive her going out with Tom even if it was before she said yes to marrying him and why did she hurry the wedding? She had her own kettle of fish to take care of without offering Crystal advice. Still, she reasoned, she might know the new Robert if he held storing. With that thought she prayed for the one who had abducted her and could have cost her baby's life.

Later, "You're quiet," Richard said. "Is everything all right in there?" he patted her stomach. She nodded. "You want to talk?" She shook her head no and he left it alone. When bedtime arrived, he pulled her close. "I don't know what's wrong, Babe, but I'm here."

"I know," she replied, quietly. "I'm so thankful for you, Richard. I'm sorry I fail you."

"You don't."

"Sometimes I think I fail everyone, you, Mom and Dad, Crystal."

"Is Crystal who is on your mind? I heard she's moving back in. Why are you worrying over Crystal?"

"She needs to get Ben in church. Would you ask her next time you see her."

"I will. I guess I'm relieved, I couldn't tell what was bothering you."

Laura thought about Crystal's visit. Their conversation. But, she knew deep inside, she wanted to tell Richard about her and Robert's conversation. She also realized within the very deepest part of her being, Richard would not be happy. He would say,

"You let him go. You are responsible. If someone else should be the victim of that man's wrath, you would be responsible." If she said but he changed, Richard. Robert found the Lord. "How can you be certain," he would ask and he would turn away from her. Worse than that, God as her witness he would be hurt if he knew about Tom.

She listened to his easy breathing. He was kind and considerate of her what if she misjudged him on this and he would listen and know her hearts unrest? But she dare not tell him, she feared the worst.

Her stomach upset she crawled out of bed and went into the kitchen. Surely there was something to settle the feeling her world was coming apart. If she were not pregnant she would consider she was getting an ulcer. It wasn't exactly nerves and yet it was, she worried over Richard's loss of faith in her and Robert's confession would implicate her part in his conversion which was a good thing but still tied her to the truth, she had led him in the plan of salvation. Then there was Mom and Dad. Perhaps that was the most saddening part of her worries, that Dad wouldn't be around and if he wasn't Mom would find it hard to go on. And she would find the loss of one who loved her devastating.

She sat down at the kitchen table, reaching for the Bible they used each morning for daily devotions. "Lord," she whispered. "Please, give me something to settle the concerns of my heart and soul, not to mention I think I've upset this little baby inside me because he or she is doing somersaults in that small space and I'm feeling them all the way up to my throat. Thank you, Lord." A paper fell out onto the table. It was her hand writing. It was the notes she had written while at the Ladies Seminar. How ironic that she had heard all the right messages before going through a harrowing experience.

John 14:1, "Let not your heart be troubled, trust God and believe in me, Jesus said. 2 Corinthians 4:8-9, "We have troubles all around us, but we are not defeated. We do not know what to do but we do not give up the hope of living. We are persecuted, but God does not leave us. We are hurt sometimes, but we are not destroyed. Hebrews 10:35-36 "So do not lose the courage you had in the past, which has a great reward. You must hold on, so you can do what God wants and receive what he has promised." Phillipians 4:6-7 "Do not worry about anything, but pray and ask God for everything you need, always giving thanks. And God's peace which is so great we cannot understand it will keep your hearts and mind in Christ Jesus." She had written AMEN in capital letters and underlined it.

"Help me, Lord," she prayed. "Allow me the peace that passes understanding, and Father if it is your will please extend it to Crystal and Robert and Richard and my parents. Oh, Lord the list is long and you know our hearts and the sadness that claims us at times, Bless those we love and those who have need. I ask this all in your name."

Chapter 9

School was going well. She loved the children in her class and Benjamin had returned to fit right in. He was such a handsome little fellow he had become the girls heart throb. Kind hearted, Benjamin never took advantage of the situation. It was on a cold rainy day she was listening to the children talk.

They were sitting in the floor, building a city with tinker toys when she heard one of his friends ask, "Where's your daddy?" Positioning herself further behind a tall bookshelf Laura listened.

"He's away. He drives trucks and I think he's on the West Coast."

"I heard he was in prison," Lannie Cooms offered, stopping what he was doing, to step up to Benjamin.

"Who would tell you that?" Benjamin was taken by surprise but still rose to question Lannie.

"My daddy's friend is on the Police Force. He thinks that. So it's probably true."

"It's not true. I would know." Benjamin held his ground. "You take that back, Lannie Cooms."

"I won't, If he's not, you prove it."

"How do you prove something like that?" Benjamin asked. "You're sick Lannie and you tell lies."

That evening driving home, Laura heard her phone buzz. She read the message. "How's my boy?"

She groaned. She could not be caught up in this. "You need to come home," she text. "He needs you."

He was quick to reply in a text. "If I come home they will put me in jail or worse convict me of something."

"Benjamin needs you. Seek legal help to see where you stand. Goodbye." She deleted the text.

He had been at work three hours when the boss called him over. "Hey, kid, what's going on? I've been watching you, you haven't spoken three words. What's up?"

"Legal matters, sir. Nothing that can't be fixed."

"All right, you don't have to tell me what's what but I got a friend might help you."

That night after regular hours while the clilentelle were behind closed doors, one of the regulars laid a hand on his arm as he sit down a drink. "You, Robbie?"

Startled, "Yes, sir," Robert replied.

"Your Boss tells me you got a problem. Tell me and don't leave out the details. Maybe I can help you."

Shaken, Robert told him the story, he had hit his wife and one issue with his son, how they'd left him and he thought her best frined knew their whereabouts. Truth is, he concluded, I was mean but something happened.

"Let me get this straight, you abducted this woman, kept her tied up in the woods but then you got religion and that makes a difference in your book?"

Robert nodded, "yes, sir, that's pretty much right and yes, sir, it makes a difference. I've changed."

"Well, Robbie, I thought I might help you resume your life with legal counsel, but after hearing your story I think maybe the counsel of common sense will be your best bet. If I were you, I would throw myself on the mercy of the woman you abducted and her family, the police and Sheriff's Department."

Robert's countenance fell, hope flew out the window. "Won't they arrest me as soon as I sit foot in the city? What about my wife and my son?"

"You ask forgiveness and spend the rest of your life proving you deserve it."

"There are legal consequences?"

"I'm afraid so. Unless there's no legal evidence it was you. That being the case…"

"They found my truck."

"I intended to finish my sentence, that being the case of no evidence other than she saw and could identify you, what does your new found belief allow?"

"The truth and pay the consequences." The Boss's friend shook his head and went back to his table. Robert returned to work. That night he wrote two letters. He never knew it was so hard to say he was sorry nor the relief he felt when he did.

J.R. shook his head, "the things we receive," he muttered, "are unbelievable." He glanced around to see if his men heard him. They were engrossed in their own case and ignored him. He was glad. Taking his hat from the hat rack, he stepped out the office door and headed toward his car. First, he'd have a visit with the woman's husband, then her and last go out to the gal named Crystal's house. What he read in the letter was utterly ridiculous, but if those duly concerned accepted the ludicrousness of it, who was he to quibble?

He found Richard Worthington stacking boxes of filters onto shelves. "Getting ready for the cold season?" He made a mental note to check his own unit, as a matter of fact he'd forgotten all summer.

"How can I help you?" Richard wiped the dust from the shelf off his hands and beckoned him toward his office at the end of the aisle. "Not often I see you in here. I want to thank you again for the way your department handled my wife being abducted."

"Mr. Worthington,"

"Richard. In our younger days, I think we encountered each other enough on the basketball courts to be on a first name basis don't you? Your team were good rivals and we scored even enough to suit me."

"Richard, I received this letter this morning and I've not shown it to another person because most would say it was a lark, not to be considered and completely out of question if anyone did, I brought it for you to read and for your opinion since it was your wife suffered at the hands of this man."

Richard motioned he take a chair as he reached for the letter, his curiosity peaked and he began to read. "This is from Robert Carrington, the man who abducted my wife because he thought she wasn't telling him where his wife was?" J.R. nodded. Richard read to the end and then read the letter again. "This is preposterous, he's asking forgiveness? Does he really think he should get off without some kind of civil punishment? He endangered my wife and the child she's carrying."

J.R.'s next question stopped Richard's indignation in its tracks. "What would your wife say? I plan to take the letter to her next. I'm waiting until she's home from school and I hope you will be there."

"I'll be there, all right." Anger was thrusting its way through his bloodstream and firing him up.

"That's all I want to know. Now, Richard, I'm keeping this confidential in the case you and Miss Laura decide to carry through in any certain way. It's your business, not the world's."

J.R. decided he'd switch visits and take a chance Crystal Carrington was home. He'd see Miss Laura after school when her husband was present. He drove on out to the Carrington home. He guessed he expected its appearance to show signs of neglect but it didn't. As he understood the woman had just returned home from hiding out all this time. One thing he had learned, you couldn't speculate on how people were going to handle a situation. You'd think you had them pegged and they'd go a different direction. He parked the car and walked to the steps that led to the front, went on up and rang the door bell.

She came shortly, out of breath, as if startled to see him in official dress. "Yes, sir, can I help you?" She fanned herself, "I was in the basement and had to climb those steps. Kind of gets me out of breath."

"No need to rush," he said.

"Oh, yes, I saw the Police car from one of the windows and the first thing I think of is my son. Is Benjamin all right?"

"I hope so, Mrs. Carrington, I came on other business. Do you want to conduct that business here on the front porch, ma'am?"

"Oh, I forgot my manners. Come on in. I just had to make sure Benjamin was all right."

"Mrs. Carrington, I received this letter this morning and felt led to bring it to your attention. Now Mr. Worthington has read it and I promised him confidentiality, as its not the community's business unless you all decide it is. My men aren't even aware of it. If you'll read it and give me your opinion, please."

"It's Robert's handwriting," she said, giving him a puzzled glance. "Why would he be writing you?" She began to read, her facial expression changing as she progressed. Finished, she handed the letter back to him. For a moment there was stone silence, then she asked, "What did Richard say?" She gave a deep sigh before he answered, then rose up to pace across the floor in agitation. "I can guess what he said and it was, "that's the man who abducted my wife and put my unborn child in danger. The answer is no, I won't forgive him and let him slide by without paying society for his mistakes." She gave him a hurried glance as she paced. "Am I right?"

"Somewhere near that," J.R. agreed. "But I take it to Miss Laura after she's home this afternoon." His expression was hard to read. "I'd say hers is the opinion that matters, am I right or wrong?"

Richard chaffed in his spirit. He had a feeling Laura would let the man off. Why? Something had been bothering her since the incident. Maybe it was remembering it could have ended badly or maybe there was more to it than she'd mentioned. Maybe he hadn't listened close enough. Was part of this his fault? All he knew was it was a profound thing they were dealing with. It was justice and wrong made right. He was so unsettled he called his parents at the other store in Walker. Then he called John and Florence.

J.R. had reason to think it all over as he drove back to the station. He'd let others in on the letter. He owed it to Miss Laura to inform her and not spring it on her that evening when she arrived home. He couldn't be responsible for that lady going into labor too soon. No, Sir, that wasn't his kind of law enforcement to scare the dickens out of a good citizen. He called the school's office and asked to speak with Miss Laura during recess if she'd call him. "Just need to check bases with her and see if she's doing all right," he explained to the office secretary.

Laura called him. "I'm doing fine, sir. But it was nice of you to ask." Mrs. Worthington, he said, I'd rather the staff not know this if you can cover for me, but I'm coming out to your house to see you this afternoon, its about that man who abducted you. Is that all right with you? She assured him it was. "Why yes, it is. Thank you, Sir. God bless you too." She left the school office with a smile on her face, "Wasn't that just the kindest of our chief of Police to call and inquire how I'm doing."

Her mind was filled with endless questions as to the reason for the Chief of Police's visit, there was more than he was saying. She had a strange gut feeling more would come out than they knew already. She needed back up and it came so quickly to her mind to call Pastor Levi Merkel and Leah that she couldn't turn loose of it. She tried through the children's reading hour into spelling and finally went in to her closet and finding their number through google made contact.

"Pastor Merkel, this is Laura Worthington and this may well be one of the strangest calls you will receive but I feel strongly the need for God's person to come to my aid this afternoon after school at my home. It has to do with my being abducted and the Chief of Police has some new piece of evidence. With complete confidentiality, if at all possible, could you and Leah drive by and drop in?" She listened to him ask his secretary if he had any appointments past four o'clock and she said he didn't. "We will be happy to see you. Thanks for calling." The line went silent, and she slipped back into the classroom feeling a weight had been lifted. "Thank you, Jesus," she whispered, putting her trust in him as she wondered what Richard would think when the new pastor and wife came for a visit that evening.

School let out as usual. Laura did duty with several other teachers seeing the children safely into the parent and guardian cars that displayed the appropriate identification. If one arrived without that piece of paper they must go to the school office and show proper identification before leaving with their child. Sometimes the person complained but became silent when they realized it was for their child's welfare and there was no way around it. There were two making delays but that was about a fifteen minutes wait.

Laura arrive to find Richard's truck in the garage and the pastor and his wife pulled in behind her.

"Come in," she called to them. "I'm sure Richard is inside. He normally doesn't arrive home until after store closing but I guess today's different." They came up the walk, smiling and giving her a hug as they exclaimed the new house was charming. "Come see the inside, if you wish," she offered. "I never know if people want to see or not. What can I say?" She opened the front door for them.

"Oh, I'm definitely interested in seeing how any woman decorates," Leah replied, entering.

"Well, what have we here?" Laura was stunned to see not only her parents but Richard's. Richard was in the adjoining room on the phone. "Mom, Dad, Julia and James Wilson, you met Pastor Merkel and his wife last Sunday. I'm surprised to see you, this soon, but always happy. How are you?"

She received as many hugs as the Pastor and his wife received handshakes. "Everyone find a seat," she invited and I'll just put my things out of the way and we'll just have a good old visit." She was making eye contact with Richard, trying to figure out whey their parents had dropped by but he seemed to be avoiding her. Oh, well, she wondered was it a good idea with the Chief of Police stopping by any moment. That thought was dismissed by Crystal coming in by way of the back door Glancing out, Laura saw her parents and Richard's had parked there, too.

"Hey, girl," She gave Laura a big old hug and said, "you got a Police car in your drive, want me to let him in?" She saw Laura's questioning look. "I left Benjamin with little ole Miss Pauline, next door."

J.R. was about as surprised as he'd ever been to see that many people in one room. Richard met him and said "I guess you know everyone. Why don't you get right to the reason for this visit?" He waited for Laura to find a seat by her daddy. Then J.R. spoke up.

"Evidently, you all know there's something has come up or you'd not be here. Now Miss Laura will be hearing this information first hand but Richard and Miss Crystal, they've had opportunity to know what its about. Miss Laura, would you like to read this letter first, before I read it out loud to everyone?"

She reached out to take the letter. The room was quiet, with every eye on her as she began to read. Finished, she hand it over to their chief of police. She didn't look at Richard, nor Crystal. Her eyes were on her parents. They had nutured and cared for her far longer than anyone else in the room and she was most grateful they were there but she had no idea what their reaction would be following the reading of the letter.

J.R. stood before them. "I want you to know, I have sworn confidentiality to Miss Laura, Miss Crystal and Mr. Richard as to the information in this letter concerning the man who abducted Miss Laura and I would ask by a show of hands that you now commit yourself to that confidentiality as this letter deals with the sanctity of not only Miss Laura's life but what happens to Mr. Robert Carrington, the abductor."

All present raised their hand.
The letter begins,

To Whom It May Concern:

My name is Robert Carrington. On September 29, after much thought to obtain information as to the whereabouts of my wife and son, Benjamin, I did cut off Mrs. Laura Worthington from traffic at the four way stop on the North End of town before entering the Interstate that leads East to Walker and the subdivision where my wife Crystal lives and the private resident of Richard and Laura Worthington. I did assist her from climbing out of the ditch where her vehicle landed and told her to get in my truck. She did resist but I persisted and she did feel threatened and did as I ask. When I tried one last time to obtain the information as to where my family was staying I was told by Laura that she truly did not know and she thought that my wife would not tell her in order to keep me from harrassing her for the information. I had not seen my family in weeks and I was terribly distraught to the point of doing reckless actions as I did in abducting my wife's friend, Laura. I would like to say I was not aware of her pregnancy but that pregnancy was obvious. Thinking she would give up their whereabouts rather than walk through the swamp basin in Oliver county, I drove there, parked the truck and made her walk with me. It is a snake infested place and the cypress knees stand tall enough to prevent easy walking of any distance. But walk she did, cautious and fearful of the snakes that lay sunning or coiled along the way. We arrived just before dark fall around the homestead where I was raised that once belonged to my family. We had begun our journey as she left school for the day and now it was dark. Because I thought she would give me the information I did not bring food. At some point I discovered she had a cell phone in her possession and took it. She was quite weary from the walking and I told her to lay upon the bed. I did not restrain her hands but I did wrap a rope around her feet and tie it to the end post of the bed. It was the next day she asked if there was a bathroom that she could wait no longer and I did allow that.

I realize the whole ordeal had set her on edge and at some point when I asked once more for the information and she declined, I reminded her that she had received a phone call from me and I told her to tell my wife I would never hit her again and I would go to counseling with or without her, I wanted us to raise our son together and if she should decide against it I would always take care of them financially, but she forgot to tell them. She denied ever receiving a phone call of that nature and accused me of being so drunk I didn't call her number and I was wrong. We were both furious with each other. I had been drinking in the months previous to abducting her, because life at home was at its worst and I sought escape but have found that was not the escape one needs. I did have a bottle with me as we walked through the snake infested forrest but felt it was not what I should do in such a dangerous environment.

We finally reached a degree of exhaustion that she slept and the bed being large I rest on the opposite side in order to keep an eye on her. She told me the next day that I talked in my sleep all the time and she listening realized what my childhood had been like and I of course denied it until she began to tell me what I said and I realized I had revealed the sorry circumstance of my life I hope for the first and last time ever. In denying it as truth, for it is embarrassing and a sad reminder of times gone wrong she and I came to the worst verbal fighting I've encountered with anyone other than close relatives, before. When I was at my wits end with tears streaming down my face because she made me face the truth, this woman I had led through a snake infested swamp, tied to a bed and taken all freedom from, sitting tied to that foot post lay her forehead against mine and said to me, words I'll never forget. "You will never be free, Robert Carrington, until you give it all to the Lord. Stop the drinking, the blaming others and leave behind the battering of your wife and child, you cannot do it alone. You need the Lord. You must let God come in to your life. Talk to him. And I replied, do you think as a child I didn't talk to him when my father beat my mother senseless, crippled my brother and made him crazy in the head and I cried out to God and he never answered? I know your childhood, she said. I heard it last night as you became the little boy remembering your daddy destroying the vegetable garden your mother lovingly attended, begging your mother to leave before he drank again and killed one of you, heard your cries when your brother hung himself from the tree the two of you were going to hand a swing on. I heard it all, Robert and you must surrender it all to God. That's the kind of woman I found Laura Worthington to be and I in my sordid worst person ever recognized God was speaking to my heart and soul through her and when she said repeat the words for salvation after her, I did. She smiled at me when the prayer was finished and I believe I smiled at her because peace came into my heart; a peace I had never experienced before. I left the cell phone within her reach and I ran, scared for my life but not ready to be locked up in prison until I proved myself to my son and wife, proved I can live a life committed to God inspite of an alcohol addiction. I believe by his stripes, Jesus stripes I've been healed of that addiction and my desire is to live for Him, to take care of my wife and child after I ask their forgiveness. This letter is my plea for forgiveness to Laura and Richard, their families and especially to Crystal and Benjamin. I'm writing to the chief of Police to see if I can come back into New Haven to see my family and make amends before it is decided what my future holds as to making right the crime of abduction I admit happened. I ask your forgiveness. May I please hear from you?

Respectfully, Robert Carrington

There were tears in the women's eyes. They could imagine the little boy that lived in constant fear of a drunken father that had beaten his mother to the point of crippleing her body, to the brother who could no longer think clearly and hung himself and they could wonder the strength that kept him from doing the same. The men were measuring the terrible act of abduction against the actions of the father and meeting out judgement that the boy could have chosen to do right rather than wrong and let it lead him into manhood. The pastor sat with his head bowed holding tightly to his wife's hand as they prayed and sought God's wisdom to be delivered on the group of people who were obviously good faith believing people but this man had taken one of their own into danger, he had mistreated his family that he loved more than any other, would he do it again or was his salvation real? It was their fate to be called into the midst of these today, it was not the first time God altered their plans; it was their job to pray.

J.R. cleared his throat, visibly moved by the sincerity of the letter, he said, "I need to know what you people decide. Judge Thrower will have to act on this regardless, but if Miss Laura chooses not to press charges, then that settles ninety percent of the outcome as far as I'm concerned. There will still be some sort of penalty but I wouldn't think prison entered into the equasion."

Julia spoke up. "How can we condemn a man who makes such admittance to wrong doing? We love our Laura, I think she is the one who must decide what should be done."

Laura glanced across to where Crystal sat. She knew Crystal cried during the reading because she heard her whimper. Laura had chosen to keep her head down, staring at the floor in front of her, rather than encounter anyone's eyes and see their personal verdict. They were not there when Robert received salvation. She was. "Crystal, would you give Robert a second chance?"

"Yes, I would, Laura but with stipulations because I want to know his being saved is for real."

"Richard, would you give Robert a second chance?"

"No, Laura, not until he proves himself."

"Pastor Merkel, as a minister of the church and God's spokesman would you commit yourself to helping Robert Carrington be accountable to all he has written in his letter?"

"Yes, I willingly submit myself to him and agree he must be accountable for the past and the present. I will help him all I can."

Laura felt the weariness creeping into her bones. "The rest of you may discuss this or make your feelings known."

"Laura Worthington," J. R. began. "Do you give Robert Carrington a second chance? It is in this room, since there is little evidence other than by his statement and yours as to his future punishment, will be decided with understanding by all Judge Thrower has the last say. Do you give him a second chance?"

"I do." She arose. "I am very weary to the point of exhaustion reliving this. Please, excuse me." Her mother and Crystal rose up, "No, I must do this alone. I am retiring for the night. Thank you all for coming to support us in this huge decision whether to forgive or hold Robert responsible. Thank you."

She was dimly aware when her mother and Julia came to kiss her before leaving. Sleep was the haven that carried her away from the discontent and judgement of others. She left it in God's hands. She was not capable of discussion at this point. Vaguely from Exodus to the unruly children of Israel she remembered God's words, "I will show kindness and mercy to whomever I decide." Yes, Lord.

She slept through the alarm the next day and Richard called Crystal to substitute.

It was past noon when she awakened to an empty house. The phone had been disconnected and her cell turned off. She saw Richard's side of the bed had been untouched. She wandered to the guest room down the hall to find he had slept there. Further notice as she stood there, was that the closet door was half opened, revealing pairs of khaki pants and shirts had been hung and shoes sat on the floor. She walked across to the chest to open a drawer and saw his underwear and socks neatly folded taking away the emptiness. Her husband had moved from their room in the night while she slept. So be it.

In the adjoining bathroom she found his razor, and bath items. The towel he used the night before hung neat upon the bar. Whatever item he might need was available and she wondered if he had moved everything himself. How were they to navigate life together when they were apart?

Laura called Crystal that evening. "I'll be going back tomorrow. Thanks for stepping in for me." Crystal was quiet on the line. "Everything okay, Crystal?"

"They told me you wouldn't be in this week, Laura. The principal."

"Really? Wonder where they got that? They don't know about the meeting here at the house, do they?"

"I think Richard called."

"If it's all right with you, I'll be there."

"It's your class, Laura. That's fine. I'll help out whenever you need me."

She wasn't happy that Richard had interfered but she wouldn't bring it up. She fixed supper that night but he didn't come home until nine o'clock and she was in bed. She had left his plate covered on the table. It was there next morning and he was gone. Thus their new routing began. He left before she was up and came in after she went to bed. Sunday would be there and she wondered what he would do.

She dressed for church, not attending the classes. Ten minutes until time for worship service to begin she walked to the door, ready to leave when he came from his room and picked up his bible and followed her to the car. She hesitated, then got in on the passenger side and he drove.

He took his place beside her in the pew. Not even through the time of greeting would anyone have suspected there was a problem between the two. He smiled at Pastor Merkel and shook hands with those who lingered, on the way to the car, as he stopped, opened the door for her and then drove them home. Once there, he went to his room and she to hers. But when she returned to the kitchen to build a sandwich, he was already in the process of eating his, sitting at the breakfast nook, his back to her. She stopped at the raised counter of the kitchen island and took a seat to stare across the field of wild flowers to the town beyond wondering what had wrought this show of disregard.

After lunch he left and she worked on the children's folders, making plans for the coming week. But that night as time to return to church arrived, Laura closed the door to her room and went to bed. He could build the farce if he wished, that didn't mean she had to participate.

That was their routine for the next month. When the date rolled around for her doctor's appointment, she went alone. Life was lonely but she could handle it if he could. If there were plans to be made once the baby arrived, that was when they would make them. For now, she would not borrow trouble.

Julia called and asked if she and Richard and her parents and Timmy would come for Thanksgiving dinner. "I'm not sure this year, Julia," she replied. "Ask Richard what he wants to do." When Julia reported Richard planned to go hunting with buddies, she made plans to spend the holiday with her parents. She wanted to be with them as often as possible and Timmy would bring his girl friend. When Florence found Julia and James Wilson would be alone on Thanksgiving, she called them, saying, "that won't do. You two come on, we've plenty food for an army." They came feeling the absence of their son.

"It's because we all voted to give Robert another chance, isn't it?" Julia whispered. "He can be so stubborn." Tears smarted her eyes. "As long as he treats you all right. Is he?" Laura nodded, "yes."

"But I feel this coldness," Julia persisted. Laura opened her arms, Julia received her hug. They all made the best of the day. Tim and his girl were engaged and they viewed her ring and shared the couple's happiness. Laura sat opposite her Dad at the dinner table and thanked God she had him this year.

Richard arrived late that night, unloading his hunting gear in the back; putting his camo suite into wash and passing through to his room as she sat in the rocker dreading yet another night alone in their room. Dare she ask him what his plans were for their future? Glancing at the large clock at the end of the hall, she decided it was late for confrontation and neither would handle it well.

She was surprised when the phone rang and decided to let voice mail receive a message. It was Crystal. "Laura," her voice sounded happy, "Robert came for dinner and of course my Mom and Dad, but Laura it was good. Benjamin was so glad to see his daddy. Thank you, Laura. I love you."

She made it through the long weekend by going with Leah on Saturday to the Cape for an early Christmas shopping. "Tell me about you and Richard," Leah said as she drove. "I see you sitting together at church but it's obvious you aren't together, are you?"

"No, we're not. Do you think everyone else notices?"

"Not really, Laura, at this time of year most are focused on their own life, what gift for this one or that and whether the funds will hold out. We've several in our church really hurting."

"Can I help?" She watched the intersection come up where Robert abducted her. "This is not my most appreciated spot," she said. "Do you think I'll ever forget what happened here?"

"Oh, yeah, when the baby comes you won't even know if you are on the right road."

They laughed. "I think the church will take up a special offering for those in need. The Jamison's are barely able to pay their electric bill since he was hurt on that three wheeler accident and little Miss Oakley has had a new medicine added for the parkinson disease that there's no way she can keep affording it. I forget the amount each month but it is just off the scale and there's others but they are the two families most needy."

"I don't know how you and Levi sleep at night hearing all the sad tales you hear and my family probably gave you one of the most puzzling, didn't we? I invited you thinking we might need a prayer at the least and counseling for the future at most, and it all went crazy and I just left everyone and went to bed. I tell you, Leah, I thought I was going to drop sitting right there in front of everyone."

"You actually needed help getting up and out of the room, didn't you. I wanted to help you but when you told your mom and Crystal no, I knew you felt you had to do it alone. So I didn't help you."

"I hate to sound like a wet blanket but it has been difficult since the abduction. Your mind never stops."

"Living in the same house is not easy when things get complicated. I know. I've been there and done that during the time we had to ease back into togetherness after I left Levi during the Revival. Don't you know that stirred the gossip?" They chuckled. "One member actually walked to the house in the dark of night to peep in the windows to see if we were in separate rooms. Can you imagine that?"

"Were you?"

"Yes, we were."

"Same here, but I don't want our parents knowing. It would kill them, I mean at this time with the baby on the way."

"Yeah, well, parents have heart aches. I imagine you and I will have a few. Don't you think?" They rode in comfortable silence awhile until Leah pulled off the interstate and there was Marigold's shop. "Want to start here? It will do us good to hear Marigold's laughter and her outlook on life." She parked and collected her purse. "Did she by any means tell you all about her birth mother when you were in her hour of the Seminar?" Laura shook her head. "No?" Leah's smile widened. "The girl is a hoot, as it turned out when she came to Missouri from Texas after her adoptive parents were killed in an automobile accident, she came looking for her birth mother and unknown to either of them, Marigold purchased the most run down house on the same block as her birth mother's prestine perfect home. Well, the rest is a comedy of two women adverse in life to about anything. They were oil and water."

"And now, how are they?"

"They surpassed the problem. Kind of gives us all hope, doesn't it?" They entered the shop to find Marigold and her mother sorting boxes of jewlrey. "Laura, meet Marigol's mother, Harriet."

"Hey, ya'll, Come on in here and shop til you drop. We got all this jewelry in for the holidays but wouldn't you know someone turned it upside down and tangled the chains and if we don't have a mess." Marigold hugged Leah first, "How's your handsome husband and that ugly baby?" Leah sputtered as Marigold turned to Laura. "Isn't that the cutest little bugar you ever seen? I just love that little boy. He should be on the baby food jar labels or maybe those ads that show the new diapers."

"So you are one of their new members?" Marigold took Laura over to the baby side of the store. "I would attend Levi's and Leah's church if I lived there. I love those people and got to know them pretty good during the renovation of their sanctuary. Here, look at these silver spoons, aren't they precious?"

"I'm going to leave you to browse, don't feel pressured to buy, just look and enjoy and if I can help you I will and if you tire, come sit up here with me and my mother and rest. We can get acquainted."

"I'm looking for something for my twenty one students, if you have any ideas it would help."

"How's the new house coming along, all decorated inside?" Marigold smiled, "I remember you."

"From that hour?" Laura grinned. "We haven't shopped yet. Still using the old sofa and rocking chair from the apartment. Why don't you come out some Saturday and tell me what to do. Any time, actually when you are up to it, since you have a shop to run and I'm gone to school the normal hours."

"Hey, Ma, do I have anything next Saturday and can you run the shop?"

"Where are your children?"

"With their daddy, he will be so glad to see me when it is time to close today." Her mother brought a small black book for Marigold to thumb through. "Nope, no appointments. How about next Saturday?"

"I'm delighted and you can bring the children if you want. I'm a teacher for heaven's sakes."

"Oh, no, I've don't that and not going to again if Daddy isn't in the field he keeps them."

I'll be ready to welcome you to New Haven, just tell me what time."

"Why don't we make it around eleven in the morning?"

"Great."

"That stop seemed to brighten your day," Leah said as they were leaving the shop.

'Yes, it did, but I did have the thought that I was going on with the house when things are precarious."

Leah pat her hand, "we will pray everything smooths out and soon because a little person will be here." She pulled back into the mainstream of traffic. "I'm needing to look for warmer clothes for Jimmy, how about we make our next stop Carters? And then lunch. There's this adorable little spot on main street down by the river. It's not too cool to eat out at one of the tables, is it?"

"We don't get to eat and watch the river flow by everyday, do we? Let's do it. Be adventurous!"

"You are such fun," Leah flashed a smile her way, intent on finding her turn in to Carters. "It is so nice when someone is agreeable and not going against you at every turn."

"Are you describing someone in your church?"

Leah grinned. "There's always one, isn't there?"

"In my case its my husband," Laura replied, her voice droll. "How long can I last?"

"As long as you have to, when you love somebody." She glanced quickly to Laura, for confirmation.

"I do, but I'm surprised he would do this."

"Does he think there was an intimacy?"

"Surely not, and if that were the case I'm certain he would have said so. It is more that I was willing to give Robert Carrington a second chance compared to his abducting me and putting me in harms way but now, instead of Robert being punished I'm being punished for believing he changed and I do believe."

"Obviously Richard doesn't and only time will tell. Carrington did agree to be in church and to use Levi as his counselor and he hasn't acted on that." Leah thought on that. "He did agree, you know."

"I know and it bothers me, but when we say we believe in someone aren't we supposed to hold tight even when it appears that trust is not appreciated?"

"Yes, but for your sake he needs to be prompt to get involved, lest he's thought to be a liar."

"That's harsh, Leah."

"Yes, my dear, life is harsh. I live it first hand as a pastor's wife and so do you as a wife."

Arriving home she was relieved to see Richard's truck in the garage. Dropping the packages in the chair by the door she went on into the bedroom to change clothes. She was midway of the process when he stood in the doorway. "Where have you been?"

"To the Cape with Leah. Why?" She stepped closer and he backed out of the door way.

His scowl was as threatening as a summer storm, his brows drawn together and his eyes mean. "I thought you'd leave a note or at least tell me if you were going to be gone all day."

Cold reasoning took hold on Laura. "Let me get this straight. You don't talk to me for over a month, you don't really have any reason to say that and you don't mean I need to check in with you, do you?"

"Yes," he thundered. "You are…" he searched for words. "You are carrying our baby, my child, too, and I should have some say on where you go. I have rights."

Laura's anger rose several degrees. "You have no rights when you have practically abandoned me in our own home. Don't push me on this, Richard. Either you trust me or we face grave circumstances."

"Like what? You'll take another walk through the woods with Carrington?"

"That was low." She turned and reached for the door knob and closed the door in his face.

"You will regret this, Laura."

"Yes, I do already and you are going to, down the road, because if it continues I'll see to it."

She sit down in the rocker, surprised to see he had moved it into their room, her room, but it was just as well, she would keep to the room rather than face his wrath. Still, she wondered, why did he move it?

An hour later she heard the door shut behind him. The hum of his truck engine told her he was leaving.

Chapter 10

$\mathcal{A}$s unexpected as always, the chimes began to play but where usually there was comfort today she felt sadness. No one explained their scheduling, they accepted them as a reminder God was at work. The house was quiet with its empty rooms. She had to do something. There were days she wondered were the chimes an omen? Picking up her purse she got in the car and headed over to her parents. Florence was glad to see her but involved in a few household chores, "It takes a lot of time taking care of your dad's needs," she explained, "and I've gotten behind, but I don't like to leave him when he's suffering."

"Do you need professional help, Mom?"

Florence gave a huge sigh, "not professional. Just someone to keep the house in better shape. I know that's not important but the church members are good to come and his family and I'm embarrassed if the house keeping has suffered."

"I understand, it's not what is important but you feel better when nothing's amiss."

"Yes. He 's asleep right now and we can talk but when he's awake he needs to see you."

"That's why I came, to see you both, just a sort of lonliness for your parents, I guess."

"Everything all right between you and Richard, Dear?"

"Of course," she lied. "Why not?"

"I guess I heard a piece of gossip I didn't like, concerning that Week's girl, the one that went off to college," She sighed heavily. "You know her mother left because her husband was so mean to her."

"Charla was named after her dad but she failed in college. Her sister married and moved away."

"Maybe it is Charla, I know you and Richard are tight but her going to work there, at the business…Well, Rose made a special trip to tell me she saw the two of them were having lunch at that new restaurant and she read more into it than should be…as long as you know, I'll try to keep my mind on a higher plain." She shook her head. "Mother's are always too protective. You'll learn."

"How's Timmy and Sherry?" Something stirred inside her, wondering if she needed to pay attention.

"Funny you'd ask, Sherry and this Charla are friends and Sherry says she has a crush on Richard. That just bothered me to no end and here you are not seeming to mind at all but Sherry says she's kind of loose."

"I hear Dad stirring, I think I'll go in and see if he needs anything." She had only a few feet of hall to blink back the tears and put a smile on her face. "Hey, Dad, what are you doing in here, napping?"

He tried to chuckle, "I''ve never had an opportunity to sit around and do nothing. It's not what it's cracked up to be so when I can sleep part of it away my days not too long. Whata ya think about that?"

"Scoot over, Pops, and let me see how that works." First she took the extra pillows and plumped them up and then scooted onto the bed beside him. "Hmmm." They lay there for a few minutes until she said, "I see what you mean, it's like we're doing something we've been taught not to do. We're suppose to be working." During the quiet time, Florence had peeped in and now stood shaking her head at them.

Suppertime brought Tim in. "What are you doing on that bed, pregnant lady?"

"Actually I'm thinking I need help getting off." She glanced around at her dad. "How're you doing, Dad?"

He grinned. "I'm kind of liking it. I try to get your mom to stop and rest with me, right here, but she don't. Guess she's afraid I'll take advantage of her," he teased. "But I won't."

"So ya'll just been laying there on that bed, not watching television or anything?" Tim couldn't believe it.

"Well, we were talking about the crop and how you got it out on time and no bad break downs."

"And I told him about my little students. They're perfect of course." Everyone laughed. "I wanted Mom to hear about Crystal's baby as she used to help with Benjamin when Crystal first started subbing at school. The little girls are very enamored with Benjamin; he's such a handsome little lad."

She was sitting up and stretched a hand toward Tim. "Hey," he teased, "you must weigh a ton."

"Make that a half-ton, and that was ugly. Dad are you staying put, or getting up?" Florence had come back, taking it all in as she smiled seeing the three of them bantering. "How about we all eat together?"

"You have dinner, ready, Mom?" She felt guilty. "I should have been in there helping you."

"This is important, Laura. Coming to see your Dad, I imagine it's better medicine than he takes."

"You got that right," John tried to rise, but couldn't find the strength needed to do so, Tim cupped an arm just beneath his shoulders and pulled his dad up while Florence pushed the wheelchair up tight and Tim picked him up to settle him into the chair, then tucked a small lap quilt around his lap. "Don't know what I'd do without you, Son. Thank you."

Visibly moved, Laura tried hard to keep her face free of frown or sadness. This was a revelation. Her father's strength was slowly ebbing away in front of their eyes. Mom needed help for physical work but she also needed emotional support and she knew she must pay better attention to be there for all three. They were all learning together what was needed and sometimes it wasn't easy to provide.

In spite of the sadness that loomed over their heads they made the most of the dinner together. John sat in the wheel chair afterward listening to the teasing among the three as they cleared the dishes and cleaned up the kitchen. "Say, Sis, how about riding over to New Haven with me to the store? I picked up all the bolts I could here in Walker but James Wilson said I'd need to drive over there to get more."

"They are closed, Tim. Did you forget?"

He grinned. "Didn't Dad ever tell you, places are good to set out parts or whatever you need after hours. There's a basis of trust when you need things, so the bolts have been sit out back by the door and no telling what else for those still getting crop out of the fields. We're just part of the lucky ones this year. I've got a truck driver coming in from delivering grain to the river. He's very reliable and if you don't mind him driving your car, he can take it to your house, you ride with me so we can talk and I'll pick him up take him to his home, then we pick up the parts and I run you back home. How does that sound?"

They did as Tim said and his employee left her car at their home, then Tim drove him to his.

"Why does your driver look so familiar?"

Tim laughed. "I wondered if you'd notice. The give away was his shaking your hand and so polite. Do you remember the State Trooper that used to come around school every year to give the safety program? That's him. He got hurt on the job and retired from serving but this spring he said he got restless and came out and ask for a job. He always wanted to drive an eighteen wheeler, so we had Old Joe teach him the basics, he got the appropriate license and that's what he does now and he likes it."

"And you ask me if I minded his driving my car?" She laughed. She felt happier than in a long time and knew it was being with family. "So tell me now what you are thinking for Mom and Dad next."

"That's why I thought we needed to talk. Mom's going to be an independent sort, in the most strenuous way because she won't want any help and if there is help, she wants to figure out what's best for her. And let's face it, Mom as a good mind; how could we decide what's best for her? I think we have to play this by ear?"

"You went the last doctor visit and Mom didn't have much to tell me. She said there was no change in Dad and yet we see he is getting weaker. Dad has never laid on a bed in daylight hours."

"But the chem is weakening him and they ask him if he wanted to stop it, and he said no."

"We wouldn't want him to give up hope. Mom says she has known people with stage four that finally rallied and are alive today." She touched his arm staring up into his face. "Isn't that Dad's hope and ours?"

"It is, Sis, but we have to realize if the cancer starts spreading to certain areas we won't get to keep him." He pulled to the alley behind the Hardware that had expanded to supply various needs for the area. "Give me a minute and I'll be right back." He was already leaving the truck.

Sitting and watching for his return, in the shadows she saw Richard's truck and wondered about his returning to work. The door opened from the back of the building and Richard and a female form stepped out. He opened the door of her car and the dome light came on. It was then, the female stood on tip toe reaching up to kiss Richard. Laura was in shock, watching, as Richard's arms went around the woman. She got in her car, he shut the door and she drove away. Laura slumped down in the seat as headlights came across Tim's truck. Richard was leaving, too.

Tim came bounding along, to deposit his sack full of bolts on the floor board in the back. Glancing across to Laura, he asked, "Are you all right, Sis?" To shocked to speak, Laura nodded. "Well, it's been good. Maybe I'll see you more now at Mom and Dad's. I just hope it goes on forever don't you, Sis?"

Her heart was beating fast and the blood pounding in her head. What was she to do? That was so unlike him. She could not fanthom her husband kissing another woman. What was she to do?

The sun couldn't shine bright enough to dull the grayness of her heart the next morning, she awoke with the image of Richard and the woman on her mind, in her heart and slowing her body's movement. She considered staying home but she wasn't physically sick, emotionally she supposed and there was no one to care. She didn't know if she wished Tim had seen the two, or not. There should be some kind of penalty for spouses who cheated on their husband or wife, but had there ever been, except hell at the end of the journey? Her own heart was black on this Sunday as she thought it would serve him right but with hell, once a person reached it, there was no turning back and Richard had not denounced his God, only his wife. She heard Levi's sermon with a stoic countenance, first Corinthians thirteen, he said, was the love chapter. "If we have not love," he said, "we are as a clanging bell that is harsh to the ears." She and Richard had fallen out of tune, they were the worst, allowing the world to think their love ran smoothly. "Scripture tells us, now abideth faith, hope and charity, but the greatest is charity, love." She and Richard had neither of the three, they were as bland as the wood they walked on and full of shame.

Laura made it through the week. Saturday arrived with Marigold Langley scheduled to come and she was at odds with whether to call and cancel or not. The rift between her and Richard should have been over by now. She had thought he would miss her as she did him and turn loose of the anger he felt that she had voted to give Carrington a second opportunity to make things right with his young family. Now, with Marigold coming she was thinking why seek help in decorating the house if she and

Richard were splitting up? And she would have the responsibility of the baby, all on her own. Men didn't see themselves with child. She sit down and listed her salary first then began to take away the expenses. If, Richard paid child support, she could use that money to keep the house payments going. It was all so new to her, frightening and unavoidable. It was happening no need sticking her head in the sand. The very thing she thought would never happen was happening. He already had someone.

She waited, to hear him whistle or sing, whatever one did when a new love entered their life, but what he did was continue to leave early for work and was coming in later to go to his room. Over the weekend she would face fact and count her money to see what her alternative was.

She knew the exact amount in the savings she had before marrying Richard, maybe that would be enough to purchase a few pieces of furniture. It it was not for the fact she would teach at New Haven in order to remain near her parents she would let the house go but she needed a home. The apartment was all she needed but the house had become a reality. Oh, she was so torn, without counsel as to what she should do. She kept pushing away the memory of seeing him kiss the girl, his arms around her. She dressed and was sitting at the kitchen island doing her class homework when Marigold arrived.

"I like." She said, all smiles. "It's beautiful but wait until we put the touch on it."

"Touch?" Laura waited for Marigold to settle. She was here and there, saying 'hmmm," and "uh huh" as she explored the rooms. She came to the guest room, finding a man's belongings. "What's this?" she questioned. "Please don't tell me you and your husband already have separate rooms."

"It's a long story."

She sat opposite her. "Tell me."

She told her. "Let me get this right. You were abducted. During that abduction you led the abductor to the Lord and your husband is angry that you are willing to give him a second chance? So much so, that he moved out of your room? And just last night you by accident or by chance saw him with his arms around another woman?"

"Yes."

"That's a hard one. I've been in your shoes but in my case, the old girlfriend conned him into spending the night, he said holding her because her parents had just been killed in a terrible accident and she was grieving and ask him to stay. It took a bit of doing for us to go beyond that episode, too."

They sat for awhile, both in their own thoughts. Finally, Marigold asked, "What are you going to do?"

"If I stay in this area I need a home."

"Good girl. Let's do this." They walked into the living room. "Do you have your heart set on the sectional in white leather? And what was the reason behind that?"

"Family during holidays like Thanksgiving and Christmas, we need plenty of seating."

"All right but white is hard to match to the secondary seating. Let's go the nuetral, soft beige, then we can pair it up with striped Queenbacks or low Club chairs in a print. How do you feel about that? Let me pull samples. Here's one of the sofa and these are for chairs."

"I love the thought of a queen back on each side of the fireplace in this stripe and the print would blend with the stripe for the two club chairs. I think the room size will carry all four very well, what do you think?"

'Nice. And here are the three different types of tables. Prices are beneath each piece."

"I seem to lean toward the beautiful wood in the traditional, it would be these and the sofa table for that empty spot that goes down the hall." She paused to stare down the hall, "There's a powder room there, with coat closet on the other side. I think it will be convenient for constant use, kind of out of the way. How did I do on making choices, Marigold?"

"Excellent." Marigold removed the unwanted photos of different style, leaving the chosen traditionals.

"I'm really drawn to the glass topped dining table but is that dangerous with young children, one anyway?" Laura glanced around the room. "With this raised ceiling, I can see a tall vase of flowers in the center of the table with a beautiful painting on that wall opposite the window, that is when we can, I mean when I can afford it."

"What about the chairs? You have to choose a fabric."

"These chairs, the wood matches the tables we've already chosen and for the fabric a nuetral because we want the flower in the center of the table to be the center piece we focus on, don't we?"

"Wonderful. What's next? You have a good eye, Laura."

"We have this room on the back, a kind of t.v., study kind of room if you can combine the two." She led Marigold beyond the kitchen to the room just beyond. "That is a half bath for convenience of our visitors, I guess I should say my visitors." For a moment she almost broke, with tears in her eyes she said, "This is overwhelming."

"What if Richard wants the house, Laura?"

"Why would he?"

"Laura?" Marigold shook her head. "Girl, you are naive. Tell me whose idea of this house came first, yours or his?" She watched Laura's expression change. "I thought so. He will want the house even if he is with another woman."

Laura sat down, bowed her head and put her hands around her face. "None of this is a good idea, is it?" The tears began and wouldn't stop. She had held them at bay so many times, now was a waterfall.

"I tell you what, let's you and I take a ride. I'll keep the notes in case everything straightens out, the two of you fall in love all over again and then I'll come and implement all the ideas we discussed today."

"I'm so sorry I've taken your time and all in vain."

"Shush. I've toured your beautiful home and I believe we've become friends. Isn't that worth something?"

"Oh, it is, but do you mind if we skip the ride? I'll be fine. Really, and you should head on back to your family." Laura stood, reaching out to hug Marigold. "Thank you. I'm so sorry you saw me like this."

"Believe me, I've been in similar situations. They aren't the same, Laura, but we understand the sadness."

She was devastated. Things had come to light that she hadn't considered. She was glad it was Marigold. She shut the door to her room, took a shower and put on her nightgown and went to bed. She didn't hear Richard come in, nor did she care. She was reaching a new plateau of not caring. The next morning she came out of her room just in time to drive to Shining Light Church. Richard was waiting as usual and drove them there. Leah dropped by and whispered, "how'd it go?" Laura merely shook her head. "We'd love for you two to join us for lunch at Sargent's. There's a group of us. What do you think?"

"No thanks," Laura replied but Richard smiled and accepted. "I think that would be great, don't you, Laura?"

Once church was over, Laura slid under the wheel. Before Richard could join her, she drove off the church parking lot and headed home. She was tired of it all. He could stay and socialize if he wished. She could take no more of his acting in front of people that everything was all right and at home ignoring her. She locked her door in case he came home angry and wanted to teach her a lesson.

Julia called. "Laura, dear, I'm preparing Christmas dinner for one thirty since it's next Sunday and I know everyone wants to attend services. That allows time to be leisurely and then we'll be together."

"Anything I should bring, Julia?" She thought Julia sounded sad when she said, "just you and Richard." She wondered how they would pull that off, lately all she felt was shame. She had wasted Marigold's time, probably Leah's. Her self esteem was taking a beating and she couldn't pull herself out of it's hold. She bought a three foot tree and sit it on the end of the island. This was their first Christmas in the new home, it should have been joyful. She knew the family would ask what gifts she and Richard exchanged. "We are so blessed with the new home we thought that was enough," she would say. He was on his own.

Open House was scheduled Tuesday before school let out on Wednesday. The children would be singing for the guests and each room would host the parents with punch and cookies. Benjamin was excited. "My Dad's coming with my Mom. Then we're going riding in the woods. Wouldn't it be fun if it snowed, Mrs. Worthington?" He leaned to whisper in her ear. "My mom says I must call you that instead of Aunt Laura. What do you think?"

She nodded and whispered back, "for school, but other places I'm still your aunt." So another hurdle to jump would appear in the form of Robert Carrington.

Tuesday arrived along with Benjamin's dad. Crystal braved the path to Laura. "You ready for this, dumplin?" She reached back for Robert's hand. "It was hard for him, Laura, he hasn't seen you since…well, you know, but he's seeing Levi on a weekly basis, and we are doing just fine." She put Laura's hand in his. "Now, Hon," she said to her husband. "Go ahead and tell her what you want."

"Laura, I'm truly sorry. Whatever I can do in life for you, I will. I'm asking your forgiveness, please."

She saw the tears in his eyes and his earnest expression and there stood Crystal happy for once with peace in her heart. This is what caused my problems she thought, but I cannot deny happiness for my friend. She reached for Crystal's hand too. "God bless us all," she whispered.

"Thank you," Robert said as his hold tightened on her hand and Crystal hugged her to her chest. "Love you, dumplin." She gave Laura a sound kiss on the cheek. "Now, lets go see our boy, he's waiting for us."

Robert and Crystal lingered at the back with Benjamin near the refreshment table where two Senior girls were serving the parents. Laura saw them suddenly come to attention their focus on a young woman studying the room number as though hesitant to enter. Laura started toward her with the intention to invite her in when Crystal intercepted, leaving Laura puzzled again. "How are you Charla?" Crystal was steering her back out the door. "What

brings you out? You got a relative in Miss Worthington's room?"
The girl broke away and hurried down the hall. Laura's blood
ran cold. So, her best friend was trying to protect her, from what?
All she realized at that moment was if Crystal knew something,
the whole town was talking. All the trips to church on Sunday
wouldn't save her husband's reputation.

She needed air, motioning to Crystal, she mouthed, take care of
all, as she pointed outside. Crystal understood and nodded. Laura
wanted to cry, to throw herself on the ground and never get up.
How could he? A young girl? Past the age that would get him in
trouble with the law, but younger and prettier than her. How dare
he humiliate her? And even now she longed for his arms around
her. She betrayed herself, willing to take him back if he would just
be there for her. She leaned against the support pole of the low
slung awning that protected the children from rain as they went
from building to bus. Wiping the tears away she stared out onto
the parking lot, at nothing, just staring, and then she saw his truck.
Her heart lurched, spasmed a time or two and caught its natural
rhythm. He had brought her? A numbness claimed her, spreading
from her head through to her toes. So it was final. The girl won.

It was past nine when she pulled into the drive of their home.
Richard wasn't there. She couldn't stand it tonight. She went in,
packed a suitcase, collected her medicines which consisted of
vitamins, grabbed a diet coke from the frig and was on her way. She
arrived as her mother was helping her dad to bed. A hospital bed
had been set up in the last few days but he still preferred sleeping
in the big bed with Florence. She felt like a waif standing staring at
her parents, no words to explain, hoping none were necessary.

"You need a bed, Honey?" He asked, seeing the suitcase. "You
can have that hospital bed, or the one in the sunroom or scoot
your brother over, I reckon like when you were young and he
scooted you over. Or come lay down with me and Mom til you
get sleepy then it won't matter where you sleep."

Florence let him do the talking but she wore a worried
expression. "We're glad you'd come home, Laurie," she said and
that was all Laura needed.

"Thank you," she replied. "I'll be here a few days." She eyed the hospital bed but it wasn't the right fit. She padded down the hall to Tim's room.

He was just putting the phone in its cradle. "Hey," he said, "What you doin' here, pregnant lady?"

"Can I sleep in your bed with you, Bub? I'll stay on my side, I promise."

He pat the mattress beside him. "Come on. I reckon it's time you collect on the times I bothered you."

"You were never a bother. Thanks, Tim. Maybe I'll sleep knowing you're there. Richard's girlfriend tried to come into my class open house tonight and Crystal turned her away. I have no idea what that was about."

"Don't jump to conclusions, Sis. It may look worse than it is."

"I figure where there's smoke there's fire," she replied. "What do you think about Sherry's friend?"

"Not always fire, Sis. Charla's kind of a messed up person but I heard she was dating someone." He didn't tell her that even with Sherry being her friend, Charla had tried to come on to him, once.

Chapter 11

He was beginning to hate himself. He should have been by her side tonight, welcoming parents, paying attention to the students. He was certain they loved her. She was easy to love and yet, he was trying to teach her a lesson. Now he questioned, was he tearing them apart rather than setting the stage to keep them together forever. He hadn't ask anyone's advice. In regard to Carrington, Laura leading him to the Lord and him taking a new lease on life…well, she needed to learn marriage meant sticking together, being loyal to one another; she should have said Carrington had to prove himself first.

What he had really done was open himself up to additional problems. The new girl flirted outrageously with him and he had to admit sometimes she caught his eye, but he always thought of Laura. Then there was the night she stayed late. When they both left together he thought to be a gentleman and open the car door for her, evidently she had a plan of her own and threw her arms around his neck to kiss him. His instinct was way off, God forbid and God forgive he did it all wrong, now he had that to live with but next day he set Charla straight. "I'm flattered you'd think you are interested in me, but I'm married and I'm not interested in you."

"You could be," she said, slipping over to his desk, inside the cubicle to sit on the desk facing him. "I know I'm young and yes technically you say you're married but why is it she never calls? Wives do that. Where I worked before the wives worried us to death. We were their message couriers. Here it's different and I think the two of you are estranged. Now tell me that isn't so?"

"That's none of your business. Now, get off my desk and go do your work and if this personal onslaught continues for me to notice you, then you will have to leave employment with Worthington Supply."

"Or what?" she ask, coyly. "I will break you and you will want me."

"That's it," he said, as if talking to a child, "I think you should go now. I'll give you a good reference."

"I don't want a reference," she whined. "I want you." Then as if to change tactics she said, "I could scream and cry rape and where would you be then?"

He had opened the desk drawer revealing the line that led to the outside and was fastened to the calendar pad given by one of the suppliers. "I was afraid for this conversation, Charla. It's all taped."

With that he had removed the tape and put it in his shirt pocket. She was not happy and left kicking the boxes that sit on the floor for emptying later. He made up his mind Charla needed to leave employment, but there need not be any problem that came back on the business.

Now, his heart ached over Laura. He was at fault abandoning her during the pregnancy. He had been so upset the day she had gone shopping with the pastor's wife he had been unable to control his temper. When she returned, unscathed, he had been angry she had not told him where she was going. Even now he shook his head remembering. Evidently she was tired, she had shut the door and gone to bed. He noticed she was retiring for the night earlier and earlier. Was she well? He was unable to tell.

Now he chuckled, remembering, she had left him behind on Sunday when he told the pastor's wife they would join the group for lunch. He had not been able to smile that day but in retrospect she was quite a woman. Maybe she was more than he could handle because she'd proven that already in every way he thought to thwart her plans she excelled. She did not cry, argue or bring attention to the matter. She outclassed him, every time. She had learned a lot in life. What part of restraint would she blame on him?

Closing the ledger and putting it in the vault, he decided to drive by the school, maybe he would go in. He had only parked when he noticed Charla Weeks leaving with a young couple and two children. Then, he noticed Robert Carrington's red truck, the signs were not good for him to go in to Laura's classroom. He put the truck into gear; he would go back to the store and return about the time it was over to help her load her car for home. The problem was, once there he sat in the big chair in the visitor's lounge and went to sleep. By the time he awoke and drove by the school the parking lot was empty.

At home, he parked in the back and entered from that door practicing in his head the words he would say to Laura. She'd left a single light on. He went to her room and opened the door. "Laura." She didn't answer. He turned on the ceiling light. The bed was made, the room in order except for two suitcases, from the set she used on their honeymoon, sitting in front of the closet. The middle sized one was missing. Why? Where would she be going? Or, was she gone? He went to the door that opened to the garage. Her car was missing. All this time, through his coldness in trying to bring sense to her, she had stayed. Why would she leave now?

The phone rang the next morning and he let voice mail receive the message. He had slept in their room, Laura's fragrance on the pillow case, her presence felt in every nook and cranny, except she wasn't there. It was his mother, "Laura, dear, you don't have to bring anything. Thank you for asking and I'm sorry I missed you, I had gone grocery shopping. Just bring yourself and my strapping son and our Christmas together will be so blessed.

James Wilson will help Tim bring your Dad over for the day. Love you. Bye."

Christmas. Christmas had almost escaped them. He'd noticed the scraggly little tree on the kitchen island and he'd seen the reminder on the pad that Marigold had been scheduled for the past Saturday. He wondered how that went over. Now he looked around the house, sterile, sterile as a house could be and what they needed was a home. Fifty percent of the problems was him. No, in all truth and honesty he was seventy five per cent the problem. Maybe more. Here he was still expecting her to conform.

Glancing out, the sky was turning a deep gray, maybe rain was coming in. He had told the employees he would be away for the day. He'd thought to make things right with Laura but that hadn't happened. He dressed and headed to town, there were items he thought they needed. On the return home, the snow began to fall, huge flakes that covered the ground and began to pack inches of white that filled in the ditches and hid the highway. From experience he knew soon the community would be snowed in.

First he put away the food items and then drug in the tree from the back of the truck, glad it was wrapped in a huge plastic bag. He then began a one man decoration with the five strands of tiny wired lights and the nine packages of ornaments he had purchased, knowing now it needed double. Next he sat out the old world Santa figurine that danced and sang a song as a body passed by. From his stash of goodies, he drew out a musical box that played Silent night and set it on the nightstand by Laura's side of the bed. Electric candles went on the empty window sills. He forgot there were two other doors until he hung the wreaths on three, and last he took the garland the lady insist he needed, placing it on top of cabinets he adorned with fake red berries and holly she also claimed necessaary. "Well, she was right," he said outloud as he viewed his handiwork. "The red makes all the difference in the world." With that he rehung the ornaments on the tree, leavin the back bare and the front more presentable. "Now for the red candles she said to sit around the room. She didn't know we don't have much furniture though." So he sat the candles on the fireplace and stacked them different heights as she instructed.

Smiling, he visualized Laura standing in front of the tree, as he went for his shot gun to do one last thing, then he would be ready to bring his bride home.

"Let there be peace on earth and let it begin in me," He found himself singing and realized it had been a long time since he'd felt happiness, he almost wondered if he was asleep or possibly at someone else's home. "Now, to call my beloved. There's one of two places I think…to find her."

He dialed her phone. It rang in the bedroom. "Well, that won't work." He dialed her parents home. Tim answered. "Tim, could I speak with Laura?" He heard Tim call her. "She said no, Richard." He thought a moment. "Tim, tell her I'll call every five minutes until she speaks to me." Tim relayed the message.

"What do you want, Richard?"

"Laura, please, come home."

"After all this time, Richard?" She really couldn't believe he'd ask. Laura hung up the phone. Tim put his arms around her and she cried quietly on his shoulder. "He's got his nerve," she said. "Thank you, Tim."

"Well, no one's going to bother us today," Tim said. "We are snowed in. It would take a horse and buggy, but tomorrow the highway department will start clearing our roads. Today they'll work in town."

"Let's crack pecans," Florence said, bringing a full bag into the kitchen. "No better time than today."

"What about Dad? Shall we pull the hospital bed back in here?" Florence nodded. "Yes, ma'am."

Laura guided the front and Tim pushed. "Feels good, us being together," he whispered.

"This is not fast work, is it?" Tim stretched, getting the kink out of his bad leg. "I think we need to move around a bit, what do you think, Sis?" He went over to the window, shaking his head at what he saw. "Dad, you better not get sick tonight, we'd have a heck of a time trying to get out of the yard, even."

"You mean it's pilin' up, huh?"

Tim came back to his side and said, "Hang on and I'll push you where you can see out."

"Mercy, the roads are impassable with this, aren't they? Well, I feel pretty good. I'm still aimin' to kick this thing. I'm just glad it's winter and not spring when we need to be busy and it would all be on you."

"Tell you the truth, Dad, I'd rather farm any day than pick pecans out of shells." They all laughed.

"What's going on, Laura? I can tell you're feeling down." He pat the side of his bed. "Come over here."

"It's Richard, Dad."

"Hon, we all have had problems. I don't know how your Mom put up with me."

"You would never have acted like Richard, Dad. I don't know what to do."

"Well, if he ask you to forgive him, and you think he means it, give him a second chance."

"That's how I got in this mess, Dad. Giving Robert Carrington a second chance didn't set well with Richard."

"But Hon, he was afraid the man wasn't sincere. Even when the chief red the letter and it stated you led him in salvation, no one knew if Carrington did it to get away or if it was real, his actions from that point on was what everyone needed to know."

"So what does that say for Richard?" Laura sniffled, the tears threatening to begin all over. "I thought he was the most honorable man in the world."

"And maybe he is. You have to listen to him tell you his side of the story."

"We don't talk."

"That bad, huh?" John was patting her hand. "You want old dad to go beat him up?"

They all chuckled. "You and all that energy," Florence said, coming to hug her man. "You warm enough?" She placed the sheet under his arms to cover his chest, smiling at him as she did so.

"Yes, always when you stop to hug me." John replied. Tim and Laura grinned as their parents kissed.

"Well, if I have to be snowed in I'm glad I'm here," Laura said, sighing as she felt the baby move. "And it's good it's not time for this baby to make appearance, in this snow, we'd have to deliver at home."

The phone rang just as he finished hanging the mistletoe over the door and he raced to answer thinking Laura had changed her mind. It was Pastor Merkel. "I've been thinking of you, Richard. How are you holding up?" He listened to Richard's model replys to his questions. "I'm supposed to give you and Laura a report on Robert Carrington, you remember? Well, he has shown up for counseling every week, not the first two mind you, during those he was working in St. Louis and stayed with his employer and minister up there, who I might say thinks the world of him. Ayway, wanted you to know he is honoring his word and seems to be gaining faith in himself that he can control his temper, he won't batter his family and he wants to make amends with you and Laura."

Richard was quiet. Pastor Merkel waited an appropriate amount of time and then said, "That's about it, Richard, call me if you need me for anything. I'll see you on Sunday. God bless you and tell Laura hello."

It was a lot to think about. Laura would expect him to turn loose of his dislike toward Carrington. He might never get her back if he didn't. He sit down to think on the matter and fell asleep.

He awoke to someone pounding on the front door and hurried to answer. The snow had stopped falling but the yard and front stoop were covered in glistening white, the sparkle enough to blind the eyes.

"Yes?" He spoke to two people dressed in snow suits with goggles on concealing their faces. "Can I help you?" On the edge of the lawn, was a pair of horses and a sleigh he thought he'd seen over at Crystal's home that according to the story had been in their family half a century.

Crystal stepped forward. "I didn't know you were here, Richard. We came to see if Laura would go on a sleigh ride with us? You could go, too."

"She's not here," he studied Crystal, she was a bit hesitant to look at him, he knew the other person was Robert. Robert must have felt his animosity, for he turned and went back to the sleigh.

"Richard, don't you miss her?" He glared at her. "I mean, she's pretty wonderful, Richard. She forgave Robert when he put her through hell. Now you've neglected her, when she's pregnant and needs you."

"Not that it's any of your business, but she wants nothing to do with me, otherwise she wouldn't be at her parents."

"Do you want her back?" He started to close the door but Crystal stuck a foot in the opening. "Really, Richard, are you ready to put this petty stuff that's pretty stupid aside and love your wife again? She needs you."

"Leave, my property, Crystal. I don't need this. I've told you she left. She doesn't want me."

"For heaven's sakes, Richard. She's pregnant. You've been acting like an ass and she has to hold up for herself because the Lord knows no one else will. The idea of your girlfriend showing up at Open House. You do know that girl goes after what she wants, don't you. You'll do well to leave her alone. So do you want her back or not? If you do, get your boots on and lets go get her."

"That is not my girlfriend." His temper flared before he realized it. "The roads are closed, Crystal."

"Not to a horse and buggy. Me and Robert and Benjamin, we're going to find her and you can come along if you want to." She held her gaze on him. "I'm going to go get under that nice warm blanket by Benjamin and we'll wait ten minutes and after that we're gone. I think if you want Laura back you're going to have to prove you want her and do something about it because Laura's about worn thin to the bone after your girlfriend…last night. She heard him sputter and say "I told you." She didn't care. "You know Laura, Richard. She don't fool around, if she decides you're not willing to bend a little, she won't either and the two of you will be history." Before he could protest, she turned toward the sleigh. "Bring a couple blankets for that back seat, Richard, if you're coming with us."

"Who do you think you are, coming here and offering your ultimatum?" He called after her.

"Ten minutes, Richard, starting now."

He was furious. That was the kind of friendship Laura and Crystal shared. They had faith in each other, not to say they didn't clear the air now and then, but they loved and trusted each other and he believed they knew each other inside out. If he wanted Laura in his life he better make a decision now.

Ten minutes passed. "Let's go, Robert."

"You sure?" He questioned, looking toward the house.

"I'm sure." She snuggled down closer to his side, pulling Benjamin into the circle of her right arm.

Robert began the circle, back out the way they'd come in. This time he noticed Richard's truck barely visible covered by snow and Richard hollering, "Wait up. I'm trying to find my other boot and my gloves." Crystal laughed, poking Robert in the ribs. "Haven't had these boots on since Thanksgiving," Richard was saying as he threw a couple blankets over and climbed into the back seat of the sleigh. "Hey there, Buddy," he clamped a gloved hand on Benjamin's shoulder and shook him. He'd made a quick decision and he'd do the best he could with Carrington. It was Laura he wanted to come home, for her he'd climb a mountain. Naked. In the snow, if need be. The burden of the last months was slipping away, let there be peace, he whispered within himself, and let it begin in me.

An hour later they were pulling into the drive of Laura's parents. Both trucks and Laura's car were totally snowed in, three mounds blending into the landscape, while Forence's jeep was parked in the garage. A curl of smoke from the chimney was all that moved. "Now what?" Richard heard Carrington ask.

"What do you think, Richard, want to brave it?"

"By that you are asking if I want to face the family? I guess I have to, don't I?"

"Want to go with me Benjamin?"

"Chicken." Crystal muttered. Benjamin was tugging at her sleeve. "Go on if you want, Son, on Richard's shoulders. Right, Richard?"

"You betcha, come on, Buddy." Standing outside the sleigh, he reached for Benjamin and sat him up high. "There you go, Buddy, wrap your legs around, let them hang down on my chest. Here we go."

It was no easy feat reaching the porch. In places the snow drifts were up to his knees. "Hang on Ben."

"I am, Uncle Richard. You think Aunt Laura is in there?"

"She better be, after this." He knocked on the door. "I don't think they're expecting us." He knocked again. They heard footsteps coming and then the door opened.

"Richard?" Tim stepped back. "Hey, Benjamin, you out in the snow, too. Come in here." Richard was stomping the snow off his feet as Tim reached up for Benjamin. "Here, Mom's got an old rug just for this purpose. Stand inside. Run in to the kitchen Benjamin and see Aunt Laura."

"Sounds like a warning needs to be done…" Richard shrugged out of his insulated wear, "I take it she is really upset with me."

"Something like that." Tim agreed.

"And you?"

"About that."

"Your parents?"

"Not happy."

"I have a full plate?"

"You bet."

"At least you let me in."

"Barely." Tim turned toward the kitchen. "You're on your own."

He followed. Florence was standing by John's hospital bed but Laura wasn't there. "Hello, Richard," her parents spoke. "She's in the bedroom and if she says you can't come in, then that's that," John said.

"Yes sir, I understand." Richard started down the hall, remembering Benjamin. "Benjamin, I need to speak to Aunt Laura, is that all right with you."

"Yeah," He went back to sit beside Tim. "I know about these things. My daddy left us…but he's back."

"Is that good?" Florence came to sit on the sofa with Benjamin between her and Tim. "Where are your Momma and Daddy?"

Benjamin slipped off the sofa, held out his hand until she stood, "Now," he said, "Lets look out the window." Florence followed his lead. "See," he pointed. "That's Daddy driving the horses and Momma wrapped up in all the blankets."

"Mercy me," Florenced exclaimed, "John, Crystal and her Robert are out at the end of the drive in that old sleigh Crystal's daddy made years ago." She hugged Benjamin. "Let's tell them to come in." She winked at John as she passed by to the door, "I'm thinking if Laura gets upset we might need some noise." John grinned. "I know what you're thinking John Noble, at least she let him in. Right?"

Richard sat on the old vanity bench, his big body seeming to perch since he was nervous and drawn into one human knot. "Say something," he practically pleaded. "I've tried to explain I'm sorry. Yes, the girl thought she like me but I didn't like her. If she bothers you, she can move on."

Laura had experienced so many feelings the last few days, not to mention the month behind them, that she didn't know what she was feeling, much less thinking but his bland excuse wasn't enough. If he didn't like her why did she see his arms go around the girl? Were all men that fickle? She remembered Leah saying Levi had mourned her leaving, mourned? This man in front of her didn't appear to mourn anything.

"What do you want, Richard?"

"You to believe I'm sorry and come home."

"If I come home, Richard, which I never intended to stay here, I just needed the comfort of someone who love me, that's why I came here." She stared at him, a solemn expression, "Do you understand, if I come home, there will have to be a time of getting used to each other again. I longed for that until the last few days and now it is as if our marriage is over…maybe it is, I don't know. I'm just being honest."

"Why?" He rose to sit on the end of the bed. "What changed everything in a days time?"

"You. You didn't acknowledge me at all, walking through the house as if I didn't exist, and then there was me witnessing, myself, you kissing her the night I rode with Tim to pick up bolts and you came out of the store together. Then last night she showed up at Open house and I had to get a breath of fresh air, but what was that about? Was I suppose to see you on the outer fringe of the parking lot when she came out of the building? It seemed you arrived to pick her up. Did she have news for me, Richard?"

"I don't know what you're talking about. I came to see you, and I did see her come out of the building and that meant I couldn't afford an encounter with her. Someone might see and get the wrong impression. For heavn's sake, Laura, I didn't sleep with her, and that night you saw, she kissed me."

"Yes, I got the wrong impression and I strongly resented what it appeared to be, whether it was or not."

"That was coincidence, Laura." His voice was low and troubled. "Please, give me another chance."

"But you don't believe in second chances, Richard. That's how we got in this mess in the first place."

"You chose to believe in Carrington." He was on edge. "I didn't. He could have hurt you."

"But he didn't. On the other hand, you chose to kiss her and that hurt me, your ignoring me, hurt me."

"I wanted to teach you a lesson." He was at loose ends again, angry two ways. She was crying softly.

"You did." She lay back on the bed. "I am extremely weary with all this, Richard." She sighed, suddenly tired to the point she didn't want to talk further. "I don't know if we can over come this."

"Only if we both want to and decide we have to." He slid down on his knees. "Laura, please, come home with me. I'll give you all the space you need and you truly do not have to worry about the girl at work."

"Call her by name, Richard," she replied, wearily. "For heavens sake acknowledge who she is. Charla."

"Come with me, Laura, if you don't it could be three days to a week before the road is cleared."

"Go. Please. And ask Crystal to come in. We steady each other, Richard, something you and I should have learned by now, instead we've held the silent war and look where it got us."

"Hey Dumplin?" Crystal slid down beside her, laying an arm across her body, looking down into Laura's teary eyes. "That bad, huh? A few days ago you wanted him so bad you couldn't stand it, didn't you, then you saw her at school last night and things changed. What do you think she wanted to tell you?"

"I don't know, you ran her off." Laura almost grinned. "Some friend, you are." Her tone became serious, "I saw him. He was parked on the outer edge, do you think he was waiting for her or it was coincidence like he says?"

"Dumplin, I'm going to tell you. It is what it is but you can make it what you want if you feel he means it when he says he's going to put all this mess behind him, get rid of her and you two become one again."

"Is that what you did?"

"It's what we are doing." Crystal lay on her back staring at the ceiling. "I could've killed him, when he threw Benjamin against the wall but then who would our son have if I was in prison? So I did the next thing I could, went into hiding scared for my life, then when I think it's clear and we can come home, I hear he abducted you and I was mad as you know what again. What do you tell me? That he's changed. Do you think I believed that, instantly? Nope. I'd been through so much with that man since he started drinking again. Busted lip, black eye, you name it…but don't hit my kid even if he's yours, too. So I had to take a few, think things over. Heck, it was my best friend telling me about his childhood, them buttin heads and finally her leading him to the Lord. Her word I trust. Him, I questioned."

"Same here. So what are you advising?"

Crystal was looming over her again, pinning her big blue eyes on Laura's serious brown. "I'm saying you got this baby together. God is giving you a gift, half yours, half his, but together all yours. See what I mean? You are going to love this baby in ways you never thought, it's just falling in love again. Give him a chance, Laura, and if he doesn't do what he says…then you can decide what's best for all of you."

Crystal hopped up from the bed, found Laura's suitcase and began searching the drawer for her things. "Come on, Dumplin', I know you want to give him a chance, after all there was a time he was the best husband ever and y'all's history aint bad either." She laughed at her own words. "Those horses are bound to be ready to hit the road, so get your shoes on and Richard can carry you to the sleigh. Now isn't that romantic, we are going on a sleigh ride and we need to get home before dark, don't you agree?"

Laura began to tidy the bed. "Mom never could stand a bed left unmade." Crystal took one side, Laura the other. "I remember," Crystal said under her breath. "I heard that." Laura grinned. "I love you."

"Well, get a move on it, it will take fifteen minutes to kiss everyone and get out of here. I am going to talk to your daddy, while you get your shoes on and I want to make sure Robert's still in one piece." She started out of the room, but turned, "You know if Robert had to break the ice getting back into society, he couldn't have had a better family, to face off with, could he?" She smiled. "It's a God thing."

For a moment Laura considered Crystal's words. She had prayed and now Richard was here and she wasn't as enthused as she should be, she was cautious. What had they done, in their cold war against each other? In her heart she knew to be thankful there had not been an affair, even if the temptation was there between Richard and Charla. She had no idea why Charla appeared at her class room door, by avoiding her she had saved herself more heart ache. Presently she was not such a good person to wonder about their heartache. Was she supposed to be ashamed of that?

"Mom, Dad, Tim," she said, leaving. "It has been good to be here and feel your love. I'll never forget."

They were bundled into the sleigh, crossing fields and on the way home as she remembered the firm grip her daddy was still able to give as he took her hand and raised it to his lips. Her mother's arms around her had said a million words and Tim, his eyes troubled with the tears in hers, said, I love you, Sis. The time they'd had together would be a cherished memory she thanked God they shared.

As though privy to her thoughts, Richard said, "You have a good family, Laura." As were his. "It's almost Christmas, and the way it looks we won't all be together. Unless the highway crews get out quicker and stay longer hours. I'll help if they let the citizens help." He reached for her hand. "Will you be terribly disappointed if we are snowed in alone at our house?"

"No," she whispered. "I've learned to make the most of wherever I am."

She didn't tell him, she had tried to remain calm throughout their ordeal, because she learned early on, the little baby inside her must know when she was at loose ends, for those were the times the movement was continuous and wore her down quickly. She didn't tell him many nights she played music to calm both her and the baby and the words from inspirational hymns gave her hope that now she was reaching for, trying to grasp and hold on to as she was unsure what lay ahead. She didn't tell him all the prayers that now seemed to be answered had become something she did not understand. She didn't tell him by the time they reached their home she was so weary she wondered if she could undress herself and slide into bed and she didn't tell him, if their baby was restless and the chimes happened to ring, their little baby would settle as though hearing a prayer and wait until the end to move again.

Just when she thought to succumb to the sound of the sleigh sliding across the snow and the steady clopping sound of the horses hooves slushing through snow, their stride flowing like electricity through the sleigh making them all one united…there was a lurch and the jerk of the horses stopping.

It was growing dark. Robert jumped out, Richard quick to follow. She heard one of them say, "There's a hole, where the pavement was thin already, has given way, and the other replied, but I think if we work together, we can do this, what do you think? Robert gave instructions, "Crystal, when I say loosen up, on the reins, I'm thinking the horses will move forward. You got that Babe? For now, hold firm until you hear me…"

"On the count of three, we lift where it's hung, agreed? Now we have to get in the right places." There was movement, then, "one-two-three, Crystal loosen up let em go."

The sleigh churned in place, the horses tried to move forward, they heard more pavement ripping away and the sleigh moved forward. Richard's voice came through the night, to the sound of a hand on Robert's shoulder, "We did it, Buddy."

Listening, Laura felt in her soul, there was where forgiveness began for Richard. He and Robert had pulled together, such a small thing if one thought about it, but most things began small. One more thing for her to register and think on. Oh, Lord, she prayed, let it be so.

She was awake now, in the dark making mental note where they were, enjoying the homes they passed along the way and glad to see electricity obvious in the lighted strands of Christmas lights. "There's your house, kiddo's." Crystal called out from front seat as Laura leaned forward, "But it can't be, that house has decoration.

Look. Inside and out. That's not ours." She turned to Richard. "Are we on our road?"

"Believe so." He was grinning as she frowned and looked again.

"Why it's beautiful and there's a tree in the window. The posts are wrapped and lights on them, too."

Robert stopped just short of the drive. "Can you make it from here?" He was getting out to help.

Richard scooped Laura up into his arms, blanket and all. "If you'll sit her suitcase over by the mailbox."

"Look, the mailbox has a garland wrapped around it and holly berries. Who would do this?"

Crystal and Benjamin were laughing and clapping their hands. "It is pretty," Crystal cried out as they were leaving and Benjamin called back, "Bye, Uncle Richard, Aunt Laura."

Her joy evolved in theirs, for a minute she forgot the trials and enjoyed the scene before them. If all was well, she was experiencing what every woman dreamed of, someone had decorated her home, it was beautiful. She was in her husband's arms. She felt like a kid from that height, her feet dangling in the air. This must be someone else's life. Hers was fraught with worry. How could this be?

And down the street, the chimes of St. Anthony's mission began to peal out a Christmas song. Richard shook his head. "Does it ever seem mystical to you how the chimes suddenly play? They have no church, just that little adobe building that always reminds me of some place in Texas and they have chimes we can hear blocks away?"

"I've always wonder if they chime for me?" Embarrassed, she explained, "I mean, does each person feel the chimes are explicitly for them?"

"Yes, I know what you mean. I hear them and they remind me, God has a plan for our lives, even when we muddle them up." He started up to the house. "I'll come back for your suitcase, remind me." After a fumble or two unlocking the door, he sit her down just inside where she stood studying the decorations that had been done with care.

"Who did this?" She groped for the right word. "I mean, it's obvious someone wanted to do this, it's done very well, I can see they ran out of ornaments for the tree possibly but who cares it's… it's good. Crystal was with you and Robert and Benjamin and you worked until noon. Julia?" She smiled. "Only my sweet Julia would think we needed this. I'll call her tomorrow and thank her."

"You've had a long day, anyway long ride home, I suppose. Go ahead. I'll go for your suitcase."

She wandered into the bedroom to sit down and take off her shoes and her eyes rest on the music box. Silent Night, Holy Night, it's pure sound rang through the air, engulfing the room and she lay back to listen, trying to let her mind soak up the sound her soul needed. He found her there, asleep, her feet on the floor, her baby belly rising up in such an awkward position he knew he had to move her.

"Laura," he whispered. "Laura?" He removed her coat, the gloves came off her hands, the scarf was wound around her neck, he removed that too, and then stood back wondering what to do? "Laura," she did not stir. "Laura. Laura, will you help me?" She nodded. Together they removed her top and slacks, put on her gown and lay her long ways onto the bed, where she took a deep breath and slept on.

He collected all her clothes and took them to the utility room. Now what was he to do? Where was he to sleep? He figured he was as tired as she, emotionally sapped from facing her parents and his fear she would not return home with him. He could sleep on a rail. Instead, he stripped down, there by her pile of clothes, showered and crawled into his side of the bed, thankful, grateful, and dead on his feet.

Chapter 12

The snow plows worked around the clock clearing the roads. Richard was home the first day, but able to go to the store the second. "Strange," he said, "to be so near and yet so far. They are asking people to stay in and I'd like to but people may be needing supplies we have. So I'll go in to open."

Laura found being snowed in a time to do the routine chores of the day and then enjoy the home Julia decorated. She found the ornaments she had purchased in early season and added them to the tree. Their home was beautiful, if only their marriage was. Was, she whispered, was it completely gone? How did it come to this? They had become strangers to one another and now it was hard coming back. Their stubbornness and strong will had brought them here; for neither was built to bend, but now someone must.

"I believe we can get through to Mother's house for Christmas," he said returning at end of day. "Have you heard from your parents? Do they need my help to get your Dad to my parent's home?"

She shook her head. "Mom tried to dissuade him going but he persists."

"He's remarkable." He wanted to add, "You are, too," but he knew she would not accept h is words.'

The phone rang and he standing near answered. "Yes, we are doing well and yes, if possible we will be in attendance this Sunday morning. Yeah, yeah, we will show restraint on the food. You, too. Merry Christmas to you and Leah and your son. Thanks Pastor Levi."

"Is there anything I should do before tomorrow? Everything is in order as far as the few gifts, right?" She nodded and he wondered if there were more words he could say to prolong her glance his way. She either avoided looking his direction or sat staring out the window onto the snow laden ground.

"Would you like to watch a movie?"

She shrugged her shoulders. "It doesn't matter. Perhaps I should bake cookies for unexpected gifts."

"We haven't made any candy, yet." He backed up to the island, turning one of the tall back stools to sit on. "I noticed all the fixings; I'll help if you're up to making a batch or two."

Placing her hands around the girth of her stomach Laura replied. "It's pretty obvious I don't need it, but if you want a taste, we can whip up the fudge and may be the white trash recipe, if we have the base ingredient." She was rummaging through the cabinets. "You know what I'm talking about? The light colored stuff, it's marked into squares."

"Oh, yeah, I actually cut a sliver off the other night. It's not bad, but pretty hard." He reached around her and pulled it from the second drawer. "Man, you show restraint, I want to taste everything. Did you read the cookie information? It says not to eat it raw, because of the eggs. Really? For years we 've eaten the mix." He knew he was talking too much in trying to draw her out, to hear her voice.

"Probably someone died and there was a lawsuit." She was growing weary of talk that said nothing.

They worked together very well, ninety minutes passed with cookies lining the top of the cabinet and the largest flat base platter filled with fudge. "You excel," she said, "The fudge looks great."

"Do we know enough people for all this?" He spread his arms wide, looking at the cookies. There's seven, no eight dozen cookies here. But you're right; the fudge is to die for." He dipped into the pan used to make the fudge. "Try this."

She opened her mouth and tasted. "Umm, that is delicious." She smiled, and then went to the refrigerator, "fudge candy and a glass of cold milk. Heaven. Right?" She sat at the island, "I'll have a full sized piece, please." Richard cut the candy and brought several pieces as he joined her.

"The cookies pale in comparison," she said, pouring milk into a glass for him. "But look what we've done to our kitchen." It was beginning to be hard to be mad at him when they worked so well together.

"Nothing's harmed. We just have to fit everything into the dishwasher, don't we?" He finished off the fudge. "I'll load the dish washer if you'll take care of putting cookies in the boxes and those tins."

Within fifteen minutes the kitchen was shining, clean. "Now, I'm headed to bed. I'll shower in the morning but for now it's bedtime, these feet are screaming." Richard glanced down at her feet. They were red above the tennis shoes she was wearing and her ankles had disappeared into a mound of flesh.

"Let me rub your feet. Looks like you've lost circulation there."

"I'm dead then," She sighed. "It had to be the fudge. Heavenly fudge was the name of the recipe."

"Go on get into your gown and I'll see if I can find a lotion to make them feel better."

"Actually they hurt badly enough for me to want to take you up on that." In a short while she was sitting on the side of the bed. Richard removed the lid from the lotion bottle and reached for her foot.

"Lay back on the bed, Laura. I'm not going to hurt you." He was concerned over the mottled color of her ankle skin. "You sure this is normal, Laura?" He was studying her foot. "Something just isn't right."

"I don't know, Richard. This is a first, probably from being on my feet all day."

"But your ankles are hanging over your tennis shoes."

"I'm sorry. This is my first pregnancy. I don't know these things. I'm learning as I go." She was trying to set her foot back down on the floor. "This is really embarrassing. Please, just turn loose."

"Is there anything wrong, as far as you are concerned? With the baby, I mean?"

"I'm fine." She saw the look on his face. "Really, we are fine."

"Lay back Laura, I'm going to rub your feet, all right, but you need to lay back and rest. Could you try to sleep with your feet elevated?" As usual, she was struggling to stay awake, and all at once sleep won.

Obviously sleeping with one's feet elevated was not an easy feat, she kept sliding off the pillows. Once she awoke to find herself resting snug in the hollow of Richard's body as he laid on his side his knees beneath her buttocks, spooning as they used to. She admit to herself it was such a comfortable place she had settled into but trying to keep her feet elevated so as not to have the fluid buildup was a chore she must try to accomplish. When she thought to move his arm pulled her in more snug to his body.

What was she to do? Were they reconciling? Or was he trying to ease her spirits until the baby was born and then he would return to Charla? If she had allowed the girl to come in and speak, she would know but Crystal had intervened and maybe it was for the best…she was becoming the mother part of herself that looked out for her baby. The question was, what did she want? What was his intention? Her eyes blinked and there, right in the middle of a thought, Laura was asleep again, her feet elevated for a time.

He awoke to realize the room was cold. What now? He untangled himself from the bed covers and went in to check the thermostat on the wall. It was sixty degrees with snow on the ground? Now, he understood, the power was off. Thank goodness they'd thought to install a backup, if it worked. He was beginning to question everything as he turned on the gas log in the fireplace. An instant flame appeared.

He settled onto the old sofa as Laura came shuffling in. "Come here," he patted the seat beside him. She didn't question, just pulled the blanket she was wrapped in around them both. "Power's out."

"That's not good."

"No, it isn't." He sighed. "But it was to be expected with the weight of the snow on the lines, I guess."

They sat there staring at the flame dancing around the gas log. He finally spoke. "It's kind of like our marriage. The weight of too many happenings nearly got us, didn't it?"

"Nearly," she asked, "or has it?"

"I don't want anyone else, Laura. Just you." He pulled her close. "I'm sorry for shutting you out."

"Are you sure about not wanting someone else, Richard? You didn't even call my name. You didn't touch me, look at me, you went from being all things a woman wants in a man to…to a figure that looked like you, a moving body that would come and go but seemed to say I didn't exist. You didn't need me."

"And you reciprocated," he replied. "For me, after you said give Carrington a second chance when he put your life in jeopardy, to me, you chose other than me and I wanted you to think how that feels."

"But I wasn't choosing him. I led the man in the plan of salvation, after I heard his pitiful childhood story, Richard, and I believed he was truly saved and ready to turn his life around. His childhood was not stable like ours, he had more reason not to put his trust in anyone, and his own parents let him down. All I was doing was saying I can forgive him, the meanness he was capable of, because I felt he changed."

"Then, can you forgive me and take the same chance on me? Do I deserve a second chance in our marriage?" Running his fingers through his hair, he tried to form the words that he thought would make the difference. "Maybe I was flattered Charla paid attention to me, but it seemed more amused because she was younger and inexperienced but being childlike she thought if she persisted I would give up our life together and move right on to her. I've loved you since we were kids. I'd rather have us together with problems than to be with someone else." He leaned forward to look into her face. "I forgot half of the equation was yours. You have to want me as much as I want you. I nearly let the same strength that loved you tear us apart by thinking you needed to be punished for your choice if it went against mine; meaning Carrington."

"Because you have always loved me, it hurt even more that you would find it so easy to ignore me."

"But it wasn't easy; it was what I decided I must do. Now I know I was wrong."

"I'm sorry it happened, Richard. I don't want to blame my being pregnant for the way I've handled things, but deep within I realized if you said our marriage was over I would take our baby and do the best I could…but I could go no further than that. I simply had no idea what lay ahead."

"You worried?"

"Yes." She thought of the many times she wondered how she and the baby would make it but always resolved they would. In the beginning she worried over the incident with Tom, who was child hood friend to both of them, but they were not married at the time. Tom had been drinking, and she had no idea what he had implied to his cousin, Robert, but Richard had no knowledge of what happened and presently their marriage would not stand the inclusion of another incident. She would explain to him someday; but now was not the time if they were to move forward in their life together for the sake of their child.

Perhaps she had acted hastily, within a month's time saying yes when he proposed marriage again when the previous month she had said no. That last trip to pull all the ends together, from her summer job and last classes she thought necessary if she was accepted to a teaching position, who knew their childhood friend would be in the same town, they would have dinner together and then everything that happened would put a smear on the friendship established when they were children?

She had handled it best she could, alone, without drawing another person's opinion into the hurt. Was that to be her lot in life? When Richard became distant and aloof she was determined the world might look on her misery but she would not share it with them. She would trust in the Lord and come through.

They sat staring into the fire, each lost in their own thought. He wondered where her iron will came from. She wondered that he was a man of strength. Together, if they directed that inner fighting spirit they could be a power house for God. He did not need them. They needed him. As they sat there some small reasoning voice spoke to their inner being. You can find happiness together if you desire. It was up to them to make the decision; God would not make it for them. They knew.

"There's something missing in our Christmas décor," Richard mused as they sit there growing increasingly warm and cozy. Do you know what it is?" He peered down into her face, a gentle smile playing on his own. "Yes? No? You don't remember?"

They actually laughed as she pointed to the top shelf of the closet. "It's still wrapped in one of your T-shirts. Be careful. It's glass, or porcelain. Just another glass, isn't it? Baked more times?" He had his hand on it and brought it down carefully. "Take it in by the fireplace where it's warm or on the island."

They unwrapped it, small but unique and perfectly formed, the colors of the costumes were painted in rich hues that glorified the very meaning of the nativity they'd brought home from their honeymoon.

"Oh, it's darling," she whispered, reverent. "Aren't you glad we chose this one?" He held the manger with the Christ child in the palm of his hand. "How could they make a form to turn out something this small so perfect?"

"That's why it cost more than the others. We said we'd read the Christmas story each year and cherish this little gem as a replica of our love and new beginning." He raised his eyes to her. "Maybe it was best that we forgot to set it out, until now, when we've made up our minds to go on together. We have haven't we? She nodded. "There's no other Christmas piece could have such hope and promise as this."

Her eyes were moist as she nodded. "I remember the shop and the shop keeper saying they sent these all over the world and most wanted this very set because its colors are so stunning."

Richard looked around. "We are limited on places to set it, Laura. It's time we bring in furniture. You had an appointment with the lady from Marigold's, how did that go?"

Her head dropped, "It went well but then realizing how things were between us, I didn't order anything. She promised to keep the list, though, and she did mention new items were coming in for Christmas."

"The day after Christmas, Laura, let's remedy this situation." He lay a finger under her chin and raised her head to look at him. Leaning down he placed his lips on hers. "Sealed with a kiss, how's that?"

She smiled through tears. He opened his arms and she walked into them. "This feels almost like home."

"Almost?" He questioned?

"Yeah, the tummy's expanded and I can't get quite as close." He pressed her head against his shoulder.

"We'll do the best we can. Is there a chance Marigold's would have tables?'

"That, they might have," She leaned back to see his face. "We do need something to set it on, don't we?"

"Next year we will have a little child to tell the story as we sit out each piece," he said as he laid his hand on her stomach. "Not once, Laura, did I forget you were carrying our child." When she was silent, he dropped down on his knees and put his arms around her, "I should have thought about that. Of course you felt abandoned." She studied his face to determine if he was sincere. "God forgive me," he whispered, "you really felt that way, didn't you?"

Strangely enough, they heard the chimes ringing out as they went back to bed. The power was on, and they felt sleepy again. "Oh, little town of Bethlehem," Richard remarked. "How appropriate that would be the song when we've just sit out the nativity set."

It was seven o'clock when she awoke again. The chimes were still playing. "Did I just go to sleep," she asked or is another malfunction the chimes are experiencing?"

Richard was perched on one elbow watching her. He grinned when she opened her eyes. "No, they started about ten minutes ago. In fact it is now seven o'clock, do we need to start our day?"

"In a minute," she said, yawning. "Merry Christmas, Richard."

"What? I was waiting to be the first to wish you a Merry Christmas and you beat me to it?"

"I love those chimes. I bet every person in New Haven thinks they are playing just for them. I do. They're uncanny; they play every time something major happens in my life"

"What are you considering major?"

"Well, first Christmas, First home decorated. I can't wait to thank your mother."

"So what time are we leaving here? Even if the snow trucks have run, what do you think?"

"Ten at the latest, maybe less so I can help your Mother?" She saw he was wearing a jogging suit. "Have you been up long?"

"Not really, but I did sweep the snow off the front porch, like if we're going to have company."

"I've got to shower, do you need in there?"

"No, I showered after scooping snow. How about I scramble some eggs while you shower."

"That would be nice."

He had the plates on the table, orange juice in the glasses and bacon and eggs ready, when she slid onto her chair. "There's jelly, if you want on your toast." He brought the toast hot from the oven. "Shall we pray, Laura?" She nodded. "Heavenly Father, we thank you for another day that is so special for many reasons in our lives. Thank you that we celebrate Jesus birthday and thank you that you have kept us safe and brought us back together again. We need your blessing, Lord as we start over. Help us to love each other with wisdom and fairness, and always listening to your voice speaking to our hearts. Now bless this food to our body and our body to thee. In your name, dear Jesus, amen."

"This is Jesus birthday," Laura said, softly. She reached for his hand, "We used to always hold hands." He brought her hand to his lips and kissed it. "We're going to have a little baby, Richard."

By nine thirty the truck was packed with food and gifts and cookies and they decided to leave early. "A car drove by slowly and Richard waved to the driver. "Do you know that person?" She asked. He shook his head. "No. But the car seems familiar." He shrugged, "Nothing rings a bell though."

The morning passed quickly as Laura helped by sitting the table, placing the napkins and the center piece on Julia's brocaded table cloth. "Everything's beautiful, Julia, and why wouldn't it be?" She kissed her mother in law's cheek. "Thank you for decorating our home. It is so pretty and we do enjoy it."

Julia stopped grating the head of cabbage where she was preparing slaw, "I didn't decorate your house, honey. What made you think that? I've been snowed in since last weekend."

"You didn't? My family didn't, either. And Richard and I were with Crystal, who possibly would have done it? It's so special and there are candles on the fireplace, a music box by my side of the bed that plays Silent Night and Julia, the tree, the tree looks so real, but it's not." She was getting excited thinking about everything. "You must come see it. There are lights on the front porch and the posts are wrapped."

Julia hugged her. "Sounds like some of your church people may have come calling. I hear New Haven's Shining Light people do just that, they shine in the community and love their neighbors."

"I can't believe they would do that for us, we've not attended the church enough for all that."

At that moment her parents arrived, Tim leading the way pushing hard to get the wheel chair up onto the porch, where he left it because Julia had brought in a day bed from the sun room just for John. It was a sad but joyous moment that brought them all together. Florence handed food into the two of them and began helping John settle onto the bed. "Thank you, Julia," John beamed. "This is a whole lot more than I could ever expect. You are a wonderful friend, Julia."

"Yes, you are," Florence second. "We could have stayed home, but you invited us and we are so happy."

"And miss being with our children?" She looked around. "Where's Tim and his fiancée?"

"They'll drop in later, but his Sherry is an only child, her parents couldn't part with her on this day and I don't blame them a bit, do you?" Florence and Julia shared an understanding glance and smiled. "Tim brought his dad in and left quietly. His heart was torn but he loves Sherry and he likes her family,"

Laura kissed her mom's cheek, finished sitting the crystal stemware on the side board in the dining room and went in to see her father. "Merry Christmas, Daddy, you're looking chipper in your red vest." She glanced around at James Wilson, "Did you two plan what you'd wear, James Wilson in his green vest?"

"Planned it a month ago," her Dad teased.

Richard had been listening to the banter, "I guess I missed out, didn't I?" He shook her dad's hand. "Good to see you Mr. Noble."

"John," her dad corrected.

"How about, Mr. John?" Richard suggested. "My folks always stressed I had to be polite with names."

"We've lined the food up on the sideboard," Julia explained and we've got a special chair for you John if you want it, but we can pillow you up and push that bed right here next to us if you prefer. How do you think we should make you comfortable for our Christmas dinner?"

"It looks like a feast, Julia. Let me see if," he paused and looked up to Richard, "With Richard's help maybe we can get me in a chair and I'll try to sit like a man and behave myself. Would that work?"

Between James Wilson and Richard they settled him into one of the arm chairs. "Thank you, Son," he said to Richard. Then patted his old friend, "Bet you never thought you'd be liftin' me did you. J.W.?" There were tears in both men's eyes. "We've been friends since little boys chewin' green leaves for tobacco," John said. "Weren't we something?"

"We've all shared blessings," J.W. replied. "When our two married, we had to be proud because we know what they're made of." He glanced to his wife, she nodded and he said, "Let's bless the food. Father God, we come before you on this special day thanking you for sending your Son to save us, and Lord we thank you for the many blessings, for our friends and family and for the years to come as we enjoy life together. Now we ask your blessing on this food, on the ones who prepared it and for our bodies to be strong in our faith for you. We pray for those less fortunate and ask a special blessing on them, where they lack physical comfort that you will give them peace. Thank you for this day to celebrate Jesus birthday together." Everyone said "amen."

They enjoyed the food and the easy banter of long friendship and family love and the time passed until the women rose up to clear the table and J.W. and Richard helped John to lie back on the bed. His strength had left him and he fell asleep. Laura had taken a dish of gravy out to empty into the kittens bowl on the back porch when she saw a car pull onto the drive, the same car she and Richard had seen before leaving home that morning. She hurried in to whisper to Richard that someone was outside.

"Dad, do you want me to go to the door, or you?" He asked. "There's a car in the South drive." J.W. rose up as the door bell rang.

Richard stepped back with Laura, as his mother came making inquiry. "Who is it?"

Richard shook his head as his father said, "Miss, can I help you?" There was silence. "Here," he said, opening the screen door, "Come in out of the cold." The hood fell away from the young woman's face. "Why, Charla, is that you?" He turned to Julia. "Honey, this is Charla, I don't think you have met her, she works at the New Haven store."

Laura reached for Richard's hand and felt him hold hers tight. Julia seemed puzzled as did J.W. "Can we do something for you, Charla?" J.W.'s voice was gentle. He was sensing the unease of the girl.

"Mr. Worthington, my Dad's out there in my car and he insists I come here, today to tell your family."

"Tell your Daddy to come on in," J.W. said, ever hospitable. "He doesn't need sit out there in the cold."

"No, Sir, he won't. He says I got to do this all myself. I got myself into it and I gotta get myself out."

J.W. was thinking what had she done, robbed the store, taken something that didn't belong to her. "What is it you need to tell me, young lady?" His voice was still kind.

"Mr. Worthington, Sir. I'm pregnant."

Laura's heart felt as though it dropped to her stomach and from the look on Julia and her mother's faces theirs did, too. Richard was squeezing her hand so tight she felt her engagement ring dig into the flesh of her other finger. John had wakened and was listening, his eyes on Laura and Richard. Florence crossed over to stand beside him. "Why does your daddy think you should come here on Christmas day to tell us, honey?"

"Because, Sir. He thinks the man who's the father should own up to the deed." At that the tears sprang from her eyes, great drops that fell onto her coat and welled up on the wool material. She suddenly was staring at the floor. Her shoulders drooped and she appeared ready to crumple to the floor, herself.

"Here, sit down in this chair." J.W. pulled a small slipper chair in front of her, took her hand and set her down. "Do you want to tell us who the father is, Charla or is that something one of our employees will have to own up to?"

"It's your son, Mr. Worthington. Richard." She said the words low, as though ashamed to admit them but Laura heard and Richard went rigid. His mother and hers were staring at him as if had two heads.

"I didn't catch that, Charla."

"Richard." She leaned back as though J.W. might hit her. Puzzled and stunned, J.W. found it all he could do to turn and look at his son. "Richard?"

"No, Sir. I never touched her. She can have a test and we'll prove it is not me."

Laura took off for the nearest bathroom, running lest she vomit on the floor, and barely making it she left the door open for the others to hear her distress as she heaved until there was nothing left.

"Richard, come here." J.W. kept his eyes on the girl. "Now you sit still, young lady and my son is going to look you in the eye and ask you why you are doing this?" J.W. stepped back and Richard stood before her. "Come, Mother," he spoke to Julia, "Come stand with us. The three of us, until Laura can join us, and we will hear what this young woman has to say."

Charla sit there, miserable, alone, wishing she hadn't come but there was no way out. She hadn't met Richard's wife, but when she came to stand with the family, Charla cast her eyes on her face with resentment and hostility. It was plain she was having a baby and why had no one told her or had they mentioned it and she was caught up in her own plan and did not hear. His wife never called him.

"What are you doing, Charla?" Richard's voice was not kind as his father's. She heard the anger and felt his wrath. His eyes were afire with rage and his voice carried the fury a man owns when he feels wrongly accused. "Have you fallen so low you would claim something like this?" He was tall, so tall when he leaned toward her she thought she would fold from the heat of his face. "If you were a man, I'd strike you but you come in here, on this day of all days when we are family and you lie. Why are you doing this, Charla?"

"Son, I thought you'd speak kinder." J.W. laid a hand on Richard, to be slung off. "This is not your way."

"It is my way, Dad. Let me speak. I have not been with this woman in a sexual way and I won't stand for it. You will take a test, Charla, and it will be negative and if it isn't we will test further. If you are pregnant it is not my baby and you can find the one who is responsible because we both know it is not mine."

Charla was crying. J.W. was becoming more uneasy by the minute, John by sheer will power was sitting up staring at the girl, while both mother's felt her dismay and wondered at their feeling of concern for her when it was Laura and Richard caught in the middle. "I'm going out to get your father," J.W. announced. "He should never have let you come in here alone."

"J.W., you need a coat and you're in your house shoes." Julia's words were cast to the wind, the door was open with J.W. striding best he could across the yard. They saw him yank the car door open and practically hall Charla's father from the seat and if they heard his words correctly, he yelled, "what kind of man are you, you're that girl's father? Get in there with her." His six foot four frame meant something.

If Charles Weeks felt a moment of fear as J.W. bared down on him, by the time he reached the door, he had a swagger, which didn't last long when Richard stepped in front of him, his fists clenched and his teeth set on edge. "Don't you touch me, Boy," Charles said, holding his hand up.

"And don't you call me Boy," Richard replied, evenly, his eyes leaving the man to settle on his daughter. "What kind of game you think you're playing, Weeks? Did you make her say these things, come here accusing me? Is she even pregnant?"

"She's pregnant, all right. I saw the test. And the only place she goes is to work and home. Who else you got workin' at that place?"

John spoke up. "Charles, is that you? Come over here and talk to me?" Surprised, Charles took notice of who was talking to him. "Come on over." John was motioning him near. "We go a long ways back, Charles. Remember that old farm truck, the two ton; I bought from you, and then that old fifty six Ford we had to put a new bed on?"

"What you doin' here, Mr. Noble?" It was plain; at that moment Charles wished he wasn't present.

"My daughter married Richard Worthington, Charles. You got a grind to pick with him?" The man didn't reply. "I'm thinkin' maybe you're hard up for cash right now. Would that be what's goin' on?"

"Now, that ain't right?" Charles blustered, but the bluster died down.

"You know, Charles, if your daughter is lying to cover for you and you can't prove a thing it's going to look bad on your part.

That boy didn't mess with your girl; he's got a wife expecting his own baby, soon. Now you need to think this over, if the DNA's not there, then you got yourself a big case against you. Knowin you, you made her admit to the first name you thought of and her bein' scared she did it, but she knows the truth and what if there's a boy out there she loves and you're here makin' trouble where trouble's not due. Now tomorrow, you take your girl back to wherever you go to find out if she is really pregnant."

"She is, I told you."

"But Charles, don't you understand, these days they got test to prove whether a man's the father, or not. What if you've concocted something so far out, you're going to be the laughin stock of the town, your daughter's goin' to hate you and you lose all the way round. These are fine upstanding folks, they're not gonna let you ruin their name just by something you said, they'll prove you wrong."

"What makes you think I'm wrong. How do you know?"

John's eyes narrowed and when he spoke his voice had a hard ring to it. "I know what you've pulled in the past, Charles. Remember the Tollison incident? He told me what you did. Remember the Alridge family's problem? That's my cousin. You tried a thing or two with me but I'd heard the story and I wouldn't let you get by with it. But I live in a different community even than Richard's folks so you weren't able to make the connection. I know you were up to serve time, but the man who informed on you died, and you got off free because there was no witness. Now you got this girl, that knows the truth in this matter; you're insistin' she blame Richard. Your girl has a chance in life, don't spoil it for her."

"I put her through college; she's just as good as your girl."

"Yes, she is and I pray she finds her young man and has a good life, but it's you I'm worried about. If you are making her lie, then clear it up, here right now, once and for all and don't look back." John coughed, weariness about to claim him. "It's Christmas, Charles; do you want this on your conscience? Straighten it up and take your girl home to her Momma."

"She ain't got a momma, my wife left us years ago."

"I'm sorry to hear that. Then you have tried to prepare her for life, giving her what you can, but tonight is about the most important thing she'll ever remember. What are you going to do?" John lay back, coughing. "If this girl is all you have, don't run her away. Make her proud of you."

Charles glared at Richard, took in Laura and the two mothers, then moved beyond J. W. to where Charla sit with the hood on her head staring at the floor to avoid their glances. "Get up, go to the car." He was out the door with the screen between them when he turned. "We'll seek counsel in the morning and let you know what we decide."

Chapter 13

They could have heard a pin drop, so thick was the silence when the Week's went down the road. J.W. rubbed his chin where a days growth was coming through. "I don't rightly know what to say. Florence. John. I'm sorry about it all and if what you said does good to turn him around, I greatly appreciate it."

"I work with that woman," Richard started to explain. "But I've done nothing. Someone is the baby's father but not me. I can't believe she would come here on Christmas day to make those accusations."

"Richard?" Laura interrupted. "I need to go home. Please." All stopped talking as concerned faces turned her way. "I'm all right, just a bit jangled in the nerves I think. We have to rise above this, too." She hugged Julia, and her mother and kissed them on the cheek.

J.W. got a hug, his voice husky as he said, "We love you, Laura."

And last she hugged her daddy, his bony arms around her as she laid her head on his shoulder. "Daddy, don't leave us. I need you now more than ever."

Richard was holding her coat and she hurriedly slipped into it and started toward the door. "She has to have time…" She heard her mother say quietly.

On the truck ride home, they were back to not speaking. She pressed down into the seat and let the warmth ensnare her. Richard was feeling the anger he'd used against Charla slip into remorse tinged with resentment that he'd been put on the spot in front of those he loved most. He'd feared any minute Charla would say "but you kissed me." Kisses did not make babies. He had felt Laura's pain, still felt it.

He had noticed these days Laura did well until confronted with despairing situations and then she was extremely tired. The emotional drain was breaking her down and he could do nothing about it. All he had done in the past, contributed to what she must deal with now. They entered the house and she kept walking to the bedroom. He wanted to follow but her mother had whispered, she has to have time.

He was at loose ends. When the doorbell rang, though it was unexpected he embraced it as relief from his solitary vigil. What if she slept through until morning? Opening the door; Crystal stood there.

"Richard, I know how you feel about Robert but we wanted to check on Laura, Florence called and said it might help if I came by, but its Christmas and we're all together. Is that asking too much?"

"She's asleep but, yeah, you all come on in. Maybe me and Benjamin could play a game of checkers."

"Well, there's a Christmas movie he's kind of set on. He usually sits over in the corner and he's quiet."

"So…Robert and I can play a game of checkers because we find it hard to talk about anything." He said as she motioned them in. "I'm making hot chocolate; you all want to test my skills?"

Once Benjamin's movie was found they settled on the stools around the island. "You said Florence called, did she tell you what happened?" Crystal shook her head no. "Well, I'm going to let her tell you, it's just a bit difficult for me. Go on in there and check on her." Just talking about it made him feel bad. "Robert, how long since you played checkers?" He placed the board between them. "Red or black?"

"I may have played a time or two last year when I was on the road. Some stops for truck drivers have cards and checkers available." He chose the black checkers. "I don't promise anything."

"Fair enough." Richard tossed a coin. "Heads or tails." Robert chose tails. "Tails it is. You go first."

Crystal had lay down by Laura, a repeat of college days when they intended to study but ended up sleeping. The ringing of the phone awakened them. Laura rose up to see the wall clock and discovered Crystal. She started to laugh. "What are you doing in my bed?"

"It sleeps good." Crystal shrugged as she wiped drool from her chin. "Girl, I was in deep, best sleep ever that nap was refreshing. How about you?"

"Amazing. I was bone weary when I lay down and emotionally drained."

"Your mother called me, both your parents are worried about you but your Dad was so tired, they knew not to risk the drive over when he needed to be back home....so here I am. I'm sorry about the whole thing but I know Charla Weeks, and I know her daddy even better. I worked for him one time. Four weeks and I quit. The man's obnoxious. Same time I left one of his friends explained his wife left him, too." She rolled onto her stomach. "He thinks he's God's gift to everyone, mostly to women, though. Why would she do that and do you think there's anything to it?"

"No. I had to flash that through my brain when she said it. Richard would be the kind of man to wait til the divorce was finished before he gave in to his temptations. Kissing's one thing, the other another."

"You sure?" Crystal grinned. "Just teasing', Dumplin. I agree. Richard Worthington is known for having all his little duckies lined in a row." She reached up to push a strand of hair from Laura's forehead. "If it's any consolation, Robert said he'd seen Charla with that handsome blond fellow that mows and weed eats the median through town. And it goes right by the hardware, he's flirty, she's flirty, and let's just say they are both attractive and probably things got out of hand. Why she'd pick on Richard, I don't know but again Robert says her daddy's in financial problems. Blackmailing someone to spill the beans, might bring in a little revenue, don't you think?"

"Isn't that a bit extreme?" Laura sat up. "You and I both know she is smarter than that, isn't she?"

"Yes, I agree, but a little time to know if the test is accurate and tongues clacking about someone else, that keeps the spotlight off her, anyway, makes her seem not so bad…if someone else is. You know?"

"I'm so glad you came." Laura hugged Crystal. "What did you do with Benjamin and Robert?"

Crystal pointed the direction as she gave a giggle of sorts. "Right beyond your bedroom door."

"And they're not killing each other, Richard and Robert?" A puzzled expression on her face, Laura asked, "Should we go out there?" Crystal's laughter increased. "If the deed's not done by now, they're safe."

The delicious smell of food assuaged them as they entered the family-dining area. "Richard, are you cooking?" Puzzled, Laura took in the plates and plastic cups and forks lined up on one side of the island, along with a pitcher of tea and ice for the glasses with the checker board still in use on the other. "Hi, Robert," she said, as he concentrated on his checkers and merely nodded.

"I put all those dishes of food in the oven that our Moms sent home from the Christmas table. It does smell good. Robert suggested we might have to wake you girls if you are going to eat with us."

"Really?" Crystal put her arms around Robert's neck, peeking around at the board to see who was winning. "Come on, you two are tied. Turn it loose and let's eat, since Julia and Florence sent it over."

"We always mentioned something we were happy over from the old year and made a remark what we hoped would happen in the New Year," Laura said. "Why don't we try that before we say grace? I'll go first." She thought a minute as everyone, including Benjamin circled the island.

"I'm happy to be home, I have found teaching in New Haven's school to be rewarding and I do love my students like this one here," she hugged Benjamin. "I'm happy to see you three here with us tonight and my hope for the year ahead, is that our baby will arrive healthy and my dad is around longer. Thank you all for friendship."

Robert was next. "I'm blessed to have received forgiveness and freedom. I pray God strengthens us to be strong in whatever way is needed, and to be kind and loving and help us to be with the right people."

Crystal's eyes were moist as she said, "I love my friends, my son and my husband. You all make my life worth living and I'm thankful. I hope and pray the New Year is easier than the last one."

"I want to thank God that my daddy and Momma are together," Benjamin spoke up quickly, afraid they weren't going to include him. "My daddy is kind and doesn't hit us anymore, he just prays." He turned to Richard. "What you going to say, Uncle Richard?" He bit his lip and his eyes grew large as he said, "I forgot to say thank you for the gifts. I can't wait for Christmas next year." They all chuckled.

"Forgiveness is a big thing," Richard began. "I praise the Lord that Laura has forgiven me. That she is the good person we all know, loves Benjamin and her family and friends. It makes me better just watching her. I pray this time next year our lives are happy and healthy and that we haven't lost anyone."

"Richard, Laura," Robert spoke to them with tears in his eyes. "Do you think, in time, you can forgive me?" Laura put a finger over her lips hoping he wouldn't say anything that made Benjamin have questions. "I humbly ask your forgiveness."

Laura stepped over and hugged him. The minute seemed long and then Richard offered his hand. "You didn't cheat at checker and you beat me several times fair and square, I think we have a friendship here."

"Listen." Laura waited. "There, do you hear?" She went to the front door and opened it. They heard the chimes. "That's for us, especially for us, tonight. "Silent Night, Holy Night, All Is Calm, All Is Bright." Benjamin was singing his heart out, "Sleep in Heavenly Peace." Merry Christmas," they all said at once.

The Carrington's left around nine. Richard followed Laura to the bedroom, but he stood outside the door, leaning against the wall. She came back, studying him. "What are you doing?"

"Just standing here, looking at something." He glanced up and back to her.

"What is it?"

"Something I found and I liked it."

She came through the door, looking up to the ceiling. A huge ball of mistletoe hung down from the ceiling on a fishing line. "Is that mistletoe?" She was almost under it.

"It is." He reached for her hand. "Do you know how long it's been since we have really really kissed?"

"A really really long time," she replied, her eyes luminous.

"So, let's correct that, shall we?" He opened his arms and she walked into them, laughing softly as the fact was she couldn't get as close as she wanted, they both bent a bit at the waist and kissed. "That was a test," he said. "If you kissed me I knew you realized there was no way Charla's accusation could be true. But if you turned away, I knew you were unsure."

"It made me sick to my stomach."

"I know and that had me worried. I thought you questioned my honesty."

"No, it dawned on me in that second that we have been through a troubled spot of our marriage and there may be more, but we have come through this one. Sick as I was and all that upchucking made me weak, I was almost one hundred per cent certain but I needed to think it over. The worry this last month has done something to me. When you gave me time to think, I wasn't as stressed.

"How's that?"

"You were confident enough you didn't pressure me, you allowed me a time of healing; I had to lie down and let my body and mind catch up with each other and while I slept God did give me peace and then to find you playing checkers with Robert?" She just shook her head, smiling and happy.

"It has been an interesting day; I don't think I could go through another one like it quite honestly. Charla's accusation is a serious thing, but all that aside," he paused, thinking, "Hey… tomorrow we are going shopping for furniture. Will that be as grueling? Will I be physically able to attend church next day?"

She had to smile, he looked so serious.

"Nah, not grueling," she said, "But I do have a question about decorating. Who decorated our home for Christmas, the lights, the candles, the sweet little music box on my side of the bed?"

"I'm not sure I understand the question. I would probably just accept it as a secret."

The Saturday furniture shopping promised arrival of a few needed pieces, on Monday. Marigold had been most helpful. Richard found Harriet, the mother, a most interesting woman. "She paid for Shining Light church's renovation," he whispered to Laura. "And she doesn't know any of the people."

"She knows our heavenly father, though," Laura reminded him.

"That is true," Richard smiled. "It's a small world. Have you ever wondered the story each person could tell?" He thought about the tid bits of gossip he heard, working in a public place. "Seems Shining Light Church and Christ Church at the Cape have ties, they help each other. They tell good stories about each other."

The next day they were coming in from church to find a new message on their machine. "This is Tom Hargrove. If you are home this afternoon, I'd love to drop by to see you."

"What do you think?" Richard waited for her answer. "I think I can take seeing him these days."

Laura thought of the scripture Pastor Merkel used that morning. "Let not your heart be troubled. Ye believe in God, believe also in me." Just when she thought life was getting better, something else came along. If trials made one a better Christian, before long she and Richard would be saints.

At the Merkel household, Levi was unbuttoning his white shirt. "I'm going to leave my shirt and tie hanging on the bedpost if that's all right with you, I may need to visit little Miss Hawkins in the hospital again this afternoon."

"You were just there yesterday?"

"I know, but she doesn't have anyone and she needs to know someone cares about her."

Leah carried Jimmy into his room and laid him down to finish his nap. "That pastor at Shining Light put my baby to sleep," she said out loud.

"I heard that," Levi came up behind her. "He is snoozing, isn't he?" He had slipped into his favorite sweat shirt that had the words, My Pastor Rocks, given to him by the youth at church. He reached for Leah's hand. "What did you think about Charla Weeks and her young man attending worship service today?"

"In all truth," she followed him out of Jimmy's room. "I don't understand the way the world works, but I will say nothing surprises me. You and I both know her name has been linked to Richard's lately."

"Maybe it was Charla's way of telling the world there was nothing to any little piece of gossip that might get into New Haven's grape vine." Levi removed his Bible from the table where he'd laid it when they returned home. He always knew more than he could tell. "You know the fellow she was with has that lawn service?"

"Well, she seemed to be having a lengthy conversation with you. What was that about?"

Shaking his head, Levi studied the floor a moment before replying. "They ask if they could be married in the church. I'm sure they can but not being members I need to run it past the church board."

"A church wedding?"

"We didn't get into that, just their desire to be married in a church and soon, there's a baby on the way."

"I'm surprised they told you." Leah wondered how much of the young couples story the community was privy to. "Do you ever wonder, Levi, why people come last to the church or in this case, to you? I mean shouldn't we all keep our selves pure in the Lord, first, then temptation wouldn't overcome us."

The phone rang at fifteen minutes til two. "I have to run down to the store," Richard said, pulling his coat from the closet. "One of the church family's water line has broken and they need a part."

"But Tom's to be here any time, Richard. You should be here."

"I won't be gone but a few, Laura. I promise."

She watched him drive away. He was just out of sight when a black Lexus pulled into the drive and Tom Hargrove came to the door. He had already seen her; she waited to let him in. Their greeting was a bit awkward and she was at a loss for words.

"Is Richard here?" She shook her head. "I heard you were pregnant, Laura. I hope you've been well through the pregnancy?"

"Why are you here?"

"I needed to set things straight, Laura. I realize I drank too much and got out of hand our last time together."

"Yes, you did and when I tried to leave you peacefully at the restaurant you made a scene." Bitterness crept into her voice. "To make matters worse, you seem to have confided your ugliness to your cousin, Robert Carrington, who made my life miserable for a matter of months." Tears of frustration welled up in her eyes, even now. "I never told Richard I betrayed him by seeing you or that you betrayed his friendship, mine as well."

"I came because I'm truly sorry, Laura. Had I not been in a state of remorse all those months I never would have told Robert but he was in depression and I trying to relate, under the evening's influence of alcohol, I might add, did speak out of my own personal regrets? I never thought about him using it against you. Especially to hurt Richard and make him turn on you."

"How could I tell Richard you, supposedly our friend…"

He interrupted. "You don't have to remind me of what I've done, Laura. I came to ask your forgiveness. It is with me every day. You are a woman any man would treasure as his wife. All these years I've been sorry I didn't claim you as mine." Embarrassed, he tried to laugh but it was a miserable attempt. "I should at least have recognized I loved you and I should have asked you to marry me. At least I would have known if you cared for me."

When she was silent, he continued. "Could we leave it at that, Laura? Must I apologize also to Richard?"

He touched on what she had questioned over and over. Were some things best left unspoken. She finally replied. "Why would you come back, now, to cause problems?"

"I won't. I'm trying to change, Laura, to get my priorities straight and I needed to start here." His eyes were pools of sadness. "I wasn't in my right mind. For years I remembered Richard once saying, "You got a chip on your shoulder, Hargrove." He was right. Once that chip fell off I began to see life is good. You can make it better. Forgive me. It's in your hands, Laura. I'm sorry for what I did. It was only a few months back, Laura, but the time has felt like years as it aged me inside where it counts and I had to take stock of who I could easily become. May I ask, how has it affected you?"

"I can answer truthfully, there have been times the worry has nearly taken me down but through it all, I know God has blessed me to be with Richard. My fear of losing him was great; I had to put that worry in God's hands." She felt the internal war being waged against Tom, but he now sought restitution. It was in her power to send him away at peace or to stir the fires of unrest in his soul. "Go in peace, Tom."

"Without seeing Richard?"

"What would you say to him?"

He stood there, thinking and finally replied, "Some things are best left unspoken." He turned toward the door. "Have a good life, Laura."

"You, too," she replied, as a great burden lifted from her soul.

He paused a moment with the door open, listening. "Chimes?" She nodded. "What's that they're playing? When peace like a river…. attendeth my way….it is well, it is well with my soul." Their eyes met, he smiled, "thank you, Laura."

Laura could not know Tom was thinking his loss was Richard's gain. They had all come a long way but where would they be had not their parents taken time to instill the love of God in their lives. He hadn't always listened and still ran the wrong direction many times but there was hope, maybe he'd make it, yet. He'd lost a good thing today; he hoped Richard gave Laura the best life a woman could have.

She watched the Lexus drive away. What had they learned; three friends from childhood? Due to God's presence in her life; she realized the small voice Elijah heard, that was in her heart because she loved the Lord, had carried her through an infested swamp, abduction, her own husband's abandonment and the uncertainty of their future together. "Without you," she whispered to God, "I am nothing at all." That strong willed girl of her teenage years had listened to her mother's words and she learned a lot. She heard the radio playing in the bedroom, "an old song perhaps," the announcer said, "But for some, it's their song; When Somebody Loves You."

THE END